Herbert Elliott Hamblen

Tom Benton's Luck

Herbert Elliott Hamblen

Tom Benton's Luck

ISBN/EAN: 9783743389946

Manufactured in Europe, USA, Canada, Australia, Japa

Cover: Foto ©Andreas Hilbeck / pixelio.de

Manufactured and distributed by brebook publishing software (www.brebook.com)

Herbert Elliott Hamblen

Tom Benton's Luck

"WITHIN A CABLE'S LENGTH OF THE QUARTER." See page 296.

Frontispiece.

TOM BENTON'S LUCK

BY

HERBERT ELLIOTT HAMBLEN

AUTHOR OF "ON MANY SEAS," "THE GENERAL MANAGER'S
STORY," ETC.

New York
THE MACMILLAN COMPANY
LONDON: MACMILLAN & CO., Ltd.
1898

Norwood Press
J. S. Cushing & Co. — Berwick & Smith
Norwood Mass. U.S.A.

To

WILLIAM STONE BOOTH

MY STEADFAST FRIEND AND LITERARY MENTOR

This Volume is Dedicated

IN TOKEN OF SINCERE ESTEEM

TABLE OF CONTENTS

CHAPTER I

CHAPTER II

CHAPTER III

CHAPTER IV

CHAPTER V

CHAPTER VI

CHAPTER VII

CHAPTER VIII

CHAPTER IX

CHAPTER X

CHAPTER XI

CHAPTER XII

CHAPTER XIII

CHAPTER XIV

CHAPTER XV

CHAPTER XVI

CHAPTER XVII

CHAPTER XVIII

CHAPTER XIX

CHAPTER XX

CHAPTER XXI

CHAPTER XXII

LIST OF ILLUSTRATIONS

TOM BENTON'S LUCK

CHAPTER I

TOM'S EARLY HOME — DEATH OF HIS FATHER — A
SURPRISE FROM THE MATE — DRIVEN FORWARD —
TOM AND THE CARPENTER PLOT MUTINY — A DES-
PERATE FIGHT IN THE DARK

FROM his earliest recollection, Tom Benton's home
had been on board the thousand-ton medium clipper
ship *Columbia*, of Portland, Maine. His father, Captain Joe Benton, had brought the boy up under his
own eye; so that, at the age of seventeen, Tom was
an expert navigator and thorough all-round seaman.
He had a dim remembrance of a pale, sweet-faced,
invalid mother; and of a certain day when, en-
shrouded in the flag, an object slid from the lee
gangway into the blue water. His father hugged
him tight and shed tears; but that was so long ago
that he hardly remembered, and seldom thought of
it now.

His father had promised to put him on the articles
as third mate next voyage, to pay him wages, and
see what he was good for. Tom was very proud of

this, and promised himself that his father should never have cause to regret his confidence in him. Unfortunately, Captain Joe, who had been ill during a stay in Buenos Ayres, died and was buried on the passage home. The day before his death, he called the two mates and Tom to him and gave them his last orders. He told the officers that he left the vessel in Tom's charge; assuring them of the boy's ability to assume the burden, and enjoining upon them to respect and obey his son as his representative. To Tom he gave much good advice and such information concerning his worldly affairs as he deemed necessary, telling him that Captain Blake, the manager of the line, would watch over his interests, and advising him to be guided entirely by the advice of that good man, who had been his own lifelong friend. Father and son prayed and mingled their tears; for, now that bluff old Captain Joe found himself entering his port of final discharge, his heart went out to the motherless boy he was leaving to fight the battle of life alone.

The main yard was backed; the hands gathered about the capstan; and, with scant ceremony, the body of the late commander, swathed in the rough canvas winding-sheet of the sea, slid from the grating and disappeared forever.

Poor Tom, his heart broken by his first great sorrow, lay on a spare spar, his head buried in his arms, oblivious to everything but his own misery. As the crew were bracing the yards to bring the ship to her course, Tom received a stinging cut from a rope's end across his bare legs. He leaped to his feet, pain and anger overcoming for the moment all other feelings, and confronted Mr. Walsh, the mate, who, with the rope raised to repeat the blow and eyes glowering viciously, snapped out : —

"Come! Git up out o' that an' lend a hand at the braces! Your skulkin' days are over, my young buck!"

Half stupefied with surprise at the indignity, and enraged by the undeniable tittering of the men, Tom stood for a moment glaring back at his assailant.

"What do you mean by hitting me?" he asked, with quivering lips and heaving chest.

"What do I mean, hey? What do I mean, you whelp? I mean that your sojerin' days are over! You'll take your dunnage forrard an' work for your livin' hereafter. I'm cap'n now, an' you'll find it out 'fore you're a week older. Come, tail onto them braces — do ye hear?" And with blows and curses he drove the boy to work.

From captain's son, the most privileged character aboard, to ship's boy, the position of lowest drudgery, is a long step to the rear. But the mate's power was absolute. There was no appeal, so Tom took his belongings forward with a heavy heart. Of a bright, happy, and generous disposition, he had always been a great favorite with the men, for nearly all of whom he had done favors; but now, taking their cue from the officers, they treated him according to the time-serving dictates of their mean natures. He was compelled to perform all manner of humiliating services for those who, but the day before, had been proud to win a smile and a pleasant word from the captain's son. Though Tom was obliged to accept the position forced upon him by the mate, and perform with the best grace possible the duties pertaining to it, he would not accept personal abuse. One of the branches of his education under his father's care had been the noble art of self-defence, and many a dog-watch had father and son thumped each other merrily about the deck with the mittens, so he found no difficulty in impressing the mongrels in the forecastle with the idea that he was a first-rate boy to let alone.

There was one man in the crew whom Tom believed he could trust. Alec Webb, the big, rawboned Nova Scotia carpenter, had been in the ship nearly five years. Captain Joe had refused to leave him to die in the hospital at Rio, though bringing him aboard the ship nearly caused a mutiny, and from that day Chips had been the firm friend of his captain, and to Tom he was like an elder brother. The mate knew something of this and kept his eye on the pair, but they eluded his vigilance and enjoyed many a quiet chat. One day Alec said that while in the lazaret breaking out a bale of oakum, he had overheard part of a conversation between the mates which led him to believe that they intended either to take her to St. Thomas and sell her, or to wreck her on one of the adjacent islets and dispose of the wreckage. They had apparently not yet decided which plan to adopt, but he was satisfied that they did not mean to take the vessel home. Tom was startled to hear of such cool villany, as he knew that his father — and therefore himself — was part owner of the ship. He thought rapidly, and turning to his brawny friend, said : —

"Chips, we'll have to take her away from them."

"I don't hardly see how you can do it, Tom; the crew ain't reliable."

"Hang the crew! We don't need their help. Too many cooks spoil the broth, always. You and I can do this job just like mice. We only need to get the upper hand of the two mates; we can handle the crew all right. Nothing would suit me better than to have a tussle with those two gentlemen. You'll stand by me, won't you, Chips?"

"Why, yes, Tom, of course I'll stand by ye," replied Alec, rather dubiously. "Mutiny is a pretty serious business," he continued, "but your ole man stood by me, an' you can bet yer life Alec is your man even if 'tis mutiny."

Tom saw that the faithful fellow had grave misgivings. He tried to explain that there was a difference between what he proposed and mutiny. The carpenter was unable to distinguish it. Mutiny, to him, consisted in taking a vessel from her officers. He argued that, if the officers were scoundrels, the crew were not supposed to know it, and if they did, it was none of their business. "But I don't care nothin' about that, Tom," he continued; "if you say the word, we'll start in right now."

"Oh, no, Chips, I ain't quite as far gone as that," replied Tom; "I don't know but that would be piracy. We must not do anything until they commit themselves. I'll keep my eye skinned. The mate won't allow me on the poop, but I can find out the course by listening to the talk of the souwegians in the forecastle. Sometimes the man at the wheel overhears the latitude; when he does, he always tells it to his watchmates, and so I hear of it. You see I almost know both the North and South Atlantic charts by heart. So the next time I hear the latitude I'll mark it down somewhere, and keep a guess dead-reckoning after that. I know they are keeping half or three-quarters of a point to the westward of the regular course now.

That is suspicious, but I want to let them get her away out of her course, so it will show on the track chart, don't you see? Then we've got proof. Oh, no, Chips, I don't propose to do anything rash. Nothing that can get us into trouble. We'll get pay and praise if we take her from them, because we won't do it until we can prove beyond a doubt that they intended to steal her."

"Wal, all right," responded Alec.

The wind fell light, the weather was perfect, and for days they held the same course. Alec had no further opportunity of hearing the plans of the officers, and as nothing leaked out from any other source, he began to doubt again.

"I may have been mistaken, Tom," said he, anxiously; "seems as if we'd hear something about it if it was so."

"How could you be mistaken?" asked Tom, a little impatiently. "You heard it yourself, didn't you?"

"Yes, that's so."

"Well, then, 'tain't as if somebody had told it to you. I tell you, Chips, they're too sharp to let on to anybody. The only way you'll ever hear any more about that will be when you get it from themselves, like you did before. All we've got to do is to be ready all the time. I won't ask you to commit yourself until you are satisfied they mean mischief. I wish I could see the chart for

a minute; I ain't quite sure about the latitude of
St. Thomas. I think it's about twenty. At any
rate, if they are bound for there, they'll keep her
away sharply to the westward before they get by
it; so you keep an eye out for the latitude. You
can find something to do round aft there at noon,
and they may mention it. Then if they don't
keep her away before passing — well, say the
twenty-second parallel, we'll give it up. That's
fair, ain't it?"

"Oh yes, that's all right, Tom, or even the
twenty-fourth. I ain't in no such an awful pucker
to git out of it. I don't say we shall give up
watchin' 'em, because, as you say, 'they're almighty
sharp,' an' if they thought we was onto 'em, they
might change their plans altogether."

Tom watched anxiously the bearings of the sun
by day, and of the Southern Cross by night, for
any material alteration of the course; but still the
old ship kept her nose in the same direction. The
carpenter shop was in the after part of the deck-
house. Chips had fitted himself a bunk in the
starboard side of it, and, as he expressed it, was
as comfortable as a bug in a rug. Tom made a
couple of soft gags, and spliced eyes in two pieces
of hambroline, handy to tie a man's hands with.
These he gave to Alec, who stowed them away
under his mattress.

The mate neglected no opportunity of showing his ill-will toward Tom by giving him all manner of disagreeable jobs, and yelling at him insultingly, but he never again raised his hand to him. There was something in the glance of the boy's clear gray eye that restrained him, big bully that he was.

One day while the mates were at dinner, the steward on coming from the cabin passed Tom, who was at work near the galley door.

"Well, Tom," said he, "I s'pose we'll be losin' the trades 'fore long now. I heard Captain Walsh say she was in 'twenty thirty-five' at noon to-day. In a week or ten days, if we have any luck at all, we'll be pretty close to Cape Elizabeth. Guess you won't be sorry, my boy?"

Tom's heart beat fast at this news. The time he believed was near now, when he would have to make the first important move of his life; and as he felt sure the mate would be pleased at any excuse to make away with him, he was indeed confronted by a serious undertaking. That night at twelve o'clock the mate—who was a poor navigator—squared the yards and kept her away due west. When Tom saw her head swing off, he wanted to hug himself and dance. He had no chance to speak to Alec until the next day in the last dogwatch, and then only for a moment. Pointing to the sun, which was dead ahead, he asked:—

"What did I tell ye, Chips?"

"By gosh! yer right, Tom! They've hung themselves, sure enough," replied the carpenter joyfully; "when shall we do the trick?"

"We'll have to watch for a chance. I'd give a big apple, if I had it, to know the longitude. I want to let them go as far as possible, and get themselves good and foul, so as to have unmistakable proof of their guilt; but if we wait too long, they'll arrive before we are ready."

"Well, let's jump on 'em right away, then."

"No, we'll let 'em go awhile. We'll watch 'em, an' I guess we can tell by their actions when they are getting pretty close in. Walsh is a poor navigator; he could hardly make the broadside of America in daylight without heaving to a couple of times; so he'll go slow when he thinks he's most there. You see it's all longitude now, an' that tangles him up bad."

"All right, Tom. You know more about that part of it than I do; but when you are good an' ready, why, just call on yours truly, that's all."

For three days the *Columbia* rolled lazily to the westward. On the third day the course was changed, so that, allowing for variation, she was heading a point to the southward of west. This warned Tom that they were approaching close to their destination. The crew commented on the strange course they were steering, but of course it was none of their business, and they did not dare ask for information. At eight o'clock in the evening Mr. Walsh told the second mate to reduce sail if the wind increased during his watch — a clear sign that he did not wish to go far before daylight. Between nine and ten o'clock the weather changed. Black squalls arose on the horizon, the wind became puffy, and then died out altogether, while the great clouds rolled up like masses of smoke from a cannonade. When the advance guard of this column of darkness reached the zenith, and was streaked and split by innumerable threadlike flashes of lightning, Mr. Wilkins, the second mate, took in the royals and flying jib. Tom was on the alert. Two men went out to furl the flying jib, and one to each of the royals. This left only the man at the wheel and the one on lookout, on deck with the second mate. Tom could not have arranged things more satisfactorily himself. He slipped round to the carpenter's window on the lee side of the house, and could hear Chips snoring peacefully. He reached in, seized him by the beard and gave it a vicious twitch. It was the signal agreed upon, as Alec said it invariably woke him quietly. With a spasmodic snort the snoring ceased. Tom could hear him moving lazily as if about to turn over for another nap.

He reached in again, but the carpenter whispered:—

"All right, Tom, I'm a comin'."

Arming himself with a couple of belaying-pins, Tom crept round to the shop door. The sky was now entirely overcast, and it was very dark, but he could see the second mate in the waist. He was leaning on the rail and looking to windward. Tom stepped inside the shop and hurriedly explained the situation to Alec. Together they stole quietly on deck, stooping to conceal themselves as much as possible. Tom crept round abaft the second mate, while the carpenter approached him from forward. When they were within three feet of him, the man on the main royal yard hailed the deck, asking to have the weather buntline hauled up. At the first sound of the hail Mr. Wilkins looked aloft. The carpenter saw his opportunity. Like a tiger he sprang upon him, seizing the bearded throat with a grip like a fox trap. They were both powerful fellows, and second mates are not the kind of men who are easily subdued. But a man with his wind shut off, though possessed of the strength of desperation, is at a disadvantage. There was a sudden, silent, and awful struggle in the dark.

Tom jumped in to help, but in the darkness he was unable to tell which head to hit. The night was close and hot. The two men perspired like

"LIKE A TIGER HE SPRANG UPON HIM."

rain, and the carpenter's hold became slippery. With a sudden jerk the second mate succeeded in freeing his throat. Before he could be silenced, he gave a gasping yell, more like the screech of a wild cat than the cry of a human being. A friendly flicker of lightning enabled Tom to jam a belaying-pin in his open mouth. The carpenter turned him over, and they soon had him effectually tied and gagged. As they were dragging him toward the carpenter shop the squall struck her. The wind roared through the rigging like a hurricane, the rain came down in a deluge, and as Tom was wondering whether Mr. Wilkins' cry had awakened the mate, there came a steelly blue flash of lightning, followed by a couple of pistol shots from the break of the poop. Oh, yes, the mate was awake.

At the first shot, the carpenter dropped his end of the second mate and, with a groan, fell on top of him. Two more shots were fired, and then — silence. Tom dropped flat on the deck and worked his way to the lee scuppers, where he lay close to the spar, in six inches of water. He was now in a fix. The carpenter was wounded — perhaps killed. He did not know whether the mate was on deck, or had fired from the window of his room; but he expected that the next flash of lightning would make a target of him. The squall was now at its height, so he crawled aft, to be in the shadow of the poop when the next flash came. He became aware that somebody was fumbling with the capstan bars in the rack on the front of the cabin. It must be the mate. Tom was tempted to spring upon him and have it out; but Mr. Walsh was a big man with a pistol, and Tom was only a boy with a belaying-pin. The squall ceased as suddenly as it had come up, leaving a flat calm. The ship was now again on an even keel. Tom could hear the last of the rain dripping from the poop scuppers. The sails flapped wetly, lazily. There were voices forward. The men had come in from furling the flying jib and were talking as they coiled the sheets and down haul.

A thinning of the clouds ahead enabled Tom to see a dark object sneaking along the weather rail, and by the faint moonlight he made out that it was the mate with a capstan bar. Carefully he worked his way along, until he was abreast of where the second mate lay, bound and gagged, but kicking his heels noisily against the deck. Mistaking the prostrate figure for the carpenter, the mate leaped toward it and delivered a vicious blow with the handspike. He missed, and as the swing of the heavy handspike nearly took him from his feet, the carpenter leaped from behind the mainmast and grappled with him.

"Come on, Tom," he cried; "I fooled him that time. Lend a hand here quick, I've got the mate!"

"You have, hey? You blue-nosed hound, you'll wish you hadn't before I get through with you," said Walsh, as he struggled with Alec.

Tom ran to the carpenter's assistance, but the man from the main royal yard, a burly Norwegian, jumped from the rail to the deck right in front of him.

"Hey, hey, vat's all dis about?" he asked, as he seized Tom by the throat.

The mate shook Alec off, fired two shots at him point blank, and ran off to his room for another revolver. When the sailor heard the shots, he dropped Tom, and ran forward, calling out that he was killed.

"Are you hurt, Chips?" Tom asked of the carpenter, who was leaning against the main fife rail and pulling off his shirt.

"I'm hurt just enough to make me feel good," replied Chips. "I'll have that Walsh now, if I tear the cabin out of her with my finger nails to get him. See if you can fasten him in, Tom," he added in a whisper.

Tom ran aft, down the after-companion and through the cabin. He found the key in the outside of the mate's door, and his hand turned just as that gentleman tried to open it. Finding himself locked in, Mr. Walsh utilized his window as a port-hole, through which he wasted considerable good ammunition. In the meantime the carpenter had dragged the second mate into the shop and lashed him to the leg of the bench. Tom and Alec now held a council of war to decide how they should dispose of the mate. It wouldn't do to leave him loose in his room, because he would take pot shots at them through the window or the panels of the door. There was no danger of his geting out; the window was too small, and the inch and a half oak door opened inward. They could starve him out, but in the meantime he might kill one or both of them. Chips was busy digging a pistol ball out of the fleshy part of his left arm, and gritting his teeth to show that he enjoyed the process. Suddenly looking up, he said : —

"Tell those fellows to stretch the hose along, Tom; we'll drown him out."

"Good idea," replied Tom. He went forward and found the crew in the forecastle, smoking, and discussing the events of the night. He stuck his head in the door, and called out : —

"All hands on deck and get the hose along — four men to the head pump!"

"Who say so?" asked Russian Finn Jake.

"I say so," replied Tom, stoutly, "and I'll give

you just five seconds to be the first man out, or I'll—"

"All right, sir, I comin'," replied Jake, as, with wonderful alacrity, he snatched the end of the hose from the reel and ran aft with it. As he passed the corner of the house, a shot from the mate's revolver whizzed by his ear. He dropped the hose and ran forward, but Tom made him come back and pull off as much hose as he wanted. All this time a great hammering and sawing was going on in the carpenter shop; so, getting the mainmast between himself and the enemy's works, Tom went in. The second mate sat on the deck, with his back to the bench and glared at him. Tom didn't care for that, but when the villain tried to kick him unawares, he warned him to look out.

"Don't talk to that fellow," said Alec. "If he bothers you, take an axe and split his blasted head open!"

"Why Alec, don't be so bloodthirsty! That would be using them worse than they did me."

"Ho! We've done that already; but they deserve it — the pirates!"

"What are you making?"

"You'll see directly. Say, Tom, you'd better keep a little watch on the crew; there's no knowing what they may be up to."

"That's so; you're right!" And Tom returned

to the deck. They need not have feared the crew, for all hands were under the topgallant forecastle. Not a man of them had the least desire to come aft. The cook was in the galley, getting breakfast as if nothing had happened. Presently the carpenter brought out a shutter, or shield, made of double deck plank. It was about eight feet long by two wide and six inches thick. There was a two-inch auger hole two feet from one end. He called four men and made them carry it aft on the starboard side and up on the poop. Then they fastened a couple of rope's ends to it and lowered it over in front of the mate's window, but about three feet away from it. When it was in place, Alec seized the nozzle of the hose, inserted it in the hole, and cried out:—

"Fire away, Walsh! Fire away now, you thief! I've got a gun too. Come, shake up that pump! Shake it up, or I'll come forward there an' set some of ye up in the boot an' shoe business!"

The men needed no urging. They understood what was going on, and such an opportunity to get square with a mate had never been presented to any of them before. The pump was double banked, and the handles flew merrily, hitting the deck at every stroke like the windlass brakes of a homeward bounder. A three-quarter-inch stream of water that would take a man off his feet went flying through the window into the little seven by nine stateroom. The carpenter, who seemed to feel no annoyance from his wound, worked the nozzle so as to completely drench the room. A few ineffectual shots were fired into the six-inch shutter, then smothered curses were heard, as, half strangled, the mate sought to evade the drowning stream.

"Dern him! I guess his powder is wet," said Alec.

The words were hardly out of his mouth, when a crashing blow was delivered on the inside of the door.

"Oho! It's axes now, hey? Here, Tom, you take the nozzle an' keep it a wigglin', while I stand by to catch him as he comes out!"

CHAPTER II

THE mate was furious, but weak. Disconcerted as he was by the drenching, and hampered by the darkness of his room, he made slow progress battering down the heavy door; for only about one blow in three hit it at all, and those were wild and had but little steam behind them. The carpenter waited for him, well out of range, with a spare gasket.

Presently the door gave way with a crash. Like a half-drowned rat Walsh floundered out, groping wildly and gasping for breath. Before he recovered, the carpenter was upon him, and had him tied.

"'Vast pumpin'! That'll do the water," cried Chips.

Tom dropped the nozzle, passed the word along to the men to "'vast pumpin'," and went to Alec's assistance. Together they dragged the mate, cursing, gasping, and threatening, to the mizzenmast, where they lashed him fast. Tom told him to stop his noise, or he would gag him. The threat had the desired effect, for after a while he relapsed into sullen silence. Tom told Alec to order all hands to lay aft. They came straggling along, hitching up their trousers, and glancing furtively from side to side. They did not relish the idea of obeying the orders of this boy who but yesterday was their forecastle drudge. When they had all tumbled together abaft the mainmast, he made them a little speech.

"Men," said he, "when my father died, he left me in charge of this ship, of which he was master and part owner. He told Mr. Walsh and Mr. Wilkins that I was to take her home; and that they should obey me as they had him. You have seen what they did to me, but you do not know that they intended to wreck her and sell the wreckage, thereby not only robbing the owners, but cheating you out of your hard-earned wages as well. You have seen how they changed the course three days ago. That was for the purpose of running her onto one of the Leeward Islands. I have regained charge of my father's ship, with the assistance of Mr. Webb, who will be my mate, and shall take her home. You will not be required to do anything but the necessary work to get her there; you will have watch and watch from now on, and will get the best grub there is aboard. Relieve the wheel, port watch! Starboard watch, go below!"

They hesitated a moment, and the Norwegian

who had grappled with Tom during the mêlée
stepped a pace to the front, and said : —

"Vell, ma hol' on; ve like to know a little more
about dis —"

"There's only one thing more that it's necessary
for you to know," interrupted Tom, pointing his
finger at the fellow while his eyes snapped omi-
nously, "and that is, that any man who fails in his
duty will be attended to by Mr. Webb and myself."

"Oho, so?"

"Yes, just *so!* Another thing for you to remember is, that we have handles to our names; and
you'll have to use them. Don't think for a moment
that because I have promised to treat you well I
am afraid of you, or that discipline will be relaxed
in the slightest degree. That's all! Go forrard!"

The faces of some of them were a study as they
retreated discontentedly. The "snap" they had
expected to obtain from the new administration
was not forthcoming. There was to be no council of all hands. Their advice was not wanted;
would not be tolerated. No matter who was captain, they were nothing but common jacks. After
they were gone, Tom and Mr. Webb looked after
their prisoners. They ironed them with their
hands behind their backs. Then they cut pieces
of chain and fastened the second mate to the carpenter's bench, and the mate to the mizzenmast in

the forward cabin. They relieved the second mate of his gag, — for which he was profoundly thankful, — and Tom told them both that, if they behaved themselves and gave no extra trouble, they should have chairs to sit in during the day, and their own bedding at night. He fed them from the cabin table and gave them two hours' exercise daily, one in the forenoon and one in the afternoon.

The mate remained surly and vicious to the end; but on the third day Wilkins expressed a desire to confess. After a consultation with Mr. Webb, it was decided to allow him to confess in the presence of all hands, who should sign the confession as witnesses. Wilkins demurred to this, alleging that he feared the crew; but on Tom's assurance that he should be protected he finally agreed. On the fourth day after the recapture of the ship all hands were called aft, and Wilkins, seated in a chair on the break of the poop, between Tom and Alec, while the crew remained down on the main deck, confessed as follows: —

"The night after Captain Benton died, Mr. Walsh called me into his room and asked me if I was as good as I was big. I thought he wanted to fight me, and I says, 'Why, what's the matter, Mr. Walsh?' 'I want to know,' says he, 'if you are a game man.' 'Well, I don't know, sir, what you

might call game,' says I, 'but I've been second
and third mate of some ships as wasn't exactly
Sunday Schools,' says I. 'Oh!' says he, 'you
don't understand. What I mean is, are you game
for a big job? Here's a fine ship,' says he, 'an'
I'm cap'n of her—I don't care nothing about that
kid; you know a cap'n can do what he likes
with his ship. If he should take a notion to sell
ship an' cargo instead of takin' 'em home, the
owners can go an' whistle. It's only a breach o'
trust, an' they can't do nothing to ye.' Of course
I tumbled right away. 'What do ye want me to
do?' says I. 'Only to put half o' this ship an'
cargo in yer pocket,' says he, 'the same as I'm a
goin' to do with the other half.'

"I was a bit flabbergastered at first, it was so
sudden, but we talked it over a good deal, an' I
made up my mind that, as long as he was bound
to do it I couldn't stop him, an' I'd be a fool not
to take half. At first we decided to take her into
St. Thomas, an' sell her there. Then as we talked
it over, Mr. Walsh said there was so much longitude to make to get to St. Thomas that just as
like as not he'd pile her up on some of these
blasted little nigger islands before he got there;
'cause he said he wasn't an expert at longitude.
But we decided that even if we had such bad
luck as that, we'd probably be able to sell the

wreck at a good figure, so we commenced to look at it in that light. Then one day I asked him how it would be if we happened to run across a man-o'-war in St. Thomas. 'By gum!' says he, 'I never thought o' that! The kid would get in his fine work there sure, and we daresn't kill him neither. I don't know but they'd make it out piracy.' So then we commenced to figger out a new plan, an' what we finally agreed on was, to beach her on one of the Virgin Islands, get the crew, all but ourselves, into the longboat with enough dead weight in her in the shape of provisions to sink her, and then shoot her full of holes from the ship's rail. If any of the men tried to swim ashore or to climb aboard we would shoot them. Then we would get out one of the small boats and go to St. Thomas, where we would either sell the wreck or bring back help to get her off, according to how badly she was fixed. There wouldn't be any witnesses against us, and we would say that the crew had cleared out in the longboat." He raised his face to the heavens and added: "That's the truth, so help me God!"

When Wilkins concluded his tale of villany, Jake made a short but violent harangue to the crew in Scandinavian. With a ferocious shout they started for the cabin door to get at Walsh. Mr. Webb leaped over the rail, and, dropping on deck in front of them, interposed his burly form in the doorway; while Tom, dragging Wilkins after him, ran down the after-companion and reënforced Mr. Webb with two pairs of revolvers. The men were raving out on deck, and swearing in a mixture of English and Swedish that they would hang Walsh. Tom and Mr. Webb, being now armed, stepped boldly out among them. Tom argued with them. He reminded them that Mr. Webb and himself had discovered the plot, and without any assistance from them had retaken the ship. He guaranteed that the prisoners should be tried by due process of law, and asked the men to go forward.

"Not till ve get dot Valsh," yelled the Norwegian.

Tom partly lost his temper. "If any one of you enters this cabin," he shouted, "I'll shoot him!"

"Shoot an' be hanged!" came from the crowd in a howling chorus. "You ain't no better vat dey are you'self!"

That made him mad altogether. He clubbed his revolvers, and Mr. Webb following suit, they ran forward at a gallop, delivering several stinging blows as they ran.

"If I had a cannon I'd blow the bows out of her. We have to fight all hands fore an' aft," said Tom as they were returning aft.

"You're feeding them too high; they can't stand it," was Mr. Webb's answer.

"I'll be hanged if I don't believe you're right," said Tom; "I'll shorten up on their grub to-morrow."

He carefully wrote down Wilkins' confession, and, after reading it to him and getting his signature, he made all hands sign it. As he was returning to the after-cabin with it, Walsh asked him to take a kink out of his chain, as it was hurting him. When Tom got near enough, the mate snatched the paper from him and tore it up. Then he had it all to do over again. Fearing the crew might surprise them, as they still acted ugly, they removed the prisoners to the lazaret, and never again went on deck un-armed.

Tom eagerly sought the track chart. He thought Walsh might possibly have been bright enough to refrain from pricking the course on it. So he was pleased on finding that the mate had possessed no such forethought. He had not only pricked the course made, but had traced a course to St. Thomas, with various branches to several islets in the neigh-borhood; thus furnishing abundant proof of his evil designs. Tom had a job teaching Mr. Webb to note chronometer time. It took him two hours to master it at all, and then he was so unreliable that Tom de-cided to make a landfall and obtain a new departure. As they were farther north than he expected, he con-tinued on the westerly course, to the crew's surprise, until he raised Turk's Island. He then set a course that would bring them into the Gulf Stream, and having thoroughly subdued the crew, they proceeded without further incident to Portland.

CHAPTER III

ONE bright June morning, Captain Rufus Blake
was busily scanning letters in his private office.
He was a rather short, square man, with thick
grizzled hair, beetling brows and a firm jaw. He
was now senior captain and manager of a line of
sailing-vessels, mostly employed in the trade between Portland, Maine, and South American ports.
While at sea he had earned the nickname of "Bully
Blake," and though it stuck to him as nicknames
will, he was now so eminently respectable that it
was never applied to him openly. It was only
used by the disgruntled, behind his back, for Captain Blake was powerful as well as respectable.

His daughter and only child, Kitty, stood near
him watching from the window the busy scene on
the wharf below, where stevedores "wrestled" with
heavy bales, boxes, and barrels; while truckmen, who

were continually bringing or taking away the valuable merchandise, drove their horses recklessly
among the men. The result was an interchange
of billingsgate that would have terribly shocked
almost any other young person; but Kitty Blake
had been familiar with it all her life. She disliked
it, of course, but would have been surprised at
missing it. It was to her merely a natural adjunct
of the scene; as much so as the red flannel shirts
and soiled and ragged overalls.

She was quite a slip of a girl, fifteen years of
age, rather tall, quick, and active. Her brown
cheeks and bright eyes told a tale of robust health,
due to abundant out-door exercise. As she stood
there, an occasional sidelong glance at her father,
and a nervous tapping of her toe, indicated her
impatience at being shut up in the stuffy office
on such a glorious morning. But Captain Blake
had said: "Come down to the office, Kate; I may
want you," and that was an order.

The office door opened noiselessly, and the obsequious head clerk, with a grimace intended for a
smile, reported: "The *Columbia* is in the offing, sir,
—colors at half-mast."

"All right!" snapped Captain Blake.

"Oh, papa!" exclaimed Kitty, with a startled,
half-frightened air, "what do you suppose can be
the matter aboard the *Columbia?*"

"How do you s'pose I know? I ain't there, am I?" He looked at his watch a moment, closed it with a snap, and remarked: "Let's see; it wants an hour yet of low water. She'll not gain much, beating against wind and tide; guess I'll get a tug and board her."

"You needn't get a tug, papa," interjected Kitty; "the *Sprite* lies right here at the wharf, and I can set you aboard quicker than you could go with a tug."

"All right then, come along and bear a hand," replied the old fellow, quickly, the cheapness of the method appealing to his economical sense. "Benton's made a long passage," he continued; "I wonder what's the trouble. Yeller Jack, I s'pose; what do they let their men go ashore for? I never did. Let 'em have plenty of scrapin' and scrubbin' when there's no cargo alongside, and yeller Jack won't trouble 'em. He ought to have been here a week ago," he added to himself as he stumped surlily at Kitty's side, who, now that she was in the open air and bound for a sail in her beloved *Sprite*, was all animation and "kinks," as her father said. The trim little sloop yacht was rubbing her nose contentedly against the piles when they stepped aboard. The *Sprite* was Kitty's treasure, her one ewe lamb. Captain Blake had bought her at a bargain the previous season, and Kitty had at

once developed into an expert and ardent yachts-
woman. The *Sprite* was the last pleasure craft
to be laid up in the fall, she was thoroughly overhauled and painted during the winter, and the first
out in the spring. Kitty passed a great part of
her time sailing the little craft, sometimes with a
merry party of friends, but oftener alone, cruising
round the many islands in the harbor, or, animated
by the spirit of discovery, investigating every bay
and inlet for miles around. It was only her
father's order that had kept her ashore on this
occasion. She knew the *Columbia* was overdue,
and had planned a long sail seaward on the ebb
tide in search of her.

Captain Blake seated himself ponderously in the
stern sheets, thereby raising her bow nearly out of
water, while Kitty, with the dexterity born of long
practice, cast off the painter and shoved off.

She hauled her jib to windward until the boat's
head paid off sufficiently, and then, hauling aft the
jib and main sheets, was off like a lamplighter.
The stern and silent man was a grim contrast to
the vivacious girl at his side, full of life and the
enjoyment that comes of youth, health, and the
pursuit of a favorite pastime.

As the birdlike craft came opposite the street
openings on her way out of the harbor, vicious little
puffs would heel her almost to the capsizing point.

Being in such bad trim, she was inclined to toss her head off the wind; but Kitty had not been sailing there all summer for nothing. She knew just where at each street she would first feel the puff. Easing her jib sheet, she would give her just a hint of lee helm. The luff of the mainsail would shiver, as, like a lady on a ballroom floor, the *Sprite* would skim safely across the treacherous spot. Captain Blake said nothing, but he saw it all.

As they drew out clear of Cape Elizabeth, they made out the *Columbia* six or eight miles to leeward on the port tack, ensign at half-mast. Kitty decided that the ship would tack within the next fifteen or twenty minutes. So, instead of heading for her, she shaped a course that would intercept her on her return. Her father observed and understood this also, but made no comment; he sat silently watching the ship with her emblem of mourning.

Kitty's judgment proved to be correct; the ship tacked just where she had expected her to. The *Sprite* sped merrily on her course, throwing the spray far out to leeward and leaving a wake like a steamer. She crossed the *Columbia's* bow a good cable-length ahead, rounded to under her lee, and with helm amidships and sails flapping dropped in alongside in such a masterly manner, that even Captain Rufus felt constrained to grunt a grudg-

D

ing: "Not bad! Not bad at all!" which was more
gratifying than a gold medal to Kitty.

Tom saw and recognized the *Sprite* as soon as
she stuck her nose round the cape. It was he who
had given Kitty her first lesson in handling the
little craft, and many a jolly sail had the boy and
girl enjoyed in her when the *Columbia* was in port.
He had a man ready in the fore-chains with a heav-
ing-line, and two more getting the side ladder over.
Kitty caught the line and dropped in alongside;
Captain Blake ascended slowly, as befitted his rank
and avoirdupois. Kitty skipped lightly up the ladder, and dropped like a sparrow on deck, in time
to hear her father ask Tom where Captain Benton
was.

"My father died at sea, sir," replied Tom, sadly.
"We buried him off Cape St. Roque."

"Who is that? The pilot?"

"Yes, sir."

"Where is the mate?"

"After father died, the mates attempted to wreck
the ship in the West Indies, sir; the carpenter and
I took her from them and brought her home. They
are below in irons."

"Humph! hoist the police flag!"

"Ay, ay, sir."

Without a word of thanks or commendation to
the boy, who, at the imminent risk of his life, had

saved his ship and brought her home, Captain Blake dived into the cabin to look at the manifest; and remained there overhauling the ship's papers until the pilot let go her anchor.

The instant her father's head disappeared below the companion slide, Kitty took both of Tom's hands in her own, and with tears rolling down her brown cheeks, exclaimed, "Oh, Tom, I'm so sorry."

Tom could hardly restrain his own feelings; but he gulped hard and winked fast.

"This has been an awful passage, Kitty," said he — "awful! It seems years since father died; and I have been through everything but death since. I feel like an old man. If Mr. Webb hadn't stood by me, we should all have been dead long ago — murdered by the mates. Then the crew tried to get the upper hand of us, and I haven't had a wink of sound sleep for the last ten days. Your father may thank the carpenter that the ship ever got here. I couldn't have done anything alone. See; this is the way we've had to go." He threw back his pea jacket and showed the two revolvers.

"Why, you poor boy! I should think you have had a hard time. You must take a good long sleep the first thing you do, or you will be sick. Then, after you get all rested, we'll go sailing again as we used to. I've found a regular cave on a little

island about twenty miles to the eastward. I took
down some dishes, and often play house down
there all day by myself. I'll take you down some
day if you're a good boy; we'll take some provisions along, and you can take your hooks and lines
so as to catch fish for the table, and we'll have a
regular dinner. Won't that be nice? How do you
like the *Sprite?* Papa let me have her all painted
up just as I wanted her. Don't you think she
looks fine? That gold stripe alone cost ten dollars."

Tom smiled at her attempt to make him forget
his troubles. He admired the *Sprite's* new paint,
praised her taste in the choice of colors and style,
and promised to visit her cave at an early day.

"I wonder what will become of me now?" he
asked. "Father was going to ship me third mate
next voyage; but now I suppose I'll have to go
before the mast, and consider myself lucky to get
even that."

Kitty's eyes opened very wide indeed. "Before
the mast!" she cried. "Well, I guess not; papa
will surely appoint you captain of the *Columbia*
after all you have gone through to bring her home."

Tom could not refrain from laughing at her
enthusiasm. "Why, they don't make seventeen-
year-old boys captains of ships," he replied.

"I don't see why not, if they're able. You
brought her home, didn't you? I'm sure no regular

captain could do any more than that, and some of them don't even do as well."

Before Tom had a chance to say more, Captain Blake came on deck and told Kitty he was ready to go ashore. "When the police get here, if they ever do, turn your prisoners over to them," he said shortly to Tom.

"Ay, ay, sir," Tom replied.

As Kitty was going over the rail, she told Tom she should expect him to dinner as soon as the ship got to her berth.

"Come, come, I'm in a hurry!" said Captain Blake. "Mr. Benton will have no time to come up to the house for dinner," he added inhospitably. Tom felt hurt by both his words and manner, for he had always been a welcome guest at the Blake home, but now he felt that somehow things were changed.

Six weeks later, Mr. Walsh was sentenced to twenty years at hard labor in State prison. Mr. Wilkins, having turned State's evidence, got off with five. After the trial, the carpenter, hearing that his father was dangerously ill, asked for his pay. He got it, and that was all, with nothing whatever in return for his extraordinary services, though Tom had enlarged on them in court, and at every possible opportunity. Before he left for home, he bade Tom an affectionate good-bye and warned him to look out for Bully Blake. "I tell you," said he, while his eyes flashed with just anger, " he's no good! He'll get the best of you if you don't watch him. I called on him and told him I was going home — thought maybe he'd forgotten himself, you know, and I'd give him a chance to remember. What do you s'pose he said ? "

" I'm sure I don't know."

" 'Well, what of it ? ' That's all he said — not another word. And I says, 'Nothin', you blasted ol' hunks; I only just stepped in to tell ye so ye wouldn't worry for fear I'd got lost.' An' he never turned a hair. Oh, he's tougher nor whale meat. Well, be good, Tom. I may run across ye sometime again. Be sure and keep your weather eye skinned for old Blake. He's the worst I ever saw."

Tom felt a sense of great loneliness come over him when honest Alec left. The last of the old ties was broken, and hereafter he would have to depend entirely on himself. He was left in charge of the ship, but after the cargo was discharged, he had little to do; business was dull, and the outward-bound cargo arrived very slowly. Kitty frequently came down and carried him off for a sail. He knew he ought not to go, but how was a fellow to resist when coaxed so hard to do the very thing he particularly wished to ? The ship could watch herself, so Tom and Kitty passed many a pleasant afternoon on the *Sprite*, skimming over the smooth water of the bay, racing with other small craft, and visiting the islands.

One day she told him her father had gone to Bath to look at a new vessel. She proposed that they should go for a sail during the afternoon, and that he should take dinner with her at the house on their return. Her father was not expected back until the following day, and she had lots of things to show him, — pictures, books, and games. There was no freight alongside nor any expected, so Tom readily agreed. They had a splendid time; they raced with a little snub-nosed tug and got beaten, and they called at the light-house and were treated to cold milk and pumpkin pie by the keeper's wife, who knew and admired Kitty. The keeper himself was a superannuated captain, who had sailed with Captain Blake years ago. They kept bees in their little reservation, and Kitty never tired of watching the busy little insects and listening to motherly old Mrs. Kimberly's tales of their wonderful sagacity. But time was flying, so they reëmbarked and took a long cruise outside the island where the long Atlantic swells made the little *Sprite* jump and rear like a spirited colt. They boarded a fisherman, and the captain gave them half a dozen fresh mackerel for their supper. They told stories, sang songs, and enjoyed themselves as only boys and girls without a care can.

When they judged that it wanted about an hour
of sundown, they started for Portland and dinner;
their appetites sharpened to a razor edge by the
salt air. It was a dead head wind, but the tide
was with them, and Kitty astonished Tom by her
knowledge of the currents in the bay. When he
supposed they were off for a three-mile tack, she
would shout merrily: "Ha-a-ard alee!" jam her
tiller down, and bring the boat round spinning.
Then when Tom asked in surprise why she had
tacked so soon, she would show him a counter-cur-
rent that would have set them half a mile to leeward if she had allowed the *Sprite* to enter it, and
go off into a long technical explanation of the
set, strength, and direction of the various currents
at this time of tide, that would have done credit to
the oldest pilot in the port. Tom listened in admiration, amazement, and something of awe.

"How many more tacks will I have to make to
get in, Tom?" Tom measured the distance crit-
ically with his eye, took plenty of time to think it
over, and answered, "Four." Kitty laughed at him.

"Can you do it in four?" she asked.

"Oh, no," said he; "I'd be very well satisfied to
do it in six; but you know the water so well, I expect you to do lots better than I could. I'll give
you five. If you do it in five tacks, you'll do better
even than I think you can."

"Suppose I do it in three?"

"Oh, you can't!"

"I can't, hey? Well, now, I'll show you, Mr. Deepwater, that there are some things you don't learn at sea. I'm going to Portland on the next tack."

"Nonsense, Kitty, you won't come within two miles of it on the next tack."

"Well, all right, you'll see — Hard alee!"

She tacked, but never let the sails fill, and barely kept steerageway on her. The *Sprite* lay there with her sails shivering, and Tom thought she had missed stays. He was going to put out an oar and swing the boat's head off the wind, when Kitty cried merrily : —

"If you don't sit down, Tom Benton, I'll put you in irons as you did the mates of the *Columbia*. I'm captain here."

Tom laughed, said, "All right, Cap', excuse me, I thought you had your *ship* in irons," and sat down. He soon saw what she was doing. She had got into a regular millrace, and was holding the *Sprite* in it, while it swept her to windward like a steamer.

"I declare, Kitty," said Tom, when he saw that she was making good her promise to go to Portland on that tack, "you are wasting your time sailing this dingy. You ought to apply for a pilot's license. Why, if old Jordan had known as much about this harbor as you do, the *Columbia* would have been at anchor two hours sooner than she was, the other day."

It was a healthy, happy pair of young people who finally rounded to at Kitty's private berth. Tom helped her to furl the sails and make all snug, though she threatened more than once to call a policeman and have him arrested for not obeying her order to sit still until she gave him permission to land. They chatted gaily on their way to the house. Kitty told him of the good things she had ordered for dinner, — to which the fresh mackerel were to be added, — and they enjoyed the feast in anticipation.

Imagine their dismay, on arriving at the gate, to see Captain Blake seated in a garden chair, smoking a huge meerschaum and reading the paper.

"Why, papa!" exclaimed Kitty, in mild consternation, "I thought you were in Bath. Here's Tom come to dine with us."

The old gentleman gave them a sidelong glance from under his shaggy brows, and asked: "What are you doing here, Mr. Benton? Are you not in charge of the *Columbia?*"

"Yes, sir," replied Tom, sheepishly.

"Go inside, Kate! what are you standing there

for? You had better go aboard and take care of your vessel, Mr. Benton; and you may call at my office to-morrow morning at ten o'clock. I have something to say to you."

"Ay, ay, sir!" replied Tom. With a sorrowful nod to Kitty, — who threw him a kiss from behind a rosebush, scowling at her father's back at the same time, — Tom returned hungrily on board. While gnawing at hard tack and cold salt horse, his thoughts dwelt with vague forebodings on the meeting with Captain Blake on the morrow. His recollection of Alec's warning, together with the captain's strange aversion, which had been so evident since the *Columbia's* arrival, worried him greatly.

Next morning, at ten o'clock sharp, Tom entered Captain Blake's outer office and sent in his name. He was kept waiting an hour. Twice during that time, he caught a glance of the captain's burly form through the partly open door, and observed that he sat by the window, looking idly out and smoking a cigar. At last Tom was allowed to enter the sanctum. He bade his employer a respectful good morning, and received an inarticulate grunt in return. The captain was now seated at his desk, scanning a very formidable looking document. He did not look up, nor waste any time on preliminaries or unnecessary courtesy; but plunged at once into the subject.

"I have sent for you, Mr. Benton," he said, "to square up the account between you, your late father, and this firm. As I shall not require your services after to-day, I will hand you the balance."

Half dazed, Tom sank uninvited into a chair and gazed open-mouthed at the back of Captain Blake's head; noting the peculiar movement of the stiff gray mutton-chop whiskers as he read aloud a long statement. Tom paid not the slightest attention while the old gentleman glibly repeated the figures. He was suddenly recalled from his wool-gathering by the harsh voice of the captain saying, "Sign there!"

He took the proffered pen and signed where he was bid. With a lordly air, and a grand flourish, the captain handed him a check for one hundred and thirty-eight dollars and twenty-seven cents. He stared blankly at the check for a moment, and then asked, "What is this for, sir?"

"Balance due you as wages, and as your father's heir," replied the captain.

"Why, father owned stock in the company!" replied Tom, in amazement.

"I have just read you a full statement of your father's account with this company, and you as his heir have signed a receipt in full. My time is valuable — good morning."

Tom was now himself again. "Do you mean to

tell me, Captain Blake," he asked, with flashing eye and quivering lip, "that this check represents my father's savings for a lifetime? I don't care how valuable your time is; I won't accept any such settlement as that." And Tom indignantly threw the check on the desk.

Bully Blake sprang to his feet, his face livid with rage. He seized Tom by the shoulder, and shaking his great brown fist in the boy's face, roared out: "What do you mean by such insolence, sir? Do you know that your father was an embezzler, a scoundrel, and a thief? Instead of paying you, I should have been justified in applying your wages to the liquidation of his indebtedness, and I might have sent you to jail."

This vilification of his dead father — whom Tom had always regarded as the noblest of men — was too much for his outraged feelings. He replied in bitterly insulting language; such language as is frequently heard on board ship, and with which Bully Blake was thoroughly familiar. He even threatened the old man with severe bodily chastisement then and there. Captain Blake thrust the check into Tom's coat pocket, and, seizing him by the throat, he yelled, "Get out!" Before Tom could offer any resistance, a door was quietly opened in his rear, a pair of sinewy arms encircled his waist, and, with the assistance of the obsequious head clerk,

Captain Blake forced him — struggling and kicking — past the grinning occupants of the outer office to the front door. The door was opened, he was kicked flying into the middle of the street, and warned to clear out or he would be locked up. He picked himself up, boiling with impotent rage. His feelings were hurt worse than his person; he had heard of people being kicked out of places, but had always regarded it as a figure of speech, — now he knew better. He brushed the dirt from his clothes, knocked a dent out of his hat, and made haste to escape from the rapidly gathering crowd.

On turning a corner he was confronted by the black and gold sign of Mr. "Theophilus Naylor, Attorney and Counsellor at Law." Tom knew Mr. Naylor, as he had frequently visited his office in company with his father, who sometimes had business requiring legal advice. He entered and asked to see the lawyer. The clerk took his name in, and though Tom told him his business was urgent, he was allowed a half-hour in which to collect his thoughts. When he was finally admitted, he found Mr. Naylor ostensibly very busy peering over a lot of papers. He had always been very affable when Tom came to the office with his father, but now he merely glanced at him, and asked coldly, "Well, young man, what can I do for you this morning?"

"You remember me, don't you, Mr. Naylor?" asked Tom.

"Captain Benton's son, I believe?"

"Yes, sir. You always attended to father's business, so I thought — "

"Excuse me," interrupted Mr. Naylor, with polite frigidity, "I have done but very little business for your father."

"Well, you knew about his owning shares in the line, didn't you?"

"I don't just recall at the moment what the nature of the business was, in which I acted for Captain Benton. I certainly do not feel competent to speak offhand in regard to any investments which your late father may have made."

In spite of his chilling reception, Tom told the lawyer — who continued to busy himself with his papers — the whole story. An awkward silence followed, finally broken by Mr. Naylor, who asked in a very discouraging manner, "Well, what do you wish me to do?"

"I want you to sue Captain Blake. He has robbed me, and I know it," replied Tom, flatly.

"I should advise you to go very slowly, my young friend," replied the lawyer, solemnly. "Litigation is an expensive luxury and a very unsatisfactory remedy in most cases. It is common talk that your father's affairs were very much involved.

Very much involved, indeed. And as for the grave
charge which you make so recklessly against Captain Blake, let me advise you to be careful. Captain
Blake's character is unimpeachable. It has stood
the test of a long business career, during which
he has lived directly in the public eye. He
has — "

"Never mind! That will do!" interrupted Tom,
impetuously. "I've heard enough! I see how the
wind lies!" and, without even bidding the wily
man of law good day, he went out, slamming the
door behind him.

CHAPTER IV

KITTY PROVES HERSELF "TRUE BLUE" — THE FIRST KISS — A STORMY INTERVIEW WITH BULLY BLAKE — TOM LEAVES PORTLAND — THE SAILORS' HOME IN NEW YORK — A BENEVOLENT EX-CAPTAIN — SANDBAGGED — A PRISONER — TO THE WORK-HOUSE — TO THE CHARITY HOSPITAL

FROM force of habit, Tom went toward the *Columbia*. As he was striding angrily along, head down, Kitty hailed him gleefully, "Ship ahoy!" She was sailing in circles just abreast of where he stood. He would have preferred not to see her just then, but she steered in alongside the wharf and said :—

"I have been aboard the *Columbia* looking for you, Tom. Where have you been? Come on and take a sail — there's a fine breeze, — a soldier's wind, 'fair a' comin' an' agoin'.' Why, what's the matter?" she asked, in a tone of disappointment and alarm as Tom dolefully shook his head. "Has papa been growling? You mustn't mind him.

I don't.   Come, get aboard if you're coming with me, and don't stand there like a loon on one leg."

Her light banter relieved the tension, and, reflecting that he was now his own master, he accepted her invitation. He sat gloomily in the stern sheets while Kitty worked her passage skilfully out of the harbor.   Once arrived in the open bay, she trimmed her sheets and set a course for Long Island, which was a favorite picnic ground of theirs, and, turning to Tom, asked : —

"What did papa say to you, Tom? was he real mad ?"

"Yes, pretty mad."

"Well, what did he say?   You needn't be so awful short about it."

"I guess you'd better put back, Kitty.   I know I ain't very good company to-day, but I can't help it."

"Tom Benton, if you don't tell me what the matter is, I'll put back and land you, and never speak to you again as long as I live.   I know papa has riled you, but you needn't be mad at me — I — I — think you're real mean — there!"

There were tears in her voice.   Tom could not see her eyes, as she kept her face turned per-sistently to windward; but her tone and manner, so eloquent of distress, subdued him at once.

"I'm not mad at you, Kitty," he replied; "the

Lord knows you are the last person in the world I could imagine myself angry with. But I'm terribly in the dumps. My cake is all dough again!"

"There! I knew it. Papa has been jawing you, and you have believed everything he said; but don't you do it. Why, Tom, he talks just the same to me, sometimes, but I'm used to it. I just let him go ahead and say nothing, and he soon gets over it. Don't you mind anything he said to you; he'll forget all about it by the time we get back — I know him."

" No, he won't, Kitty, nor I won't either; I s'pose I may as well out with it: your father has paid me off — I am discharged and —"

" Discharged! Tom Benton, what are you talking about? Discharged! Do you mean to say that my father has discharged you after the way you brought the *Columbia* home ? "

"Yes, Kitty, that is just what I mean to say."

"Why, I can hardly believe it; what did you do?"

" You know as much about that as I do, Kitty; you heard him tell me to call at the office this morning, and when I called, he discharged me."

" I'll tell you what I think, Tom ; somebody has been telling papa lies about you. I'll bet it's that Jorkins, the head clerk. He don't like it because you and I go out together. I hate him; but he's always smirking and smiling, and trying to talk to me — "

"Down helm, Kitty! Down helm!" cried Tom excitedly; "I'll go back and punch the head off that Jorkins; I owe it to him on my own account, anyway."

"Pshaw, Tom! never mind Jorkins; I don't care anything about him, and I'll talk to papa this evening and make it all right — you see if I don't. You call at the office again to-morrow morning, and I bet it will be all right. I know how to come it over him. I've done it lots of times."

"You can't do it this time, Kitty. It's no use, and you mustn't try. Your father an' I have had a big row; he said things about — about my dead father that I wouldn't — wouldn't take from the — the President of the United States — " Here, in spite of his seventeen years, Tom buried his face in his hands and sobbed aloud.

"What did he say about your father, Tom?" asked Kitty, soothingly.

"Never mind; I don't want to tell you; he's your father, an' it wouldn't do any good for us to talk about it; but, Kitty, he angered me so that I talked back to him as I never did to a grown person before. So you see it's all over, and Portland ain't big enough to hold us both. He won't go, so I must. I think I'll go to New York and work my way up. I can do it. Thousands of other boys have; my father did."

"Oh, don't go away off like that; I can't bear to have you. We'll never see each other again, I know we shan't." Kitty was crying as if her heart would break. Now that the prospect of a permanent separation obtruded itself upon them, they each realized how much their happiness had depended on each other's company. Tom tried to comfort her, but his own feelings were so dismal that he made but little progress. They sailed in silence for a while, then Kitty said : —

"I don't think you ought to go away, Tom. It isn't good for you to leave all your friends and go off among perfect strangers."

"Friends!" said Tom, cynically, as he remembered his reception by the lawyer. "What friends have I in Portland? When it becomes known that your father has discharged me, nobody will care to be my friend. No, Kitty, outside of yourself, I have no *friend* to leave. I tell you I've *got* to go, and the sooner the better."

They sailed around Long Island — neither caring to land — and returned to the city. Kitty's sound sense enabled her to see the force of Tom's argument. So, like the brave girl that she was, she subdued her own feelings of sorrow at the loss of the only companion she had, and applied herself to the task of cheering him. While they were still a mile from the harbor he said to her : —

"Kitty, you are the only person in the whole world — now that father is dead — that cares for me. I ain't afraid to go — I can make out. Thousands of other fellows have gone off, as I am going now, and come back rich. That is what I'm going to do; I'll never come back until I'm captain of as fine a ship as your father ever commanded. It will be an uphill job, I know, and it will be a great help to me if I can remember that somebody is thinking of me and wishing me success. You will, won't you, Kitty?"

"You know I will, you poor boy; I'll think of you always and remember you in my prayers every night; and, Tom, I want you to write to me every chance you have, and I will to you, too."

"I don't suppose I'll have much chance, Kitty; you know sailors don't as a rule; but say, Kitty."

"What is it, Tom?"

"We are getting pretty close in — I'm going away to-day —"

"Yes?"

"Do you mind — kissing me good-bye?"

Tom's face was as red as the sun on a hot summer's morning. Kitty blushed, too, but she had the courage of her convictions. Without a word she put her disengaged arm around his neck and for the first time their lips met in a kiss of innocent boy and girl love. After that, they both felt differently.

There was a sense of mutual ownership ; they were closer to each other than they had ever been before. Tom was now sure he could safely have told Kitty of all that had passed between her father and himself, but he would spare her. Kitty felt that it was *her* Tom who was going away, and she talked to him in a motherly way, giving him lots of good advice, and calling him *dear*. All of which Tom found very gratifying, and he wished that he had made the proposition hours — ay, days and weeks — ago.

As Kitty jammed her helm alee and luffed round the head of the wharf to her berth, Captain Blake — his usually surly face like a thunder cloud — stood on the stringpiece, looking straight at them. They furled their sails and made the boat fast, while he stood silently glaring down at them, then, hand in hand, they came up the water-soaked steps. Kitty's cheeks were flushed, but she went up to her angry father fearlessly.

"Go home this instant, Kate!" said Captain Blake, his voice trembling with rage. "And you, sir," he continued, turning to Tom, "if I ever catch you with my daughter again, I'll cane you till you can't stand. Do you hear?"

"Oh, papa!" exclaimed Kitty, pleadingly.

"No, you won't," replied Tom, stoutly; "I'm not in your employ now, and I won't take any orders from you."

Captain Blake raised his heavy cane. He was livid with rage. Flecks of foam dropped from his purple lips upon his beard. He was a horrible sight. Kitty rushed to her father's aid, at the same time begging Tom to go. Desiring to spare Kitty the annoyance of witnessing a quarrel between her father and himself, Tom turned a corner, and, calling a dray, hastened on board the *Columbia*. The sooner he left now, the better, he decided; so he soon had his dunnage on the dray, and, telling the driver to wait for him at the Boston and Maine station, he cashed his check at the ship chandler's, and was soon miles away from Portland.

The next morning on arriving in New York, Tom inquired of the line of vociferous hackmen who formed a gauntlet across the exit from the railroad station, if any of them could take him to the Sailors' Home. They swarmed about him like flies, each declaring himself the only one capable. With genuine Yankee shrewdness, Tom demanded to know the fare. "Five dollars!" "Take ye fer four, boss! four dollars an' de finest hack in town!" "Tree dollars, boss! Hey, mister, I'll take ye fer tree!" And so they haggled, beating each other down and abusing each other shamefully, until a bright young fellow forced himself through the crowd, and, seizing Tom's sleeve, said: " Hey, boss, don't ye mind none er dem ducks; dey don' know where de Sailors'

Home is. Come wit Barney. I'll take ye fer *nuttin!* Now, den, wat's de matter wit dat?"

Tom laughed. "You're the man!" said he, "Do you mean it?"

"Dat's wat I does! Come 'ere!" He led Tom to his hack. Opening the door, he waved his hand grandly toward the interior. "W'at's de matter wit dat, hey?" he demanded. "Fit for an alderman, ain't it? I should say so! Git right in dere an' make yerself comfortable! Put yer feet on de seat if yer wants to! It's your hack! Got any baggage? Gimme yer checks!" •

He returned shortly, accompanied by a porter; between them they had Tom's chest and bag. When the baggage was loaded, the driver stuck his head in the door and said: "I had ter give de porter tenpence ter help carry de trunk; but dat's all right, I ain't kickin'." Without waiting for an answer, he slammed the door, jumped on the box, cracked his whip, and away they rattled. It was a long ride across town from the station to James Street. Tom employed the time watching the strange sights, and wondering at the disinterestedness of the hackman. If all business in New York was transacted on a similar basis, he reflected that he had come to the right town. After driving through blocks of squalid, filthy streets, they stopped in front of the worst-looking den Tom had yet seen. The driver jumped down, opened the door with a flourish, and said: "Here ye are, boss! How's dat fer a free ride, hey?"

"Is this the Sailors' Home?" asked Tom, surveying the vile rookery with frank disgust. Its appearance was indeed far from prepossessing. The front room was a gin mill of the lowest type. There was a show window streaked with dirt and festooned with "Irish pennants," and one pane of it splintered, and fished with a brown paper patch. Inside it, by way of ornament, there was a stuffed penguin, with a heavy starboard list, as though the squall that sprung the glass had shifted its sawdust ballast. This derelict bird was supported on one side by a swordfish's sword, and on the other by a pot-bellied demijohn — both equally flyblown. There were two wooden settles, one on each side of the door, and end on to the street. Their black, grease-polished backs were ornamented by numerous jackknife carvings, representing notches, stars, anchors, and crucifixes. Further than this, the nautical amateur artists had not ventured. One of them was occupied by a filthy brute lying at full length, his head hanging nearly to the ground, his purple and swollen face covered with flies, while from his open mouth he emitted a series of drunken snores. Two rather decent-looking fellows occupied the other one.

They utilized the space between them on the seat as a card table, and were playing a game of bluff.

The interior of this kennel was, if possible, less prepossessing than the exterior. A low ceiling was festooned with scalloped and many-colored fly-paper, fancifully perforated, and dingy with age, having evidently served its purpose with the flies. There was a low bar at one side, which harmonized with the general filth. The floor was covered two inches deep with a fragrant mass of sawdust, saturated with beer slops, tobacco juice, and such other bar-room flotsam as had accumulated during the week. Four men, clad in cheap cotton trousers, and shirts of varying shades of weather-beaten blue, slouched against the bar, gazing stolidly — anywhere.

In answer to Tom's question, the Jehu replied, that it was indeed the Sailors' Home, and a finer place couldn't be found in a day's ride.

"Hey, youse!" he cried to the card-players, "w'y don't ye's lend a hand wit de cap'n's clo'es? Ye's won't hang back w'en it comes to bracin' agin de bar an' drinkin' 'is healt', will ye's?"

"All right! All right, boss; yust as you say," answered one, as they came cheerfully to the front and carried in the dunnage. Tom followed the hackman — who was greeted by the ruby-nosed, black-moustached functionary behind the bar, as an old acquaintance — into the place.

"Hey, Mike!" said the driver, "dis bloke was astin' for de Sailors' Home, so I brung 'im along."

"Dat's right, Barney! Dat'll be all right, me boy!" replied the bartender. "Now, den, gen'lemen, step up an' 'ave a wet wi' yer new shipmate. W'at'll it be? No beer dis time; all hard stuff."

"Oh, set out the bottle," called out the worst looking of the four. "What are ye guffin' about? Wanter make us think this is Delmoniky's?"

While they were drinking, the hackman confided to Tom that the proprietor was his cousin. "An' he's got a heart in 'im like a bullock," he added. "Fine place, ain't it?" he asked, with a comprehensive glance of unmistakable pride at the vile surroundings. Tom asked the proprietor his terms.

"Five dollars a week, me boy. Dat's all I ast any man, an' you has de privilege of de whole house. I treats my boarders jes as if dey was members of me own family; eats at de table wit 'em meself."

"That's what he does," chimed in the fellow who had spoken before; "they ain't no lugs about Mike; I don't care if you was the cap'n of the *Great Eastern* or cook of a Philadelphy coal schooner, it's all one to Mike."

"As I don't know how long I may be here," said

Tom, "I should like to pay a couple of weeks' board in advance; if I ship before that time, you can refund whatever is owing to me." Mike nearly fell over the bar. Board in advance! The time-honored customs of sailor town shattered by a boy! But he recovered himself by an effort.

"W'y cert'nly, of course," he replied when he could catch his breath. "Dat's w'at we are here fer. Two weeks' board; ten dollars. De drinks is on me, gents."

It was some relief to get out in the street and walk about; but the sun was hot, and the odor from the overflowing garbage boxes so overwhelming that he was glad to return. After dinner — which to Tom's surprise was both good and bountiful — he had the luck to secure a seat on one of the settles under the awning. Here he was joined by a decent-looking elderly man whom he had not seen before, and who explained that he had but just risen after sleeping off a load of Mike's "benzine." During the conversation which ensued, the old fellow said that he had sailed with Captain Blake, "years ago," and had been robbed by him of half his pay. Tom asked him why the hackman had been so generous.

"Oh, he knows the ropes, that's why. He knew if he offered to carry ye free, he'd git the job, an' he knew Mike would pay him, an' take it out of your month's advance when ye ship. The other fellows didn't know that, so he got the job."

"I always thought the Sailors' Home different from this," said Tom, with unconcealed disgust.

"So 'tis, sonny, altogether different. That's where you'd ought to have gone."

"Why, isn't this it?"

The old man looked at him a moment, and then burst into a loud guffaw.

"Say, bub, who give ye that?" he asked.

"The hackman."

"Well, I swear! Say, boy, that's worth a treat. Come on, fellers, an' have one on the new ship-mate!" Thinking it advisable to keep on the right side of the crowd, Tom submitted with the best grace possible, though it was contrary to his prin-ciples to buy liquor, to say nothing of the vile com-pound which Mike retailed. As he pulled out a roll of bills to pay for the shot, he observed a tall, thin old man, clad in a long threadbare black coat and an equally threadbare silk hat, watching him hungrily. When the old man saw Tom looking at him, he slunk away. The boarders also observed the wad, and immediately became friendly; but Tom refused to be bled further.

At about nine o'clock that evening, the seedy individual reappeared. Tom was standing near the door. The old man handed him a tract and entered into conversation. When he learned that Tom had but just arrived, he became interested. He urged the boy to come with him and pass the evening at the Seamen's Bethel. A prayer meeting was in progress there, he said, and it was a much better place for him than among the profane and drunken sailors in the boarding-house. Tom readily assented. He was disgusted with his surroundings, and the prayer meeting offered an air of respectability.

The old gentleman, pleased to see him acquiesce so readily, took his arm with an air of fatherly solicitude, and beguiled the walk to the Bethel with a short account of himself. He was, he said, an ex-captain. After following the sea for forty-five years, he had the misfortune to lose his ship, and being an old man he found himself crowded out. No one was looking for old men who lost ships. Having always kept a sharp eye to windward, he was not destitute, and by strict economy, his means would last until he should moor in that port where the windlass brakes are thrown overboard, and the battered hulk may find permanent rest. To occupy his time in a fitting manner, he had volunteered to distribute tracts, and try to induce sailors to attend the Bethel meetings, rather than pass their time in the numerous hell-holes with which sailor town abounded.

Tom wondered, mildly, how such a self-sacrificing and beautiful spirit came to be associated with a a phosphorescent nose and chemical breath. He decided that it was the result of early vagaries which had become crystallized into a settled habit, and therefore should not be charged against the good old man. They had now arrived at a lonesome place. The street was occupied entirely by closed warehouses, and the sidewalks encumbered by old boilers, iron buoys which had outlived their usefulness after years of faithful service, and rust-eaten anchors and chains which, like the old captain himself, were now laid up for good.

"There, my dear young friend, do you see that green light?" asked the old gentleman, pointing as he spoke across Tom's hawse toward the river. Tom looked in the direction indicated by the lean and shaking forefinger; but, seeing no light, he turned in time to catch a fleeting glimpse of the venerable captain's right arm describing the arc of a circle, which, if indefinitely extended, would bisect his own cranium. His astonishment prevented him warding off the blow. He saw myriads of stars — and then — some one shook him roughly, and a voice said: "Come, come! Rouse up! the Black Maria is waiting. Git up, d'ye hear?"

He was dragged unceremoniously to his feet, and, opening his eyes by an effort, he found himself in the grasp of a policeman. A dazed glance at his surroundings showed him that he was in a cell. Having got him on his feet, the officer pushed him through a grated door, up half-a-dozen stone steps, and through an outer office to the street. The bright sunshine dazzled him and hurt his head. He was vaguely glad when he was thrust into the semi-obscurity of the Black Maria. Here, among samples of the city's human refuse, which the police drag-net had gathered during the preceding night, he stumbled to a seat in the corner, and promptly relapsed into unconsciousness.

"Ye're a drunk short, Barney," said the court officer, whose duty it was to tally off the prisoners and see that Barney had not lost any on the way.

"How am I? How manny does the recate call for?" asked Barney, partly in fear, but alert to resent any imputation upon his character.

"Fourteen: five faymale an' nine male."

"Here, Barney, where's that drunk o' mine?" asked a burly officer, as he forced his way through the crowd of dishevelled and miserable creatures who had just debouched from the sombre vehicle. Without waiting for an answer, he looked inside. Perceiving the limp heap in the corner, he dragged it out. "It's all right," he continued, "I got him. That Water Street benzine has a great holt on him. He's drunker than he was when I brought him in

F

last night," he added, as, puffing vigorously, he dragged Tom to the pen. When the officer released his hold, Tom fell to the floor an utter outcast, trampled underfoot by the vilest dregs of the great city.

His captor partially aroused him by dint of much shaking and many objurgations, and arraigned him at the bar.

Tom laid hold of the grimy rail, swaying dizzily as he blinked at the blinding glare of the window at the magistrate's back.

"Pretty tough case, yer hon'r," remarked the officer, with a grin.

"Well, I should say so!" replied that high-salaried politician, as he surveyed Tom's reeling form over his gold-bowed glasses. "Where did you find him, officer?"

"Southeast corner of Roosevelt, near Water, yer hon'r. He was layin' square across the sidewalk. It's rather dark there, an' I nearly fell over 'im."

"What is your name, young man?" shouted the magistrate.

Having expended the last of his energy, Tom let go the rail and fell to the floor by way of response.

"Workhouse! Ten days!" said his honor, in a tone of deep disgust.

To the workhouse, therefore, Tom was taken ; but

before he passed the doctor, that luminary discovered that alcoholism was not his sole ailment, so he had him transferred to the Charity Hospital, where for two months he hovered between life and death, as a result of the sandbagging he had received at the hands of the venerable land pirate, for the sake of the few dollars in his pocket.

CHAPTER V

WHEN Kitty rushed to her father's side, it was solely for the purpose of interfering in Tom's behalf, to save her friend and playmate from her father's fury. She clasped him round the waist, crying, "Oh, papa, don't, don't!"

Captain Blake threw up his arms, swayed a moment, staggered a few steps ahead, and fell heavily. With difficulty, Kitty disengaged herself in time to avoid being crushed under him. He fell like a log, flat upon his face, on the stone-paved sidewalk, while his daughter, frightened nearly out of her senses, screamed wildly for help. There were many people about, and a crowd soon gathered. All offered advice, but none acted. Kitty regained her composure quickly, and requested some of the men to carry her father to his office, which was near by. She followed the dismal procession, weeping and wringing her hands. The captain was laid on the lounge in his private office, and messengers sent in different directions for physicians. The first to arrive, Captain Blake's own family physician, saw at a glance that it was a case of apoplexy. "I have been expecting this for five years," said he. "He had no control over his temper — I have warned him many times."

But little could be done, as recovery was out of the question. The doctor gave a few instructions to Mr. Jorkins, who assumed charge of the office, and said he would send in a nurse. He invited Kitty to go home with him, but she declined; she would not leave her father, as he might regain consciousness, if only for a moment. She dried her tears, and took charge of the sick-room, doing carefully the few little things that the doctor had said might be beneficial to the patient. The trained nurse arrived later, but there was nothing for her to do. In the gray of the early dawn Bully Blake, without recovering consciousness, passed from human ken. He died as he had lived, — a man of domineering nature, and fierce, ungovernable passions.

In this, her first great trial, Kitty Blake, the brave, motherless New England girl, showed herself a true heroine. While there was anything to do, she never faltered. And when the last great change came, and the nurse drew the covers over the dead face, Kitty, overwhelmed for a moment, staggered, clutched at the wall, gasped, and in an incredibly short time was herself again. Her father's death was a terrible blow, but her training and the traditions of her family taught her to repress all unseemly exhibitions of grief.

Captain Blake's funeral was a solemn pageant. He was one of the best known men in Portland. For a lifetime he had been prominently connected with its principal business industry, — foreign commerce. The shipping, foreign and domestic, displayed their ensigns at half-mast. An eloquent eulogy was pronounced over the remains of the man who, fifty years before, had walked into Portland a barefoot boy. The holy man who officiated drew a lesson and pointed a moral from the well-spent life so recently ended. It was an enduring monument to the conquering power of industry, energy, and thrift, when combined with, and controlled by, the sterling integrity and unwavering honesty which had been the dominant characteristics of the deceased. Representatives of numerous organizations, civic, political, and philanthropical, followed the body of their late brother to the grave. Many who had regarded Bully Blake as a close-fisted old skinflint now saw their error. Some even acknowledged it. Captain Blake had cared for the savings of many of the employees of the line, notably of the captains, because they had more to save. Some said that all the captains were obliged to leave a certain percentage of their pay in his hands as the price of their employment. But these were found to be only the vaporings of the disgruntled who had failed to secure employment in the line.

An administrator was appointed to settle up the estate. So many interests were entwined with those of the late manager, that the settlement assumed almost the proportions of a municipal function. It became the leading topic of conversation. Among other items it was learned that the late Captain Joe Benton had left twelve thousand dollars in Captain Blake's keeping. Where was young Tom, the sole heir? Kitty told what she knew of Tom's intentions, and when it became known that an account properly rendered to the boy, and his receipt in full, had been found, the old stagers shook their heads dubiously and feared he was squandering his patrimony in riotous living.

Lawyer Theophilus Naylor had a grievance of many years standing against Captain Blake. Shortly after his arrival in Portland, fresh from college, Captain Blake had tried him. He gave him a small case, just to see what he was made of. The young lawyer, unable to win against the facts, lost it, and was at once thrust into the obscuring shadow

of the captain's disapproval.   He felt the ill effects
ever after, but dared not rebel.   This wholesome
dread of the magnate's active ill-will had restrained
him when Tom told his tale of woe.   Now he saw
his chance; by a master stroke he could accomplish
several things.   He could expose the man who had
ruined his prospects for life; the man whom he
knew to have been a scoundrel, but whom an admiring populace seemed about to canonize.   He
could pose as the champion of the robbed orphan
and bask in the resulting glory.   He would no
doubt receive a fat fee from the grateful beneficiary
of his efforts, and, incidently, cause an act of justice
to be done.   But better far than all these results
combined would be the fact that he, Theophilus
Naylor, would be known far and near, as the
obscure but learned — very learned — lawyer, who,
single handed, had challenged and defeated mighty
Wrong, in behalf of puny, helpless Right.

He was so elated with the prospect of rapidly
approaching distinction that he lapsed into indis-
cretion.   He hinted to his intimates that a sensation
was soon to appear in the matter of the settlement
of the Blake estate.   Such heresy could not be
kept secret.   It spread from tongue to tongue, —
in strict confidence, — and expanded as it went.   Having acquired scandalous proportions, and reached the
ears of the faithful, it could not be overlooked.

Being pressed to make good his words or publicly
retract, he incautiously published the whole story
in the *Transcript*, signing the article boldly, and
paying space rates. He was promptly prosecuted
for malicious libel. Popular opinion — as usual
— was divided, and feeling ran high. Mr. Naylor
asked for and obtained time to procure his witness.
The evidence of the ship chandler's books bore out
that part of the statement relating to the check,
but that was of a negative character. While it
proved that Tom had such a check, it did not
prove that he had been robbed of the remainder
by Captain Blake.

Mr. Jorkins, Captain Blake's head clerk, mindful
of the fact that he needed another position, merely
remembered assisting at Tom's ejectment for insuf-
ferable insolence. A stub corresponding to the
check appeared in the check book, but that merely
corroborated what was admitted. The fact that
no stub was found for any other amount proved
nothing. The receipt was there.

Mr. Naylor hired expensive private detectives, and
set them on Tom's trail. They sent in expense accounts with discouraging regularity; but learned
nothing. Having failed utterly to sustain with facts
his shameless attack on the character of a reputable
citizen, he was disbarred and became utterly dis-
credited in the town. He shook the inhospitable dust

of Portland from his feet forever : wondering why, even from his grave, Bully Blake should be able to blight his life.

During these troublous times, Kitty did a great deal of thinking. She had loved her father with the blind, unreasoning love of a child for a parent. But she also thoroughly believed in Tom Benton. She knew Tom had not received twelve thousand dollars. She *knew* that. Therefore, by some means, the money must still be in the estate. Mr. Naylor having received his just deserts, and no other questions having arisen, the estate was settled, and Mr. Hiram Hayward, a staunch friend of Captain Blake, was appointed guardian of the orphan during her minority.

One of Kitty's first acts was to tease Mr. Hayward for twelve thousand dollars. This modest demand struck the old gentleman flat aback. That was a splendid beginning, he thought. Of course he refused to entertain the idea for a moment. It was too absurd to merit serious consideration. But Kitty persisted. Morning, noon, and night she urged, pleaded, and coaxed. She talked of nothing else until, worn out and half distracted by her persistency, he told her the court would never sanction such an act.

"The court allows you to give me a reasonable amount of spending money, suitable to my station, doesn't it?" asked Kitty.

"A reasonable amount? Yes, certainly, my dear. But twelve thousand dollars to start on! You are not a millionaire, Kitty."

She promised to sign an agreement — any kind of an agreement — binding herself never to ask for another cent as long as she remained under his care. She also consented to have the *Sprite* — her sole valuable possession — sold, and to accept the money so received as part of the twelve thousand. The result was what might have been foreseen. Mr. Hayward's heart was not as tough as perhaps it should have been. He was very fond of Kitty, who succeeded in gaining Mrs. Hayward's prompt support. The *Sprite* was sold advantageously, and Kitty received Mr. Hayward's personal check for twelve thousand dollars. Within the hour, the valuable scrap of paper was deposited in bank to the account of Thomas Benton, and Kitty felt the gratification that comes of the knowledge of a just deed.

Surrounded by such home comforts as she had never known before, and cared for by a woman of warm affections, Kitty rapidly recovered from the depressing effects of her father's sudden death. But she was never again the merry hoyden whom Tom Benton had known. Separated forever from her beloved *Sprite*, her recreations under the thoughtful guidance of Mrs. Hayward assumed a character more suitable to her sex and to the position she was destined to occupy. Her sweet, generous nature and true heart remained unchanged, or rather, under improved surroundings, the beauties of her character were developed and strengthened. Living in comfort and moderate luxury, she never forgot the playmate who, she honestly believed, had been wronged by her father. She thought of him continually. She hoped he was prospering. She knew he would never discredit himself or any one; and every night she, his only friend, prayed that he might succeed, and return to refute the slanders that many had spoken of him. Sometimes, when she thought of the misfortunes that might so easily befall him, out in the world alone, with no one to speak a kind or encouraging word, her heart was very sad, and her pillow wet with honest, loving tears.

CHAPTER VI

WHEN Tom regained consciousness in the hospital,
they asked his name, age, residence, and occupation.
Nothing more. He answered them, but volunteered
no information, for he understood that, among such
universal misery, his affairs were of no moment.

At the expiration of two months he was discharged, not because he was well and fit to en-
gage in the fierce struggle for bread, but because
the poverty-stricken horde of invalids crowding the
limited accommodations necessitated vacating the
beds as soon as possible. An orderly brought his
clothes. Faintly hoping, he searched the pockets.
The dim recollection of his walk with the benevolent old captain was verified. His pockets were
empty. His clothes had been good, for they were
his best suit, but now they were little better than
rags, as, like himself, they bore evidence of their
experience in the police cell, the prison pen, and
the hospital.

No one asked him what he would do on regaining his liberty, nor what were his prospects of obtaining subsistence. That is no part of the work of municipal charity. He was turned adrift ragged and half sick, but with the ravenous hunger of convalescence — an hour before dinner. Thereby he contributed his poor mite to the making of the economical record of the new commissioner. He wandered miserably about, becoming momentarily fainter. He sank wearily upon a doorstep — and was ordered away by an offended citizen who disapproved of his presence. He leaned for a moment against a lamp-post to rest his dizzy head on the cool iron. A pompous, well-fed policeman moved him along. He could not beg; and never knew how to steal. He could only drag one foot after the other, and wonder inanely where he was going. Instinct kept him near the river. He saw ships; they were familiar. He arrived at Fulton market. The appetizing aroma that floated out from the coffee and cake stands nearly overcame him. Why did he not snatch even one from the great stocks of crisp, brown doughnuts so temptingly displayed within easy reach? It may have been heredity; he was of puritanical descent. He feebly hurried through the market and plodded along South Street. It was evening. He had been long on the way. The six o'clock whistles had sent forth their screeching note, warning insatiate capital that it had squeezed the last drop of perspiration from needy labor for that day. The street was alive with workmen returning to their homes.

Sturdy 'longshoremen swarmed up from the piers, rolling down the sleeves of their red flannel shirts, or lighting their pipes for the long-wished-for first smoke since one o'clock. With their coats thrown over their shoulders, and cotton hooks stuck with a technical twist in their leather belts, they trudged sturdily along, talking together about the day's work, or heartily cursing the foreman for a slave-driver. Their dull faces expressed, if not pleasure, at least contentment. They had a job.

A gang of riggers who were employed in setting up the rigging on a new ship, followed half a dozen caulkers, all smelling wholesomely of tar, all homeward bound, and all safe, at least from starvation. The mate of a small schooner, who was "keeping ship," locked the cabin door, took a final glance about the decks and leaped lightly ashore. He squared his necktie, straightened up his hat, and went into a restaurant to get his supper.

In all that throng of hundreds of men, men to whom for the most part the multiplication table would have been an unsolvable puzzle, Tom Benton, lately son of a well-to-do sea-captain, was the only one helplessly and hopelessly hungry.

On a half-tide rock, or in the middle of a desert, he could not have been more alone. He was rudely jostled by the thoughtless laborers, any one of whom would willingly have shared his supper with him. To avoid the crowd, whose very energy wearied him, he crossed the street and went out on the pier. At last! Why had he not thought of it before? Here he could rest. He sat down on the stringpiece and leaned against a pile. It was heavenly. He drew his tired legs under him and eased the aching cords and muscles. But relief from one source of misery enabled him to concentrate his attention on another. He was terribly hungry.

From where he sat he looked directly into the galley of a small coasting schooner. The cook was busy clearing away the débris from his day's work. A dim lamp suspended from a bracket on the bulkhead threw his shadow out to where Tom sat. He gathered up a pan of scraps — bits of stale bread, bones, bits of gristle and fat, potato peelings and tea-leaves. He approached the rail within six feet of where Tom sat. Divining his intention, Tom, his shame covered by the kindly darkness, cried: "Hey, doctor! Don't throw that overboard; give it to me, will you?"

"Ven you don'd goes avay from dere, I gif you somedings vat you don'd like," replied the cook, as he threw to the East River eels the scraps for which Tom would have been so grateful. Returning to the galley, he picked a lump of coal from the scuttle, and, holding the lamp above his head, he threw it at the starving boy, cutting a painful gash in his cheek. Those wharf rats would steal anything they could lay their hands on.

There was no fight in Tom Benton now. Without a word he arose painfully and retraced his steps up the wharf. Having tasted the sweets of temporary rest, he resolved to have more of it. Presently he came to a place where at some time there had been a fire. A few tottering walls and a high chimney were surrounded by a dilapidated high fence. A loose board showed where some one had effected an entrance; probably the street boys in pursuit of a lost ball. It was now quite dark, though a crescent moon, fighting its way through the flying scud, threw fitful gleams of deceptive light on the chaotic scene which confronted him as he emerged from the broken fence. A tangle of weeds and thistles flourished among the débris of bricks, mortar, twisted iron pipes, and shafting. Here and there, a pulley or other piece of machinery, had, by the inertia of its dead weight, successfully defied the marauders. A ray of moonlight showed a well-defined path leading from the place of entrance. Following this instinctively, Tom found it led him

G

to the interior of the ruin, and while groping in the darkness he fell, through a hole in the rotten floor, to the cellar. He was bruised and shaken, but not disabled. As he regained his feet, a kindly moonbeam, penetrating the mass of wreckage above, fell upon the open door of a boiler furnace. It seemed like the finger of a friend pointing the way. He felt within and found that the grate bars were covered with a mass of dried weeds, old bags, and other refuse. Without a thought that he might be trespassing, he crawled in ; and with a deep-drawn sigh of thankfulness, fell at once into a restless, feverish sleep.

He dreamed horribly. He thought he lay on his belly in an immense dish-pan. He was greedily devouring the swill with which the pan was partially filled, when a gigantic German cook discovered him, and with frightful curses seized the pan and dumped the entire contents into the fire. As he was clawing wildly at the slippery edge of the pan, a husky voice said in a whisper, "Is dat you, Patsey ?"

Tom opened his eyes, to be partially blinded by a blazing lucifer match held close to his face. Behind it was a frowzy head and a pair of fierce eyes. The German cook's, he thought. The match was hurriedly extinguished, and he heard some one backing hastily out of the boiler. There was a consultation on the outside. He heard the scout say, "It's one o' de Gouverneur Street gang."

A short whispered colloquy ensued. Then he was seized by the heels and dragged violently out. More bumps and bruises, and sundry patches of skin removed. The moon was now obscured by an adjoining building, but he saw that his captors were three boys, smaller and more ragged than himself. They pitched into him at once, thumping and kicking him roundly. He was unable to resist, and fell from sheer weakness. Finding him so easily subdued, they desisted, stripped off his coat and shoes, and ordered him, with much profanity, to "light out o' here!" As he did not comply immediately, two of them took him by the shoulders and one by the legs. They carried him, cursing horribly at his weight, to the hole in the fence, swung him, — once, twice, three times, — and tossed him through.

He fell heavily on his back upon the stone pavement. A pedestrian who was hurrying along with hands in his pocket and bowed head stumbled over him. He was a slim, under-sized, poorly dressed man of forty. He recovered his balance, and grasping Tom by the collar, raised him to his feet.

"'Ullo, me lad," said he, in an undeniable English accent, "w'at's hup?"

Tom looked at him in stupid blankness for a moment. It was a kindly, sympathetic face that he saw by the rays of a neighboring street lamp. His resolution gave way at the first expression of kindly interest he had heard. His overpowering hunger so dwarfed all his other troubles that he lost sight of them entirely. Tears of honest shame suffused his eyes as, for the first time in his life, he begged.

"I'm nearly starved to death!" he cried desperately.

"Starved, is it? Well, I can 'elp ye there, lad. Come down to my place an' 'ave a cup o' coffee an' a plate o' cakes. I'll not see ye starve, anyway. W'ere did ye come from?"

"Portland," replied Tom, weakly.

"No, no; I mean w'en ye shot out ther' on the walk like that."

"I dunno."

"Ah, poor chap!" said the man to himself, "'e's that 'ungry as 'e doesn't feel like chattin'. I'll just wait till 'e's 'ad a bite."

Presently, they stopped before one of the coffee and cake stands in the market that had been such a sore trial to Tom the day before. Jerry was the proprietor of this one. He soon had the coffee boiling on the gas-stove, while Tom glared ravenously about, inhaling the delicious odors of yesterday's fried fish. In a minute more — or was it a dream?—he sat in front of a plate of butter-cakes, flanked by a cup of steaming hot coffee.

It was good. It was glorious. But, oh, there was so little of it! Jerry guessed where the trouble lay, and he produced another plate of cakes. Though greatly refreshed, Tom's aching void was far from filled. His appetite was merely whetted. But he was so grateful that he restrained, as best he could, the wolfish looks with which he regarded his new friend, who was now regaling himself on ham and eggs.

"Ye can 'elp me a bit, if ye will, lad, w'en the men comes in fer breakfast," said Jerry.

Tom told him he would be only too happy. Presently they began to come; great, fat, rosy-cheeked market-men; dressed in long, woollen smocks; loud-voiced and jolly. Some had big diamonds in their shirts or on their fingers.

"Come, Jerry," shouted a burly butcher, "what's the matter now? Cook on strike? Or has the grocer shut down on ye at last?"

"Now, then, where's them cakes?" came from a fish-dealer, as he entered the door; "I ordered them half an hour ago. If you don't git a move on ye, we'll all git filled up with smell, and won't have no bill to pay."

Jerry's uniform answer to all this good-humored chaffing was a cheery: "Comin', sir; right away, sir." Being both cook and waiter, he was extremely busy for an hour or so; but from long experience he had become very deft. He could keep half a dozen orders cooking, wait on tables, and allay the impatience of his customers, without becoming in the least mixed. He set Tom to washing dishes. A continual stream of dirty dishes slid along the oil-cloth-covered table towards the sink; but Tom hustled, and fairly kept his end up. Jerry showed him a tub under the table into which he could throw the refuse; but no refuse more edible than egg-shells found their way into the tub that morning. Sometimes, but not often, a whole cake would reach him, and once he got a rind from a beef-steak. It was the most delicious morsel he had ever eaten, only too tough to masticate, so he gulped it down whole; merely coughing and choking a little.

When the breakfast rush was over, Jerry gave Tom instructions, previous to going out to do the marketing for dinner. He told him where there was a large tub, into which he could dump the refuse from his small one. Tom found the large tub nearly full, and on top there were many pieces of stale bread, on which lay a great, juicy, boiled ham-rind. The stuff was not dirty nor in the least fermented. The raw edge had not yet been taken from Tom's appetite; so he hurried through the duties that had been assigned him, and then, rubbing the bits of bread on the fine, fat ham-rind, he proceeded to enjoy himself right royally. He was startled by hearing Jerry's voice right behind him.

"W'at ye doin', lad?" it asked.

Tom felt the hot blood rush to his face. He was thankful for the store he had found, but he was ashamed to be caught browsing in a swill tub.

"'Ere," said Jerry, handing him the potato-masher, "take this, an' give me a good beatin'! The hidea o' me, as gets me three squares hevery day, a stuffin' o' meself wi' 'am an' heggs, an' leavin' a Christian w'ite man to rake over my swill barrel!"

Tom protested that he was not hungry now, as he had picked up quite a good deal from the breakfast plates.

"Ay! There it is agin! Wuss an' more on it. Sit ye down there now to that table! An' if ye let up w'ile yer able to 'old another mouthful, s'elp me I'll cut yer 'ead off wi' this 'ere dish-clout."

Such a feast as followed this dire threat, Fulton Market has seldom seen. Jerry fried "'am," "heggs," and "taters." He piled the doughnuts and butter-cakes on both sides of Tom's plate, and maintained a generous foot-bath in his saucer. Tom shovelled and ground for dear life. At last, what seemed to have been an impossibility was accomplished. He was full. Oh, the joy of it, to be able to decline food!

When this record-breaking meal was finished, Jerry raked out from somewhere a pair of old shoes, — very old they were, and holey, — a coat which had long ago been discarded and had only escaped the ragman because it wasn't worth bothering with, and a hat which in all respects matched them.

"Put 'em on, lad," said he; "they're not that fine as ye needs to be ashamed on 'em, an' no cop will ever arrest ye on suspicion of 'avin' stole 'em from John Jacob Hastor. So there's good p'ints about 'em, a'ter all, ragged as they is."

They now had an interchange of confidences. Jerry admitted that it took about all he could make to keep the "hol' woman an' the kids." Consequently he could neither afford the luxury of an assistant nor a reckless indulgence in charity; but he would do what he could to set Tom on his feet. At dinner that day, he informed his customers that any employment they could give Tom he would consider a personal favor. Nobody promised anything, while a butcher remarked that there were "too many bums around the market now, stealing everything they could lay their hands on." Yet he was the first to give Tom employment and put many a dime in his way.

Jerry permitted him to sleep in the shanty and gave him his breakfast for washing the dishes.

Tom hustled for work early and late. No job was too hard or too dirty for him; and as he never dickered with his employer, but cheerfully accepted such recompense as they saw fit to offer, he became well and favorably known. That he was strictly honest goes without saying. He was also obliging, polite, and grateful for small favors. Before a month had passed, "Jerry's boy" was constantly in demand. He was a feature of the market. He paid Jerry regularly for his board, and tried to pay him for that first grand meal; but Jerry said he had enjoyed it more than Tom had, so, if there was any balance, it was the other way.

Never for a moment did Tom lose sight of the fact that he was to go to sea and win for himself the command of as fine a ship as floated. Many a rose-tinted dream he indulged in while lying awake on Jerry's table. He fancied himself sailing into Portland Harbor, proudly pacing the starboard side of the poop with the pilot. And when the ship ——, Benton, Master, was reported, he knew just how Mr. Bentick, the ship chandler, and Mr. Ridgeway, the rigger with the big wart on his upper lip, would peer inquiringly into his eyes, and, hoping to establish a claim of previous acquaintance with the captain of the fine, big ship, ask, "Cap'n Bent'n, hai'n't I seen you before som'eres?"

But, of all the prospective pleasures in which,
he indulged, that in which he took the most delight, and over which he hugged himself, was to
be the look of surprise, pride, and happy congratu-
lation in the brown eyes of Kitty Blake, when he
should welcome her on board; thereby proving
himself true to the promise he had made her when
he left. But Tom was blessed with the rare virtue
of common sense. Winter was approaching. He
had no clothes. He would hang on to the market
until spring at least. One day, while on an errand,
he recognized across the street the building known
to him as the Sailors' Home. Hooray! Here was
luck! He would demand his clothes. But the
place was now a junk shop. He entered and
found an aged Hebrew busily sorting rags. His
red, watery eyes and tangled black beard were
all that distinguished him from the frowsy mound
on which he was enthroned. Tom inquired for
the former occupant. "Vat?" asked the old Jew,
stupidly blinking at him through the dust. Tom
made his request for information concerning Mike's
whereabouts a little more explicit. "I know nod-
ings," truthfully replied the descendant of Moses.

During the holiday rush, Tom increased his
slender stock of money to fifteen dollars. He
continued to help Jerry, although he now paid his
board regularly, and when the biting blasts of

winter gave way to the gentle airs of spring, he began to consider his seagoing plans in earnest. Jerry told him plumply that he was a fool.

"W'at better could yer arsk, than w'at yer gittin'?" he asked; "three square meals a d'y, an' money in yer pocket. Does sailors git that? Yer knows better. Leave well enough alone, say I. Yer learnin' the business; yer quite 'andy all ready. W'at's the matter wi' another coffee an' cake stand down ther' at the corner? Better'n goin' ter sea, I lay."

But Tom was ambitious. Coffee and cakes? Bah! He would be a captain. Having learned the ropes by conversing with the sailors on South Street, he entered his name in a boarding-house, and paid a week's board in advance. He told the proprietor he should remain at Jerry's, and desired to ship for China, or round the Horn. Although he called at the house daily, it was three weeks before the boarding-master had a ship for him. He told Tom that he had waited to get him a good ship, and had succeeded beyond his expectations. She was a fine one, he said; the captain was a nice, fatherly, old man, and the mates, his sons, were just like him. Sunday services at sea, watch and watch the whole voyage; the finest of grub, and no profanity nor abuse of seamen permitted. She was bound for Bombay, so, when he got back, he would

have nine or ten months' pay to jingle in his pocket.
"And when you come home with money, don't fur-
get Andy Mason, who got the best ship in New York
for you," he added.

Tom promised that he certainly would not, and
thanked Mr. Mason very heartily for his kindness.
He also apologized for any impatience he might
have manifested during the previous three weeks.
Mr. Mason assured him that he had not taken the
matter at all to heart, and to prove it, he generously
furnished a mattress of shavings, a tin pot and pan,
an iron spoon, sheath knife and belt, and a huge
plug of navy tobacco, in lieu of Tom's month's advance of fourteen dollars.

When the wagon drew up at Jerry's, and Tom
handed up his new, neatly painted chest, it was
greeted with drunken jeers by the ragamuffins in
the wagon. Jerry bade him a reluctant adieu.
Tom promised that, on his return from Bombay,
he would set his friend up in the finest stall in the
market. His parting from this one true friend,
this heart of gold, was the only drawback to his
pleasure at being once more afloat. He was·thor-
oughly disgusted with his new shipmates, who
were the most disreputable gang he had ever seen;
drunken, ragged, and dirty. The ship having been
anchored on the Jersey flats, they were transferred
to a tug at the wharf. Tom understood that he had

signed for the ship *Chanticleer*, of Boston, but he was put on board the *Montezuma*, an old rattle-trap Liverpool packet. He protested, and was told to shut up or have his head knocked loose.

Packet-ship lore was no new story to him. He had heard it over and over, so, knowing he was in for the trip, he philosophically decided to make the best of the bargain. When they were lined up at the capstan, the mate asked the shipping-master if he called *that* an able seaman, indicating Tom by a contemptuous jerk of his head. "I think you will find me quite as able as any of them, sir," Tom piped up boldly. "I will, hey?" replied the mate, with a surly scowl.

The crew having answered to their alleged names, the windlass was ordered to be manned. Then the regulation packet scenes were enacted. The fatherly captain contented himself principally with roaring curses at all hands, though he was not averse to filling in with fists or boots, when any of the drunken wretches came conveniently near. His equally refined mates, being from the nature of their duties, in the thick of it, hammered, kicked, and cursed the men for everything or nothing; and not a man returned even a protest. Tom, being sober and agile, found no difficulty in evading the abuse. He made it his business to jump at the word, and, being the only thorough seaman in the crew, the mates

spotted him before the ship was under way. When
the pilot called for a man at the helm, Tom was
half-way up the main rigging.

"Come down here, bantam, and take the wheel!"
shouted Mr. Burlingame, the chief mate.

Not having distinctly understood the order, Tom
dropped lightly from the sheerpole behind the big
mate's back, who was now attending to something
else.

"Did you call me, sir?" asked Tom, stepping
round in front of him.

"Git aft there to the wheel!" yelled the mate,
furiously. He raised his acrobatic toe, but Tom
was half-way up the poop ladder.

That was the nearest he ever came to receiving
bodily chastisement aboard the *Montezuma*. The
mate, in whose watch he was, came to depend on
him unconsciously. When he knew Tom — or "the
bantam," as he called him — to be on lookout, or
at the wheel, or on a yard, furling a sail, he felt that
his profanity could be reserved for a more fit occasion.
Tom escaped the heaviest of the pulling and hauling incident to getting a big ship under way, and
no doubt many a stray thump, by being at the
wheel. The crew were inclined to practise on each
other the treatment served by the officers to them.
Tom being neither drunk nor ragged, they despised
him. The fact that he had passed through the

ceremony of initiation with a whole skin, while they
— veterans though they were — had all been soundly
drubbed, exasperated them. He was young to be
rated as an able seaman, and small, so they decided
he should be their meat.

The port watch were ordered to supper. As
they hungered only for whiskey, the big pan of
hash was slighted. Having no whiskey, they entertained themselves by cursing the ship, her officers,
and their own bad luck in being there. One
bleary ruffian, seeing Tom sitting on the only chest
in the forecastle quietly eating his supper, seized
him by the collar and threw him half-way across
the place, saying: " Git up, you! Time enough for
you to set down when they ain't no *men* stannin' up."

Knowing them to be more or less under the influence of liquor, Tom said nothing, but seated himself on the edge of a bunk to finish his supper.
Presently the bully tried to open the chest. Finding it locked, he glared savagely around, and, in
a tone intended to be terror-inspiring, asked:—

" Whose donkey is dis ? "

" Mine," replied Tom, quietly.

" What's it locked for ? "

" Because I chose to have it so."

" Ye do, hey? Wa't's de matter? do ye t'ink
we'se t'ieves? Unlock dat donkey, 'fore I kick
it open ! "

"I'll unlock it when I see fit, and you won't kick it open, either," replied Tom, jumping down from his perch, and laying his pot, pan, and spoon down on the deck.

Without more ado, the big fellow raised his foot to kick the chest open. In doing so, he was obliged to turn his back to Tom, who leaped lightly upon his shoulders. The ship gave a lurch in the nick of time. Together, they pitched over the chest into the empty bunk beyond. The bully's head struck the side of the house and knocked him senseless. Tom dragged him out, and, tumbling him on the deck, asked, as he stood defiantly on his chest, "Anybody else want to take a hand at kicking this donkey open?"

Just then, the third mate flung the door open, and called them to relieve the starboard watch. He took in the situation at a glance, and indorsed the mate's sagacity in christening Tom "The Bantam." Tom's accidental victory over big Bryan by no means subdued the watch. As they sobered up, their true characters appeared. While arrant cowards, they were equally arrant bullies — when they thought it would work. They felt Tom's locked chest a reflection upon their characters. He, believing his clothes safer under lock and key than they would be entrusted to his watch-mates' sense of honesty, kept it locked. To soothe their tender feelings, he licked them one after another, when they expostulated. Before the *Montezuma's* anchor grappled with the Mersey mud, he had relieved the overwrought feelings of nearly all of them, and his chest was taken ashore still locked.

As Tom had no intention of sailing in any other than American ships, he returned to New York in another packet. He passed through a very similar experience, and arrived, about three months after his departure, without a cent of money, and his clothes much the worse for wear. He was ashamed to call on Jerry; for that good soul was not above the weakness which derives comfort from repeating the moth-eaten phrase "I told you so!" He pursued the only course open to him: he went with the rest of the crew to a sailors' boarding-house, where they were received for what could be got out of their advanced wages when shipped again. During his brief stay in port, Tom came across Mike, the former proprietor of the "Sailors' Home." Tom asked Mike eagerly if he remembered him.

"Why, sure!" replied that worthy. "What ship?"

"The *Raven.*"

"The *Raven?* Why, she's been in port a week."

"Yes."

"Oh, then you've got a boarding-house?"

"Yes; I'm stopping at Kelley's. Whatever became of my dunnage that I left at your place?"

"Dunnage ? I don't know nothin' about no dunnage. You didn't leave no dunnage here. I never
saw ye afore. I thought at first ye was Billy Adams
what went to Frisco las' year in the *Gamecock*. I
guess you've made a mistake in your bearin's, young
feller. Best thing you can do is to go back ter
Kelley's ; I don't want ye round here. I got no
time ter listen ter cock-and-bull stories 'bout lost
dunnage. Come, clear out ! "

In ten days Tom was off again, bound for Havre,
where he repeated his Liverpool experience ; remaining a week ashore, and shipping for Galveston. He had a long passage to Galveston, with
the result that there were a few dollars due him
when he arrived, enabling him to partly replenish
his wardrobe. Tom despised the miserable wretches
with whom he sailed in these ships, but he loved
the western ocean. He was young and strong, and
it filled him with enthusiasm to see the gallant old
ships bang and buffet their way to the westward.
Fighting their way through the northern passage, that region of continuous gales, of fog,
snow, and ice, they challenged the endurance
of the toughest men in the business, and it delighted him, rousing all the fire and combativeness
in his nature. When reefing, he never allowed
any man to get ahead of him at the weather earring.
Astride the yard-arm, high in the air, the gale

howling and shrieking at his back, the sleet driving past like a volley from Gatling guns, filling his seaboots, and penetrating every rag on him, Tom Benton was in his glory. With a half-turn of the earring round his neck, he would straighten his powerful back, and bawl out, "Haul out to wind'ard!" and, when he had the dog's-ear fast, he would send the word flying like a trumpet-note along the yard, "Haul out to leeward!"

At such times he felt like a young storm-king, and would not have exchanged places with the captain. He became fairly well known, and was invariably well liked by those who had sense enough to treat him fairly. He stayed nearly two years in the business, but the sturdy Puritan blood that flowed in his veins saved him from becoming contaminated by his vile associates, while the training he received was of incalculable value to him in after years. Occasionally an ambitious second or third mate would attempt to use him according to the custom of packet ships, but they soon learned that he was a first-rate man to let alone. He was offered promotion, but declined. Packet-ship style did not appeal to him. He knew he was in the business only temporarily, and when the opportunity offered, he would quit it.

CHAPTER VII

ONE day as Tom was idling along West Street, he met a former shipmate.

"Hello, Tom!"

"Hello, Larry! What's the good word?"

"Oh, nothin' much! Got a ship yet?"

"No, I don't bother about ships; let the boarding-master attend to that. He's more interested than I am — he gets the money. All I get is the privilege of doing the work."

"I jest shipped for Boston."

"Boston?"

"Yep, — by the run, ye know, — fifteen dollars for the run, — *Jane Spofford*, — deep-water ship, — b'longs in Boston."

At the name of Boston, Tom's heart gave a bound; it seemed almost like home. He asked Larry if the ship had got her full complement of men.

"I b'lieve not," replied Larry. "Ye see the old-timers don't care to leave York, not for Boston, anyway. Pretty slow town, I've heerd."

"Where are the articles?"

"In Van Hoesen's ship chandlery, jest this side o' Washington Market."

"Guess I'll go up and see. We may be shipmates again. Will ye come along?"

"No, no, Tom, you're a good shipmate; but no tectotalers for me. There's a homeward-bound crew down at the boardin'-house, and booze to swim in. I'm goin' to have one more good blow-out 'fore I leave for Bean Town."

"All right, then; so long!"

Ten minutes later, Tom signed his name to the *Spofford's* articles right under Larry's. The ship being in ballast, and Captain Beebe in a hurry to get home, there was lots of sail drill during the four days' passage. With his usual ardor, Tom took the lead. He gave out the "shanties" on the topsail halyards, and showed the runners the way aloft. As Captain Beebe worked the ship himself, he noticed and liked the young fellow; but he had his doubts of the possibility of any good thing coming from "York." The short run over, and the ship fast, the crew were called into the cabin and paid off. Tom's name was the last.

"Thomas Benton!"

"Here, sir."

The captain fumbled with the bills until all the others had left the cabin. Then, without looking up, he asked carelessly : —

"Where do you hail from, Benton?"

"Portland, sir."

"Portland, hey? I used to know some Bentons down there. Ever know Cap'n Joe Benton?"

"Yes, sir."

"No relation, I s'pose?"

"He was my father, sir," replied Tom, quietly.

"Hey? Your father? What Joe Benton was that?" asked the old fellow, craftily.

"Captain Joseph Benton, of the ship *Columbia*, of Portland, sir," replied Tom, proudly.

Captain Beebe turned and faced Tom squarely. "You don't say!" he exclaimed. Then, as he gazed for a moment into the honest, gray eyes, — "Yes, I might ha' known it. It's a wonder I didn't notice the resemblance before; but you see I didn't know any of your names till I come to pay off. Sit right down here, Tom Benton! Your father and I went to school together, and went to sea together, too, when we were boys. I haven't seen him but once in fifteen years; that was five or six years ago in Rio. Were you with him then?"

"Yes, sir. You may have heard that our carpenter was sick in the hospital with yellow fever," replied Tom, desiring to identify himself beyond a doubt.

"Yes, I remember, and Captain Joe wouldn't leave him — took him along in spite of the protests of the whole crew. Did he live?"

"Oh, yes, sir, he lived, and remained in the ship till father died, three years ago next month."

"Sho! You don't tell me Joe Benton is dead? I never heard a word of it. You have lost a good father, Tom! I'm awfully sorry! Joe Benton was a good square man, and as fine a seaman as ever stepped aboard a ship. Did he teach you navigation?"

"Oh, yes, sir. I was only seventeen when he died, but I took the ship home."

"Well done, my boy, well done! I'll bet you're a chip of the old block. But how is it you're out here in York before the mast? I should have thought Cap'n Blake would have hung on to ye."

"He didn't," replied Tom, bitterly.

"Well, that's strange! Did ye sell out your father's stock in the line? Or do you hold that yet?"

"It's a long story, Captain Beebe. I believe, and always shall, that Captain Blake robbed me. I can't prove it, though, so it's hardly worth while to talk about it. At any rate he discharged me, and drove me out of Portland, after I had, with the help of that same carpenter you spoke of, taken the ship from the mates, who were going to wreck her near St. Thomas, and brought her safe home. For the last two years and a half I've had a pretty tough row to hoe down there in New York. That's why I took this run — to get away from there. I thought I might do better in Boston."

"What ye been doin'?"

Tom related his adventures, and the old gentleman remarked: "My, but I should say you *had* had a rocky row to hoe! What ye goin' to do now?"

"Ship again, sir."

"Don't ye think you've been 'fore the mast most long enough?"

"Yes, sir, I think I have. I knew the business just as well before I ever went before it, as I do now; though I do believe that the experience of these last two years has done me good. I've had the actual practice now."

"Yes, that's right, and in a hard school, too — the hardest there is. Well, now I'll tell you what I think you'd better do. You stay right here and keep ship for me until I'm ready for sea. Then I'll — well, I'll do something. What do you say?"

Tom not only accepted the offer, but thanked the captain heartily, and entered with his usual vigor upon his new duties at once.

Captain Josiah Beebe was a typical Yankee skipper. Long, lean, and leathery, he was as tough as a hickory knot. He was a humane man to his crew, provided they had sense enough to allow him to be so. But, though of a kindly disposition, he was by no means lacking in those prime qualities in a ship's officer, — rapid decision, fearlessness, and the ability to exercise necessary severity, — which are frequently called by well-meaning but ignorant persons on shore, brutality. Had he been otherwise, he would not have commanded the *Spofford* for twenty years as he did.

Mechanical refrigerating not having become a commercial factor in those days, the cabalistic initials B. I. C. (Boston Ice Company) were familiar in nearly all tropical countries; and the wealthy East Indian nabobs gladly paid gilt-edged prices for the clear, sparkling ice which the severe New England winters froze to a depth of several feet. For years the ice trade with India was an important industry.

A venturesome skipper took fifty barrels of Baldwin apples out "on spec'." When he returned, he reported an incipient riot in Calcutta on the news of his venture becoming known. The Anglo-Indians — their appetites jaded by years of rich tropical fruit — hailed the advent of apples with eagerness. This report caused a flurry in the maritime circles of Boston, Salem, and Portland. Several ships were laden with full cargoes of apples and despatched to India. Owing to the long tropical voyage, they arrived with their cargoes completely decayed, and thereafter apples were a delicate subject with down-east shippers.

Captain Beebe proposed taking a cargo of ice and apples combined, arguing that the ice would preserve the apples. An objection was raised that they might arrive frozen. To this he replied that he hoped they would, as he would then be able to dispose of them at a dollar apiece. Having gained his point, he stowed the apples in the fore peak and the after-run, securing them by bulkheads. He took up the between-deck planks in the midship section of her, and stowed the ice from the ballast up. This would allow it to drain to the pumps, and settle down as it melted, keeping her stiff for the passage round the Cape, and through the monsoons.

Before the cargo was half in, he assigned Tom to the second mate's berth, and shipped a young fellow by the name of Gregg for mate. Mr. Gregg was an Englishman, but he had always sailed in American ships, and was a fine young fellow. He and Tom became quite chummy at once. The cargo being in, a crew were shipped, and once more the *Jane Spofford* took the familiar road to

TOM IN HIS GLORY.

India. She had light and baffling winds from the start. When she finally dawdled out of the north-east trades into the doldrums, she should have been across the line, but was not within a dozen degrees of it. She rolled about for two weeks in the warm water, under the broiling sun of those latitudes; the pitch frying out of the decks, and all hands gasping for breath. Morning, noon, and night, there was the same clear blue sky overhead, and the same glassy, unruffled sea below. The sea had lost even the gently heaving swell, which, like the feeble pulse of an invalid, proves that life at least remains. Not a sail flapped. A lighted candle would have burned itself out on her main truck. Her jibboom end would hardly sweep a quarter of the horizon in twenty-four hours.

It was a horrible, sickening, raging calm — and HOT. The ice melted rapidly. The men were required to pump, but not asked to do any other work. As Captain Beebe saw the profits of the voyage pouring from the nozzle of the pump, he gritted his teeth and abused the weather with a Yankee heartiness that was good to hear, in that enervating, depressing, killing calm.

One afternoon a slight dinginess appeared on the western horizon. Between the pumping spells, the men would lean, gasping, over the rail, and argue

in a desperate, hopeless way, on the prospect of a
breeze. A little after six bells, a great black head
rose out of the smudge and rapidly approached
the zenith. Tom had the watch stand by royal
and topgallant halliards. The port watch crawled
out of the stifling forecastle, where they were vainly
trying to sleep, and lent a hand. The squall was
furious while it lasted, — only a couple of minutes,
— but the deluge of rain revived all hands.

The backbone of the calm was now broken,
and they entered upon that ever-varying, yet dis-
tressingly similar, succession of drenching squalls,
succeeded by broiling spells, which are the distin-
guishing feature of the doldrums. As it is on these
unreliable little spits of wind that ships must depend
to fan them across this ocean Sahara, the *Spofford's*
crew now had to brace yards, and haul sheets, and
tack constantly to catch every whiff of it. To
save the men as much as possible, Tom and the
carpenter rigged a windmill to operate the pump.
There was not wind enough to do it all, but it
helped.

One morning, a little after three bells, there was
heard a strange, hollow roaring, or rather moaning.

The ship trembled, and the blocks and gear
rattled, as though she were scraping over a reef.
All hands scrambled on deck. As Tom came upon
the poop, Captain Beebe's bald head rose through

the after-companion like a harvest moon. The sea, which was rolling in a lazy ground-swell, had become churned to froth. It spurted in jets as though a thousand whales were spouting. Mr. Gregg was clutching a backstay and looking as though he had seen a ghost. A second shock threw Tom, who had no hold on anything, to the deck, bruising him painfully. The wheel got away from the helmsman and flew round like a buzz saw.

Mr. Gregg ran to the helmsman's assistance, and Captain Beebe shouted to Tom to clew up everything. He later ordered her put under close-reefed topsails, saying the disturbance was due to a submarine earthquake, and there was no telling what might come of it yet. The stars were becoming obscured — not by clouds, but by a thin, smoke-like haze, although it was perfectly clear at the surface of the sea. While shortening sail, the obscurity overhead became complete. The captain had gone below, and Mr. Gregg was forward. Tom stepped aft and took a look at the compass. The early tropical dawn was just beginning to show, although the stars were obscured. As Tom glanced ahead, the horizon appeared unnaturally near. He watched it wonderingly, when suddenly he saw a line of white foam extending across the bows. Then he remembered that tidal waves frequently accompany earthquakes. The line of foam was nearer;

he could see it curl and hear the roaring of it.
He shouted to all hands to hold fast, took a turn
around himself with a rope, and hung on for dear
life, just as Captain Beebe leaped on deck and
caught hold of a backstay.

Although it was a flat calm, the wave came on
like a cannon shot. The side toward the ship was
concave, like the surf that runs in on the beach,
and its frothy top appeared above the topsail yard
before it struck. As the ship lay there inert —
dead, it washed clear over her. The helmsman
was driven through the taffrail, overboard. Mr.
Gregg and three men were washed away — killed
instantly, probably; and four other men were injured. These casualties were learned afterwards;
for during the next few minutes, no man had a
thought for his shipmates. The first sea set the
ship to pitching slightly. She rose almost perpen-
dicularly on the next. As Tom hung on, gasping,
blinded, and half dead, he felt a solid shock in the
hull under him. The ice had fetched away and
slid aft into the run, ripping out stanchions, springing beams, and sending a tremor through the
masts. Tom thanked Heaven fervently that the
run was filled with apples. Otherwise, the force
of the wedge-shaped mass of ice might have split
the old ship in two.

When she pitched over the crest of the wave

and plunged headlong down the other side, the ice shifted forward, stove the forward bulkhead, and mashed to pulp the apples stowed in the peak. On account of its previous movement aft, it had sufficient leeway to strain her and start a leak. The third and last of these awful seas caught her, and, as she climbed wearily over it, that internal iceberg could be heard and felt, as it slid back and forth, trying to ram the bows and stern out of her. Captain Beebe ordered the carpenter to sound the well. A stiff gale had come on while the big seas were occupying the attention of the crew; so, being shorthanded, everything was furled except the fore topmast staysail and the main spencer. The helm was lashed alee, and all who were able went to the pumps, for the carpenter had reported twenty-six inches in her.

The crew were in bad shape to make a long fight of it. Besides the fact that their vitality was low, owing to the long spell of hard work during the recent enervating weather, nearly every man had been more or less bruised by the first sea that boarded her. As they wearily clanked the pump brakes up and down all day, the carpenter made a discouraging half-hourly report: the water was gaining — slowly but steadily. The gale increased until it blew with hurricane force. Captain Beebe hoped to keep her afloat through the gale, when he might make a port, or even an anchorage. While daylight lasted, however, he resolved to prepare for the worst. He took two men from the pumps and provisioned the long-boat. After hours of infinite labor, hooking his tackles "luff upon luff," and taking the falls to the main-deck capstan, he got her overboard and let her ride astern by a long line.

Just before dark, Tom, who was doing yeoman's service at the pump, noticed a bit of apple come from the nozzle and go rolling about the deck. As he watched he saw more. Presently they came thick and fast. He gathered up a handful and took them down to the captain.

"Aha!" exclaimed Captain Beebe, as he rubbed some of the mashed apples anxiously between his thumb and finger, "I've been expectin' that. Have the men noticed it?"

"I don't know sir; at any rate, I haven't heard them say anything about it."

"Well, we must keep the pump goin' as long as we can. When we can't do any more, we'll leave her."

When Tom returned to the deck, he found the apples already coming up in a thick, mushy mess, like apple sauce. Inside of twenty minutes, the pump was choked. Tom reported to the captain, who ordered him to hoist it out and clear it. The carpenter again sounded the well and reported six and a half feet in her. Since the apples began to come up, the water had gained rapidly, the limbers being choked. When Tom called for a tackle to hoist out the pump, the men stared at him without offering to move. It was eleven o'clock at night; the gale was coming in heavy squalls, and it was pitch dark. He repeated the order emphatically; though he sympathized with the poor fellows, who, half dead with fatigue, knew the utter futility of the proposed task.

They stood huddled together under the weather bulwarks. Presently two of them rolled out into the feeble light of a lantern hanging inside the pantry window.

"Mr. Benton," said one, "ye can tell ol' Beebe that we're done tearin' our insides out pumpin' his ol' basket. We'll man the long-boat if he says so, an' that's all we will do. If he wants the pump h'isted out, he can h'ist it out himself an' be hanged to 'im." And away they went forward.

Tom reported their answer to the captain. Captain Beebe sprang to his feet, his face as red as the British ensign.

"What!" he roared, "do you dare come down here an' tell me that your rascally tar-pots refuse duty? *I'll* turn 'em to, an' you with 'em!"

He rushed into his stateroom and returned directly with a revolver in each hand and his eyes blazing.

I

Tom led the way on deck without waiting for an invitation.   Not a man was to be seen.

"Go forrard an' git them hounds out!   I'll turn 'em to fer ye, quick!" said the old man.

As Tom swung along from pin to pin, on his difficult way forward, he noticed that the wind was coming in vicious gusts.   While this might betoken the breaking of the gale, it was exceedingly dangerous to the *Spofford*.   Her cargo was now afloat in her, which made her terribly "logy," and as the squalls struck her, she would roll nearly to the capsizing point, recovering herself very slowly.   With difficulty he made his way forward.   There was a light in the forecastle, and he peeped in the window to see what they were up to.   Every man jack was stretched comfortably in his bunk smoking.

The sight enraged Tom.   He jerked the door open, and ordered them in rather uncomplimentary terms to lay aft — the captain wanted to see them.

"To blazes wid de cap'n an' you, too!" answered a six-foot Liverpool Irishman.

Tom's blood was up now.   He leaped lightly inside the door — he would have that Irishman out if it was his last act.   A heavy sea-boot, wet and soggy, took him between the eyes, and he tumbled backward, through the door on deck.   A fearful squall was howling through the rigging. He fell on his back in the water and struggled spasmodically. Once, twice, his feet touched the deck. Then there was a hell of swirling, roaring water over his head, and he went down, down, down, as it seemed for miles.

CHAPTER VIII

KITTY BLAKE had not, to her knowledge, a
relative in the world. So she was easily persuaded
to allow the old home to be rented, and to take
up her residence with the Haywards. They were
a childless couple, and Mrs. Hayward, a mild-
mannered and affectionate lady, lavished on merry
Kitty the wealth of maternal love that had been
pent up in her heart for forty-five years.

The fact that Mrs. Hayward had arrived at this
mature age no doubt prevented her spoiling the
girl; if, indeed, such a sunny nature could have
been spoiled. Mrs. Hayward's judgment had so
ripened with the passing years that not even her
engrossing love for Kitty could blind her to that
young lady's shortcomings, or to what was for her
best interest.

Mrs. Hayward had once had a younger sister
who was a very brilliant scholar. Even at the

early age of twenty-three, when her promising career was cut short by death, she had become prominent in Boston's literary set. As these two had no brother, their father — not without many misgivings — mortgaged the old farm and educated his youngest daughter. The venture proved such a signal success that Mrs. Hayward had ever since retained an overwhelming respect for education.

Throughout her married life she had longed for a son — that she might educate him. Bearing this fact in mind, it is easy to understand why, when Kitty Blake fell into her kindly clutches, she was foredoomed to drink deeply of the fountain of knowledge. For an entire year the good lady gave herself up to the delightful companionship of her charge. The novelty of a mother's care brought out all the latent sweetness and beauty of Kitty's character, and she returned Mrs. Hayward's affection with a love and devotion as deep and strong as the nature she had inherited from her sturdy sire.

After many tearful struggles with herself, Mrs. Hayward decided that the time had arrived for Kitty to enter upon her studies. A sorrowful scene ensued. Kitty objected to wearying her brains with French and music, mathematics and literature. "What was the good of it? Papa never knew such things, and he was proud of it." But, after Mrs. Hayward had explained her life-long ambition, and how, through Kitty, she hoped to satisfy it, Kitty surrendered at once, and promised herself to burn the midnight oil if necessary, that her friend's wish might be fulfilled. But, when she learned that it would be necessary to leave home, — to go to Montreal, where Laura had studied, — she nearly rebelled. Again her desire to please her kind guardian won; and with many tears and a breaking heart she bade adieu to the only real home she had ever known.

It was at the opening of the winter term, after a long cold ride, that Kitty arrived in Montreal. A handsome, high-backed sleigh, drawn by a pair of strong, mettlesome grays, was waiting for her. Her spirits rose mightily as, tucked warmly under the voluminous wolf-robes, she was whirled swiftly through the clear, keen air, to the merry jingling of the sleigh-bells. Next to the graceful careening of a swift boat, when the breeze is stiff enough to hint a spice of risk, Kitty Blake admired the flying heels of a lively horse.

She was received by Miss Lavinia Randolph, the elder of two sisters who conducted the famous seminary for developing sweet girl rosebuds into severely erudite, spectacled blue-stockings. Miss Lavinia was a buxom, rosy, jolly lady of sixty. She greeted Kitty with a kiss, the heartiness of which was beyond the shadow of a doubt, and

personally removed her wraps. She drew a chair
to the blazing log fire for the new pupil, and at
once made her feel that she was among friends.
After the old lady had gained her confidence, and
put her perfectly at her ease, a few of the other
pupils were introduced. With the rare tact acquired during years of experience with strange
girls, Miss Randolph kept Kitty by her all the
evening; showing her the thousand and one little
attentions that would have been so sadly missed
this first night among strangers.

Before Kitty had been a week in the school,
her schoolmates pronounced her "jolly," and her
teachers took to her. She studied hard: at first,
to please Mrs. Hayward; afterwards for the pleasure her vigorous mind experienced in overcoming
difficulties and acquiring knowledge. Her fallow
brain absorbed instruction like a sponge, and her
healthy body enabled her to endure hours of the
closest application. Flattering reports of her progress were sent to Portland, and the doting heart
of Mrs. Hayward swelled with maternal pride.
Kitty soon found her affinity in the person of
Nellie Druse, a slight, gentle, and somewhat backward English girl, six months her junior. They
were attracted to each other by their differences,
like the opposite poles of a magnet.

Kitty took Nellie under her wing, helped her

with her lessons, preached independence of spirit
to her, and mothered her generally. She asked
Miss Lavinia to allow them to room together.
That shrewd student of human nature, observing
that each was the complement of the other, readily
agreed.

In the delightful hours that intervene between
going to bed and falling asleep, the two girls
opened their hearts to each other. Kitty told
Nellie of Tom — all about him, not even hiding
what she believed to have been her father's villany toward him, and Nellie listened with absorbing interest.

"Is he pretty?" she asked.

"Pretty?" repeated Kitty, in a sort of dismayed
surprise that she had been confronted with a question that must be answered to Tom's discredit.
"Tom Benton pretty? Why — n — no; at least,
you see, Nellie, I never thought about him that
way, nor you wouldn't either; you'd like him right
away. Tom is good!"

"I know he is, dear, and I know I should like
him because you do. Are you going to marry him
when you grow up, Kitty?"

"I should like to," replied Kitty, frankly, "if —
if — I only knew whe — whe — where he is now.
Poor Tom!" And these two innocent lambs
mourned the unknown fate of Tom Benton.

Nellie's father was a very wealthy man, with innumerable interests in many parts of the world. He owned immense lumber districts in Canada, and tea plantations in China and India, besides sugar and coffee plantations in the West Indies and on the Spanish main. He owned or controlled great fleets of ships which found almost continuous employment in handling the products of his various industries and supplying them with the necessary tools and stores for the business. He was a director in numerous boards, controlling great interests all over the world. He travelled almost constantly; sometimes with his family, at other times alone. While in Montreal on a business trip, he became acquainted with the establishment of the Misses Randolph, liked the old ladies, believed their methods were right, and entrusted them with the care and education of his only daughter, — the apple of his eye.

Nellie never tired of telling her bosom friend about her father. Her love for him overshadowed all else. He was handsome, generous, kind, and, to sum it all in the one phrase that to her expressed perfection, he was "awfully jolly." Both girls received letters regularly from home, and it is safe to assume that the correspondent of each read a great deal concerning the other's chum. When the second vacation arrived, Nellie's father

was away, and would not be able to see his little
girl for several weeks. The natural result was
that those intervening weeks were spent in Portland with Kitty Blake. Here Nellie saw the very
places where Tom and Kitty had spent their few
pleasant hours together, and heard all the old tales
retold, living the scenes over in her strong sympathy for Kitty.

As the vacation season approached again, Nellie
told her father of her wish to have Kitty pass it
with her. "Where would he be?" He was unable to say positively, until about six weeks before
the time. He then wrote to her that he had decided
on a trip to La Guayra, where he had purchased
a large cocoa plantation. He wished to inspect
the property, and, if she and her chum cared to
go, he would call for them at Halifax and guarantee
them a good time.

Would they go? They could hardly sleep with
excitement at the prospect. Atlases and histories
were conned for information concerning La Guayra,
but about all they learned was that it was the
seaport of Caraccas, and terribly hot. "But
pshaw," said Nellie, "I know papa; he'll not
take us to a place where there's no fun; or, if
he has to go to such places, he'll only stay as
long as he's obliged to and then be off somewhere
else. We'll have a good time, you see if we don't."

There was only one drawback to their prospective happiness. Kitty feared she would be unable to visit Mr. and Mrs. Hayward if she went so far away, and she couldn't slight them, not even to go with her friend. Nellie said little, but the next mail carried a very urgent letter to her indulgent father. "He must invite Mr. and Mrs. Hayward, or she and Kitty would not be able to go." The return mail brought the requisite document, couched in such a well-bred manner that it put the invitation in the form of a request for a great favor.

Kitty now found herself with a big contract on hand. The Haywards could not think of such a thing for a moment. It was absurd to expect them to accept an invitation like that from a perfect stranger. But sometimes the fates conspire to be kind. Mr. Hayward had been particularly successful in business for the last three years and had not had a holiday in twenty-five. Under the circumstances it was not difficult for his wife to persuade him that he needed a good long rest; so they had arranged to treat Kitty to a trip through the West during her vacation. The proposed sea voyage upset all their plans. They knew the dear girl had her heart set on going with her chum, and would not enjoy anything else. It was an extremely delicate situation.

Kitty, of course, showed all her letters to Nellie, and explained, while Nellie corresponded with her father. As he was a man whose life had been devoted to solving riddles and overcoming obstacles, he soon straightened out the tangle and managed to overcome the scruples of his sensitive guests, so that when the five-hundred-ton British bark *Albatross* sailed from Halifax, she carried as merry a party of pleasure-seekers as is often seen afloat or ashore, including Mr. and Mrs. Hayward.

CHAPTER IX

WRECKED AGAIN — THE CATAMARAN — THE HOME OF
THE WARUNAS — LIFE ON A MUD-BANK — A QUEER
FUNERAL — UP THE GREAT RIVER — A STRANGE HAR-
VEST — ESCAPE

As Tom partially lost consciousness, he thought
Captain Beebe was yelling at him from the poop.
He could not understand the order, but dared not
ask for a repetition of it. He heard a confused
roaring, his head was bursting, and he saw stars
and flaming swords. Suddenly he shot half his
length out of water. His lungs were filled with
life-giving air, and he struck out instinctively, and
opened his eyes. There was no ship visible — nothing — nothing but blackness, made lurid by the
phosphorescence of the breaking seas. He swam
aimlessly about, swallowing the salt water that was
flung over his head by the gale. This could not
last long. He was becoming momentarily weaker,
and with the increase of bodily weakness his mind
became resigned to his fate. Tom Benton had
never been of a religious turn. Few seamen are.
In this, his extremity, no thoughts of the future tor-

"

mented him. He did not wish to die, but, there
being no hope, he was resigned. In that supreme
moment, he had but one regret. Kitty Blake would
never know why he had failed to make good his
promise. This troubled him. He could not decide
to cease his struggles and voluntarily drown, though
every labored breath — consisting of a large percentage of water — was torture.

Suddenly, in the darkness before him, a spot or
patch of denser blackness loomed. He was sensible
of shelter. The wind passed over him. The sea
was smooth enough to permit his getting an occasional whole breath of air. He swam towards
the dark spot, and, as he was unable to gauge distance, he received a severe blow on the head. He
put out his hand — it was the long-boat. She was
clinker-built, and so high out of water that it was
impossible to climb into her. He remembered that
she had been in tow. There would perhaps be a
bit of the line yet fast in her bow. Slowly and
wearily — his sodden clothing dragging him down —
he swam along her side: she seemed half a mile
long.

When he reached the end of her, it was her
stern; he must have started from near her bow.
He was nearly spent, and had neither the strength
nor the will-power to work his way back along that
dreary road. Probably there would be no rope

there, anyway; it would be just his luck. He had
about decided to let himself sink, when the boat's
rudder hit him a sharp crack on the side of the
head. That roused him. "Be hanged if I'll ever
say die, while there's a shot in the locker!" he remarked to himself, and started to swim ahead again.
He reached the stem and felt about for the dan-
gling end of the rope. There was nothing.

Bitterly he repented the useless exertion. He
might have been dead now, and had it all over.
As the sea tossed him about under the boat's nose,
he thought that, by watching his chance, he might
breach from the crest of a sea, and secure a hold
on her gunwale, as he had seen seals climb upon
an overhanging rock. He waited for a good chance
— he could not afford to waste an effort. A round-
backed sea, not yet ready to break, raised him. He
leaped as far as he could, threw out his arms, and
caught — the rope. She was still fast to the wreck.
As it sprang taut again, it nearly got away from
him. It seemed as if it would tear his arms from
their sockets. But there is such a thing as a death-
grip. When the rope slacked again, he worked his
way a little nearer to the boat; and so, hope playing see-saw in his heart, as he was alternately dragged
half his dripping length from the water and soused
back again, he edged along, until his hand — one
hand — was on her rail. The sharp edges of the

wood hurt his lacerated hand, but a twenty-foot shark could hardly have broken his hold. The time came when, with his body balanced on the rail, it was an even bet whether he would fall in or out. A friendly sea raised his booted legs, he shoved with his hands, and fell in board.

He lay a long time resting and regaining his breath. Then he sat up and looked about. The squall that had capsized the ship was the last expiring blast of the gale. Here and there a star-studded patch of blue sky showed smilingly through the surly masses of heavy black clouds that were rapidly breaking up and drifting away. With the suddenness pertaining to the tropics, day dawned. The ship lay, bottom up, a few fathoms ahead of the long-boat.

What a satire on the puny efforts of man to dominate the sea! The ship, representing the crystallization of all the maritime knowledge gathered during the centuries that man has sailed, lay there a useless wreck — the coffin of her crew — while this fragile open boat, in which no one would willingly undertake a voyage, was sound and whole.

Tom hauled up to the wreck and shouted; over and over again he called his shipmates by name. He knew it was useless, but there are certain traditional forms that one does not willingly omit. With a heavy heart he cut the rope; and after

ALONE IN THE LONG-BOAT.

several attempts, — nearly falling overboard twice, — he stepped the heavy mast and set the sail. The sun was up now, and the breeze had fallen quite light; but as the sea was still running high, she bobbed about and shipped considerable water. This kept him busy baling until noon. After that she did very well. Tired, hungry, and thoroughly disheartened, Tom sat at the tiller and thought bitter thoughts. He was not a bit thankful for his escape. He envied his shipmates, who, now that it was over, were at rest. He called himself a fool for having exerted himself — for this. He was hungry and thirsty. There was a breaker of water and a bag of hard bread in the boat.

The bread had suffered from the salt water, but he found several biscuits near the centre that were dry. He ate a biscuit and drank sparingly of the warm water in the breaker; for he knew that economy was now the golden rule. His bodily wants having been partially appeased, his spirits rose, and he began to take an interest in himself. The wind having died out, the heat became intense. The sun glared down angrily at him, and its rays were reflected from the glassy surface of the gently heaving sea. He was tempted to drink continually, but restrained himself. He lowered the sail and made an awning of it. The motion of the boat caused a slight circulation of air under the

K

awning, but it was hot air. He dipped himself over the side, and from the rapid evaporation experienced a delicious sense of coolness. Being thoroughly worn out, he disposed himself in an easy position, and slept as only sailors can under such trying circumstances.

When he awoke the sun had set, and a pleasant, cool breeze was blowing. He jumped up, feeling much refreshed, set his sail, and headed her about SSE. as nearly as he could estimate it by the stars. Although he did not know the longitude, he knew that the latitude, the day before the gale, had been 10° 56′ N., and he knew from the conversation of the captain and mate that they were farther west than they wished to be; so, by what he could remember of the general trend of the South American coast, he figured that he needed to make a southerly course to raise the land, and as there was apt to be a trace of the great ocean river here, that makes up through the West Indies, he gave her, as near as he could guess, a couple of points of easting to offset it.

He had no plan. In case he failed to fall in with a trader, he would make the coast; that was all. As long as he got away from the boat before the water gave out, he was satisfied. He sailed all night; and there, alone in the boat, under the brilliant tropical stars, he thought of many things. At first he thought of his lost ship-mates; of Captain Beebe, from whose influence he had hoped so much. Now his plans were entirely upset again. He was just where he started when he left Portland. Worse — much worse. He had often heard his father say that his long life at sea had been as uneventful as it would have been had he passed it on a farm. Why did he have such terrible luck? He almost wished he had been drowned with the rest.

With the return of daylight his buoyant nature reasserted itself. He decided that he had been spared to enable him to try once more to make good his promise to Kitty Blake, so he took a fresh grip on himself and silently renewed that promise to come home captain of as fine a ship as ever her father commanded. Captain, indeed! He was in a fine way to become a captain. He was more likely destined for shark bait. Then he remembered that even now he was captain, ay, and owner too, and he laughed loud and long at the merry conceit. He enjoyed the sound of his voice, so he talked to himself. "All you need to do, Tom, my boy," said he, "is to get a good deal bigger ship and you are all right. If you ain't Yankee enough to do that, with the start you've got, you are no good, and I'll shake you the first chance."

He dowsed his sail at sunrise, hung a bowline over the stern, and took a swim — keeping close to her in case of sharks. As the wind still held, he set his sail again, and continued on his course until three or four o'clock in the afternoon. The breeze died out then, so he rigged his awning and went to sleep. He awoke sometime during the night and got under way again, and again he had an attack of the blues. He was lonesome, terribly lonesome, and for the first time he began to worry. Perhaps, after all, he should have steered to the westward of south. He might not be as far west as he had at first thought. If there was a current, he might be in an eddy of it. The more he thought about it, the less positive he was as to the general formation of the coast-line; it was years since he had seen a chart, and just as likely as not he had been sailing all this time away from the land instead of toward it.

Thus he tormented himself with doubts. Finally, he changed his course to due south, as nearly as he could judge. He wanted to make the land — any land; if it was uninhabited, he could take a run ashore, and then coast along until he found inhabitants. That he might see where he was going, he decided to sleep nights; so, an hour after sunset, he spread his awning and lay down. He would doze off, and wake feeling cramped and uncomfortable. He would turn over, try to find a position in which the boat's timbers would not punch holes in him, and fall asleep again. He dreamed all sorts of things, waking with a start, and towards morning he reënacted the capsizing of the *Spofford*. He was standing in the forecastle door calling the men. He heard the roar of the squall as it struck her in its fury. He felt a shock — there was a crashing of timbers, and he awoke floundering in the water.

He heard strange voices shouting wildly in a strange language. A great coarse-looking sail was disappearing rapidly to leeward. He had been run down as he slept. He shouted lustily for help. The queer-looking craft bore down on him, its occupants calling out in their outlandish lingo. He yelled to them not to run him down. As they held to their course, he dived deeply to clear her bottom. On returning to the surface, he called out again. They appeared to be bewildered by the new direction from whence the voice came. There was a great jabbering, the big sail jibed, and, just as the first level rays of dawn glimmered across the water, Tom saw the craft that had wrecked him. It was a catamaran, manned by three Indians, and consisting of three logs lashed together with thongs of fibre, rigged with a bamboo mast and a sail of coarse matting. It was

unsinkable, and, while the thongs lasted, inde-
structible. No wonder the long-boat had gone
down before it; it had a ramming power almost
equal to a man-o'-war. She was steered by a very
old and wrinkled Indian with a paddle. There
were two young men, one little more than a boy,
with him. They pulled Tom aboard, chattering
all the while like monkeys. No doubt they wondered how he came there; but, being unable to
converse with each other, he could not tell them.

They resumed their voyage, heading to the westward, the old man steering, the others squatting
silently on the logs. Tom noted that the water
had changed from a deep sea blue to muddy yellow,
a sign that they were approaching the mouth of a
great river. About ten o'clock, the peaks of a
distant mountain range were dimly defined in the
clear blue atmosphere. Immediately after, long
lines of low bushes on either side proved that they
had already entered the river, though Tom had
supposed them to be still several miles at sea. The
old man now gave up the steering paddle to one
of the others, and talked long and earnestly to
Tom, who understood never a word. He then made
motions equivalent to asking him if he was hungry.
On being answered by affirmative nods, he produced from a corner of his untidy waist-cloth a
handful of dried turtles' eggs. Tom looked at

them dubiously. He recognized the hospitality of the act, but he shook his head with a smile. "I guess I'll wait for the pie, Cap'," he said. The Indians ate the queer-looking provender with undoubted relish.

In spite of her clumsy appearance the catamaran made remarkably good time, and as they neared the bank Tom observed that it consisted of a dismal strip of mud. Alligators basked in the sun and birds innumerable pattered or flew screaming overhead. Tom pointed upstream, and said to the old captain, "Amazon?" The old fellow regarded him stupidly. Then he remembered that they could not possibly be so far south as that, so, pointing again, he asked, "Orinoco?"

Now they understood; they all bobbed their heads vigorously, and shouted in reply: "Si, si, Rinoke, Rinoke." So this was one of the mouths of the mighty Orinoco, and these were Waruna Indians. Tom had read of them, and knew they were not savages. But what was to become of him now?

Before night they arrived at the island home of the Indians. It was a mere mud-bank, like all the surrounding country. The village — if it might be dignified by such a name — consisted of five huts, or rather shelters. They were built upon piles stuck in the mud, and were simple structures of bamboo and reeds, thatched with palm leaves. At each hut, a catamaran, or a canoe, or several of the latter, were moored to the piles. On the raised platform that served as floor there was a mud fireplace. This was the kitchen. Between the posts grass hammocks were slung. Nearly every hammock had an occupant swinging lazily, but some were too lazy even to do that.

The arrival of the catamaran created hardly any stir. A few heads languidly rose above the gunwales of the hammocks, only to fall listlessly back again. The catamaran had been on a trading voyage, though the sum total of their homeward-bound cargo would hardly amount to a dollar's worth. When the few bundles were passed up, the owner's wife and children became interested enough to sprawl out of their hammocks and admire the bits of bright calico and cheap trinkets that "papa" had brought them. The presence of a white man created a mild excitement. Only the grown persons were familiar with the appearance of white people, the children — mud larks, Tom called them — not having yet travelled to the outer world. The odor of boiling fish which saluted Tom's nose when he arrived in "the sitting room" was most welcome, for he was famished.

The old gentleman remembered that Tom was fasting. He spoke to one of the girls, who immediately brought him a calabash of chowder. Remembering his manners, Tom neglected to analyze it. He took it on trust. Barring some unfamiliar flavors, it was good and very filling. The oldest daughter, a young lady of sixteen or seventeen years, took a great shine to Tom — which he did not reciprocate. She admired his fine white skin and coaxed him to *peel*.

As she evidently considered him her personal property, she sent some of the younger children — of whom there were eight or nine — to call the neighbors. She collected a gang of fishy-smelling young aborigines, who crowded around him, staring with all their eyes and commenting on his outlandish appearance. When he could stand it no longer, he backed to the far side of the platform for air. The young ladies followed him up, handling him quite freely. They passed their unclean paws over his hands and face and toyed lovingly with his hair. They begged him to remove his shirt, that they might feast their eyes on a larger area of white pelt. Tom's bashfulness disappeared in the face of their earnest pleadings. Who could hold out against the wiles of such guileless charmers? He yanked off the old blue shirt. Their admiration, expressed in high-flown Waruna, was boundless.

They slapped his shoulders, pinched the white

flesh, and tickled him, until he could stand it no longer. Convulsed with laughter, the tears running down his cheeks, he turned to dive off the platform overboard. They divined his purpose, and surrounding him held him back, while they pointed to the water and shouted in tones of horror, "Caribe! Caribe!"

Not understanding, and thinking they merely wished to frighten him, he broke away and dived off. The instant he touched the water, it seemed as if a hundred hot pincers were tearing the flesh from his body. Frantically he climbed aboard the catamaran. He was bathed in his own blood from the merciless attacks of those voracious little devil-fish — or fish devils — the caribes. It was fortunate that the raft lay so handy, for the caribes would have stripped the last morsel of flesh from his bones in very short order. The girls dressed his wounds, consoled him, and gave him much valuable advice — which might have benefited him had he understood it. Tom put his shirt on, and declined to oblige the ladies after that.

The Indians passed nearly all their time in their hammocks. Tom wondered when the houses and canoes were built, and how they procured food. He soon discovered that generous old Dame Nature did nearly all the work. The palms and bamboos produced nearly everything they required, very little labor being necessary to complete and fit the articles for use. They were too indolent to wear anything out except the hammocks, and they were pretty tough. As for food, thousands of fish of many kinds were swimming at their very doors, begging to be caught, while the trees among which they slept were alive with birds, monkeys, and other animals. The Indians, being experts with bow, arrow, and blow-pipe, had no occasion to fear a meat famine; and, as the teeming forest was full of fruit and vegetable-bearing plants and trees, their menu was only limited in variety by their laziness.

Tom was provided with a hammock, and before morning he appreciated the wisdom of the Indians, who slept during the day. Howling monkeys, owls, tree-toads, birds, beasts, and insects kept up a distracting clamor. Mosquitoes, fleas, bugs, caterpillars, spiders, and small snakes made it their business to see that he should not lack for diversion. He rolled and squirmed, scratched, slapped, and grumbled at his tormenters all night. He heard an occasional half-surprised, "Caramba!" from a native, when an extra lusty gallinipper succeeded in penetrating to the quick, but as a rule the Indians slept well and did not appear any lazier or more exhausted than usual.

Tom kept a good lookout, and a couple of weeks

after his arrival he was made happy by the sight of a distant sail. The vessel was so far away that it appeared merely as a white speck, but it looked like civilization and home. He shouted and pointed it out to the Indians, who merely grunted and rolled over for a fresh nap.

Having picked up a few words of their language, he signified his desire to go. They declined to allow him to leave. He had nothing with which to bribe them, and was unable to explain that they would be rewarded for delivering him aboard a vessel.

Tom wondered if he was to pass the remainder of his life with these dirty savages on their mud-bank. He was exceedingly weary of the uneventful life, and worried about his wasted time. As he paddled the canoe when his owner fished, he became quite an adept at handling the awkward craft. He decided to steal a canoe and escape at the first opportunity, but a certain favorable combination was necessary to make the undertaking a success. There must be a vessel, for to sail off into unknown waters would be foolish. There must be — at the time of the vessel — an opportunity to steal a boat, and that was the most unlikely part of it; for, aside from the fact that some one was nearly always awake, they had a most reprehensible habit of stowing their oars and sails on the bamboo rafters over their hammocks. This place being also the storehouse of their ancestor's bones, it was a difficult feat even in daylight to get anything from there without upsetting the beaded baskets of human relics. During his stay on the island he had an opportunity of witnessing one of their strangest of funerals. His owner's mother — a very aged squaw — was found dead in her hammock one morning. As soon as the sad news became known, her dutiful son tied a manatee-skin rope about the neck of the deceased and lowered her tenderly into the river. The water became instantly alive with caribes, and next morning the orphan drew up a beautifully cleaned skeleton — all that remained, outside of the caribes — of his parent. This he proceeded to cut apart and stow carefully in the basket prepared to receive it. When all the separated bones were snugly packed, there was just room for the skull, which grinned gleefully over the edge at the mourners. The basket was then filed away in the garret, there to remain until accidentally disturbed.

The blazing days and stifling nights dragged along for two full months. Not another sail, nor anything but birds and alligators, had Tom seen. Suddenly a strange activity pervaded the colony. This was brought about by the passage of three west-bound canoes loaded with Indians, who hailed the village. Much shouting and excited waving of arms ensued. Tom understood that the strangers were admonishing his friends that the time had arrived to go turtling. Hasty preparations were made, and the next morning all the grown people, except a couple of aged squaws, and all the children over fifteen years of age, embarked in canoes and catamarans. The trade wind was strong and steady. They set their sails, and, in spite of the four- or five-knot current, made very fair progress to the westward.

They told Tom they were going far up the river for turtles' eggs. He welcomed the change heartily. The catamarans, being fine sailers, took the canoes in tow, and they skimmed merrily over the yellow water. During the first few days, the change affected even the phlegmatic Indians, and an air of joyful activity pervaded the fleet. This soon wore off, however, and they relapsed into their normal state. Tom forgot that he was virtually a prisoner. He was greatly interested in the tales they told of the great turtle country. He learned that they expected to be two or three weeks on the way, and would pass a great city of white men, called "Angostura." He wondered if he might not be able to escape when they arrived there, but he found they had no intention of stopping. They sailed continuously, night and day.

As the Orinoco is more like an inland sea than a river, and the Indians kept well out in the stream, Tom saw but little of the land. Occasionally a palm-thatched hut could be seen nestling under the luxuriant foliage, but the inhabitants were either asleep in their hammocks or off to the turtle harvest. Before they had been a week out, they began to see an occasional "Bonga," or "Lancha," making its way between river ports. The sight was reassuring. It reminded him that they were away from the mud-bank at last, and he promised himself never to return to it.

One day a big American schooner came beating down against the trade wind. She passed so near the little fleet that Tom could see the man at the wheel and the captain leaning on the corner of the cabin. He shouted and waved his arms. The captain looked listlessly in their direction, saw an Indian boy waving his arms, but paid no further attention.

Tom's heart sank and his eyes filled, as the handsome schooner glided gracefully away, gently courtesying to the ripples.

A couple of days later they passed Angostura, or Bolivar, with a small place called Soledad on the opposite side. Tom gazed longingly at the dome-shaped hill and the buildings. They were the first he had seen since leaving Boston. He begged the Indians to put him ashore. Had it not been for the caribes, great as the distance was, he would have swam for it. The Indians paid no attention to his pleadings, but held stolidly to their course. Tom wondered if he would ever speak to a civilized man again. His position seemed almost ridiculous.

This long river trip came to an end at last, and they arrived at their destination, — a group of sand-bars uncovered by the falling river. For several days there had been many turtles in the river, all swimming in the same direction, upstream. On the morning of their arrival the river was almost impassable, so numerous had they become. There were hundreds of Indians ahead of them — for they were a little late, and the harvest was in full blast. The instant the canoes reached the shore, the younger members of the party jumped out on the sand, shouting and yelling with glee; they rushed to the shallow pools which the first-comers had scraped in the sand and stocked with baby turtles. These they seized and thrust in their mouths, all squirming. They crunched and swallowed them with the same zest that Tom would have eaten strawberries. The turtles were so numerous they were unable to wait until night, or even to dig holes for nests. They scrambled out of the water in all directions, jostling each other and scattering their eggs all over the place. The blazing sun shrivelled and spoiled them by thousands, and one could hardly take a step without trampling eggs and young turtles under foot. The Indian boys played ball with the eggs, and pitched young turtles into each other's open mouths. Such lavish abundance of natural wealth Tom had never seen anywhere, not even in this land, where nature spontaneously produces everything in extravagance. He had seen the river teeming with countless varieties of fish, and the forests and mud-banks crowded with birds and animals, but here was a scene of prolific animal life the like of which is probably not to be found elsewhere on earth.

All hands commenced work at once. Fires were built, at which the women dried the turtle flesh and eggs for future use. While a part of the men slaughtered turtles, others proceeded to build straw huts for the party to live in during their stay. The boys and girls gathered eggs. Tom was of this party. At first they simply picked up the eggs that lay about, but as many of these were addled, having been exposed to the hot sun of the previous day and afterwards to the cool night air, they let them lie, and dug from the nests. In each nest would be one large egg, — a male; these they invariably threw at each other.

When they saw an unusually large turtle, they would turn her on her back and leave her vainly waving her flippers until the arrival of the men. As the supply of eggs was inexhaustible, the

L

women soon had more than they could dry in a day, so a couple of canoes were washed carefully and blocked up level on the sand. The eggs were washed until perfectly free from sand and thrown into the canoes. Water was added, and then the boys got in with their bare feet and mashed up the eggs. On this mixture being left in the sun, the oil would float to the surface, and was afterwards refined in pots over the fire. The daily food consisted of turtles and turtles' eggs, and Tom was surprised at the culinary skill which the squaws exhibited, as they cooked the delicious morsels in an infinite variety of ways, each apparently better than the other. In spite of the richness of the eggs and meat, they appeared perfectly wholesome, and did not cloy on the appetite. All hands got fat, and were as jolly as aldermen.

During the passage up the river, Tom had noticed many fires on shore. The Indians, in answer to his questions, had told him they were built by the " Llaneros " to burn off the dead grass. " Llaneros ! " They would be white men.

About a week after their arrival, a big fire was seen away to the northward on the great treeless plain, or Llano. In the evening, while the women were skimming the oil pots, and the men were lying about in the warm sand, Tom strayed down to the beach. There were few Indians away from their camp. Jaguars roamed the beach at night. Tom watched the sparks flying through the dense black smoke, and the great sheets of flame that shot up like fiery tongues as an extra heavy bunch of grass, or perhaps a small bush, contributed its mite to the grand spectacle. He had a small bag of dried eggs. A canoe had just been emptied of oil and lay on its side, draining. He put his shoulder to her, dug his toes in the sand, gave a mighty heave, and she was afloat. Cautiously he boarded her, on the dark side, confiscating a paddle which was sticking in the sand. He gave her a shove, and lay down quietly in the bottom. Presently he heard voices. Then the firelight flickered across the canoe above him. Presently a voice — the voice of the old Indian who ran him down in the *Spofford's* long-boat, — cried in startled tones: "Whose canoe is that adrift?"

CHAPTER X

TOM heard and understood. He decided to put
on a bold face, and raising his head above the gunwale replied in, as he flattered himself, excellent
Waruna: "She's not adrift; I'm going up to the
other island on a visit."

His old friend recognized his voice, raised a
howl, and two canoes were at once launched in pursuit. It was now or never, so Tom seized the
paddle and plied it as no Waruna had ever done
since they fled before the cannibal Caribes to the
mud-banks of the great delta. He had a little start,
and his pursuers could not get up enough enthusiasm to entirely overcome their natural laziness.
Tom's canoe shoved her nose in the sand a half
dozen lengths ahead of his foremost pursuer. He
dropped the paddle overboard, seized his bag of
dried eggs, and leaped ashore. Turning, he gave
the canoe a sturdy shove out — it was a lucky
thought — and sprinted for the interior and liberty.

The Indians, valuing the canoe more than they did him, never landed at all. Without even a glance over his shoulder Tom ran while his breath lasted. Then he walked towards the fire, which had now burned itself pretty well out. He fell into several armadillo holes, — frightening both himself and the occupants,— floundered through small puddles of water alive with fish and *Bavas*, a species of small alligator, but escaped all harm. Becoming too tired to proceed, he decided to lie down and wait for daylight. In the vast Llano there seemed to be no choice of places, so he was about to throw himself on the ground, when he heard an ominous rattling, saw something move, and by the faint starlight he discovered that he had nearly lain down on a six-foot snake.

This sight rested him so much that he continued to walk until daylight, when he discovered a clump of small palm-trees. With a handful of grass he swept the ground under them, disturbing many small animals. He walked around the group and carefully inspected the tops. Seeing nothing more ferocious than squawking birds, he lay down and dropped asleep at once.

He awoke, lying flat on his back. The hot sun was blazing, the perspiration was pouring from him, and he was nearly hidden by a swarm of flies. He sat up, brushed the insects away, and looked forth on the great level "Llano of the Apure." He heard a rumbling like distant thunder and felt a tremor in the earth. Remembering the famous earthquake of Caracas, he scrambled to his feet. It was only a herd of cattle on the other side of his clump of palms, driven by a couple of men on horseback. Tom stepped out in full view and shouted, waving his arms and running toward them.

A brawny mulatto, with a wide hat that flapped as he rode, and a pair of cart-wheel spurs strapped to his naked heels, galloped up to him like a whirlwind. As he came tearing on, with his long black hair flying in the wind, and doing a lot of entirely unnecessary yelling, Tom began to fear that he had made a mistake and was trespassing on the grounds of a lunatic asylum. The vaquero rode straight at him. Tom's Yankee was up, and he stood his ground. The wild man nearly threw his horse on his haunches, as, swerving a bit to one side, he stopped within four feet of him, and asked in Spanish who he was and how he came there. In a mixture of English and Waruna, Tom gave a brief account of himself, but the vaquero, not understanding, ordered him, partly by signs, to mount behind himself.

Although the horse stood like a rock, Tom was unable to accomplish the feat, never having been on horseback in his life. With a grunt of disgust, the yellow giant seized him by the collar, and before he knew it he was seated. The vaquero dug his spurs into the animal's ribs and let out one of his unearthly yells. They darted forward as though fired from a gun, Tom barely saving himself from a tumble over the stern by clutching wildly at his captor's waist. Away they went at a terrific pace, right in among the cattle, who were rearing and plunging in frantic fear. The dust was blinding, and in spite of his death grip Tom could hardly retain his seat. As the mulatto swayed about continually, shouting and yelling at the cattle, Tom expected every minute to be thrown off and have his brains dashed out. He was so busy hanging on, that he was unable to look where they were going, and when the headlong race came to a partial stop, he was surprised to see a number of low, palm-thatched buildings. This was the headquarters of " El Hato de Santa Barbara," one of the great cattle farms of the Apure. The stock were frantically rushing and jostling into the Majada, a corral formed by driving heavy posts into the ground, thus forming a great pen with a funnel-shaped entrance.

The mulatto leaped lightly to the ground, and as Tom had not relaxed his hold, he was dragged after him, falling in a heap. This caused a hearty

laugh from the assembled vaqueros, who fired a
rapid volley of questions at "Juan Amarillo," as
to where he had found his queer prize. They
invited Tom to breakfast. The fresh beef, seared
at an open fire, "Cafe con leche," and tortillas
tasted wonderfully fine to him after being so long
confined to the diet of the Warunas. To the great
surprise of the vaqueros, Tom declined their offer
of aguardiente. Such men were unfamiliar on the
llanos.

After breakfast some of the men entered the
majada and drove a lot of the animals into the
corrallejas — which was a smaller enclosure. They
packed them in as tightly as they could stand, and
the majordomo, who was to boss the job, several
vaqueros armed with garrochas, — a ten-foot combination goad and rattle, — and all the boys on the
place, including Tom, mounted the fence. Three
men, armed with lassos, then entered the corrallejas
among the frenzied wild animals and commenced
lassoing calves. Tom thought they would all surely
be killed. The cows resented the attacks on their
offspring, and when a poor little calf, bellowing
piteously under the merciless prods of the garrochas
and the cruel tail-twistings to which it was subjected,
was dragged toward the gate, its mother would make
frantic efforts to get to it; but being packed so
tightly, the poor parent's efforts were unavailing.

Once through the gate, the unfortunate was seized and thrown, and when half a dozen were ready, a white-hot brand was stamped hissing upon their flanks. Again they bellowed and kicked, their protests being answered from within. Sometimes they discovered a young bull, two or three years old, who had so far escaped. Then there was fun. He could not be so easily lassoed and dragged out. He would fight.

After the crowd on the fence had goaded him with their garrochas, and yelled until they were tired, one venturesome fellow leaped nimbly into the seething pit of tossing horns, and gave the princeling's tail a furious twist. He may have defied all other methods, but the tail-twist is a convincing argument, and, with a snort of fear and pain, he dashed through the open gate. The fellow with the lasso had preceded him, catching a turn around a post like a man snubbing a canal boat. As the infuriated animal rushed blindly about, the llanero improved every opportunity of taking in slack, until he had the bull safely moored by a very short warp to the botalon. One brown-skinned mass of bones and sinews grabs the animal by the hind legs and another by the tail. They tug and sweat, the dust of the fray envelops them, and the excited spectators on the fence shout encouragingly to men and bull: "Bravo, Juan!" or "Bien hecho toro, da le una patada mi hijo!" ("Hooray, John!" or "Well done, bull! Give him a kick, my son") and so on with the utmost impartiality. Suddenly there is a crash, and the voices of the wrestlers are heard pantingly making disparaging remarks concerning the characters of the bull's female ancestors for several generations back; the dust settles, or thins a bit, and the proud young animal lies prostrate. After maiming and disfiguring him, he was let up, and then he had his innings. As there was no more to be done to him, the llaneros desired him to leave, but revenge is sweet. Leaping to his feet, his eyes rolling in a frenzy of fear and rage, and lashing his sore flanks with his recently outraged tail, he charged wildly on his tormenters. The crowd on the fence cheered him lustily; but his blind rage was no match for the nimble heels of his foes. They jeered at him as they deftly stepped aside, allowing him to charge vainly on the empty air. A new and inexplicable sorrow had come into his young life. He left the place dehorned, branded, and an ox.

At dinner time, Tom was introduced to Don Rosario, the majordomo, who was a magnificent specimen of the Venezuelan llanero. Big, broad-chested, and muscular, his fine face was brightened by a pair of flashing black eyes and ornamented with a fierce-looking moustache. He questioned Tom, but of course learned nothing. The dinner was enlivened by much loud and excited conversation, good-natured jokes, and hearty laughter. Tom regretted his inability to understand the conversation, for it would have been pleasant to talk once more with *people*.

The branding was continued after dinner, and finished about three o'clock. Several young bulls were then collected in the corrallejas, and some of them were tied to the botalon. The boys immediately jumped down from the fence. Tom was pushed off from behind. A couple of lusty vaqueros seized him and tossed him astride one of the bulls, backwards. The tail was handed him, and the bull prodded to frenzy with the garrochas. Mechanically Tom clinched his legs around the neck of his charger, who tore round the enclosure like an animated whirlwind. By the time Tom was started, all the boys had received mounts, and, as the gate was open, the bulls made a break for liberty. Scared though he was, and sore from his morning's ride, Tom knew he must keep his seat. It would never do to be beaten by the boys. To his surprise, after the lapse of ten or fifteen minutes, he was not only alive, but still on board his uncomfortable craft. Through the clouds of dust he caught fleeting glimpses of boys and bulls, as they flew across his field of vision like shooting stars. The shouts, yells, and roars of laughter of the vaqueros, accompanied by the rattling of the rings on their garrochas, stimulated the bulls to wilder bursts of speed. They kicked, bucked, and shied in their efforts to be rid of their burdens.

Having discovered that he could stay on, Tom now wondered how he was to get off. His steed was now circling around the bunch at some little distance, which enabled him to obtain a pretty good view of the performance of the others. A young fellow suddenly leaped from his bull, while in full career, and, without letting go of the tail, he seized a horn with the other hand, and ran by the beast's side. Tom saw him twist and jerk the tail to make the maddened bull increase its speed. There appeared to be a scuffle, a great cloud of dust was raised, and other animals and their riders intervened and cut off the view. When Tom again caught sight of the pair, the bull was on his back, and the young vaquero sat upon him in triumph, holding the bull's tail between its legs. Now Tom knew how to dismount.

His own playfellow was as lively as a newly caught skip-jack, and getting fuller of kinks every minute. The volley of "bravos" that greeted the other successful young fellow encouraged Tom to try. He had not had a good view of the whole performance, and had grave doubts of his ability; but he was ambitious to get out of the boy class.

Successive bravos were wafted to him through the din of his own performance, telling him that the boys were dismounting one after the other. He must hurry up. There seemed to be no choice of time or place, or if there was, he was unable to recognize it. He was becoming tired of the strained position. It must be now or never. He let go with his legs, and, remembering that he was progressing backwards, attempted to vault off.

He was conscious of a great noise, a flashing of lightnings, and of swallowing a quantity of dust, and then he lay on a pile of hides in one of the houses, sore all over, his clothes torn to rags, and himself more or less covered with blood, and raw spots. Painfully, after many trials, he rose to his feet. A short inspection proved that he was all there, and possessed of many newly acquired protuberances. He limped to the doorway just as old Manuel, the lame cook, hobbled past with a calabash of water. He wondered if Manuel had received his injuries from riding, or rather dismounting from a wild bull. The old fellow leered at him, muttered something, and beckoned him to follow.

He followed Manuel to his cooking place. The old fellow chattered in his incomprehensible lingo, taught him to drink "mate" through a tube, and helped him to cleanse and repair himself. When the vaqueros returned for the night, they chaffed him and laughed at him good-naturedly. They sat up late, whiling away the time with music, singing,

dancing, and telling stories. Tom gave them " Hail
Columbia," "Yankee Doodle," and " Haul the Bowline," and they learned the chorus of the latter, join-
ing in heartily. By the time they were tired of their
diversion, and ready to turn into their chinchorros for
the night, Tom believed he had partly effaced any
bad impression made by his fluke in bull riding.

Before daylight they were up again, saddling their
horses. Tom made Don Rosario understand that he
wished to go with them and make himself useful.
The majordomo called up a bright young fellow,
Santiago Nuñez by name, and, after giving him some
instructions, turned Tom over to him.

Tom Benton, the Portland sailor, now entered upon
a course of education as a vaquero, which continued
for nearly a year. He never became as expert as the
natives: they are bred to the business from their childhood, and know nothing else ; but he learned to ride
as only cowboys can. He got on well with the entire
outfit, but Santiago was his bosom friend. When
Tom acquired enough of the language to converse
intelligently, he was in great demand as a story-
teller. The hardy llaneros would ride miles from
neighboring hatos to listen to the strange tales told
by the " marinero Americano," and as they knew
absolutely nothing of the world, outside their own
llanos, Tom's stories interested them as fairy tales do
children.

He enjoyed the life exceedingly. Aside from the excitement of the cattle business, the plains, pools, and rivers teemed with strange and beautiful forms of animal life. Hardly a day passed without a new and interesting discovery. He became familiar with animals, birds, and fishes, of which he had read and seen pictures; crocodiles and electric eels, the great anteater and the armadillo, monkeys and parrots of many kinds; vultures, toucans, herons, wild ducks, and turkeys, an infinite variety. Then there were jaguars, boa constrictors and poisonous snakes, reptiles and insects galore; while wild hogs and deer furnished them with sport and a change of diet from beef, fish, and fowl.

He had many painful falls, and was subjected to much good-natured chaffing, before he learned to ride perfectly. He had also many narrow escapes before he became sufficiently expert with the lasso and garrocha to protect himself and master the wild animals; but he stuck to it bravely, rubbed his hurts and tried again. After the third trial, and much coaching from Santiago, he threw his first bull. To seize a wildly fleeing bull by the tail, and when necessary leap from one's horse's back and throw the animal, is an art that requires practice, and Tom felt quite elated when he accomplished it. Santiago told of it that night, and the old vaqueros slapped Tom on the back and congratulated him heartily.

"Now, indeed," they said, "he was learning to be a man."

The rainy season came, and they drove their stock to the high land, the "*matas,*" which seem to have been especially provided as refuges in these vast plains during the time of the annual drowning out. The wild inhabitants accompanied them. This was not an unmixed pleasure; for the scarcity of food made them overbold, and necessitated keeping a strict watch night and day. The vaqueros were obliged to make a careful search of the camp before retiring, and to kill or drive out the snakes, scorpions, centipedes, tarantulas, etc., who made themselves entirely too neighborly for comfort. The dreary wet nights were made hideous by the screeching and howling of owls, monkeys, and jaguars, who seemed bent on keeping every one else awake as well as themselves.

This dreadful season was very depressing to the spirits of the men. They slouched through their duties in a half-hearted way, and there was no fun in them, so that all hands, including the animals, rejoiced when the rains ceased. When the sun once more appeared, the mud quickly dried, and the tropical vegetation grew in leaps. It was a joyful day when Don Rosario ordered a return to the plain. With whoops and yells, swinging lassos and brandishing garrochas, the herd was rounded up, and the two days' drive to the ranch began. But little damage had been caused by the flood: there was a deposit of mud over everything, but the new grass was already springing up, and within a week the only trace remaining of the inundation was the high-water mark on houses and trees.

About six weeks after their return, the vaqueros were surprised by a visit from Don Ramon, the owner, who came with a party of friends from far-off Caracas. He was received with shouts of welcome by his men, who galloped madly round and round his little cavalcade, displaying their daring horsemanship, and yelling to their hearts' content. After bowing gravely, hat in hand, in acknowledgment of their welcome, the Don, who was a handsome old gentlemen with long white moustache, withdrew with his friends to the house of the major-domo for dinner. Swift riders were dispatched to the distant parts of the hato, to call the rest of the men in for inspection.

Before sundown they were all drawn up in front of the house — a hundred and fifty as tough-looking bashi-bazouks as were ever corralled at once. When Don Ramon appeared, they rent the hot air with vivas. He and his friends bowed again and again; but it seemed that they would never be done. Their enthusiasm was so spontaneous, so hearty, so full of life and vim, that it seemed a pity to

M

cut it off; but the old warrior had something to
say. He raised his hand for silence. When they
choked back their noise and quieted their horses,
he said in a strong, deep, melodious voice — a
voice that one could imagine rising clear above
the din and clash of arms: —

"My children, it gives me great pleasure to find
you all well and prosperous. It is a little more than
a year since I was here last, and Don Rosario has
given me a very gratifying account of your services since that time. But I have not come here
simply to compliment you on the faithful performance of your duties: that would be the merest
idleness, for when have you been otherwise than
faithful? No, my sons, I have come on a much
more important mission. Important to you, to me,
and to Venezuela. Don Jorge, who promised so
much when we installed him in the presidential
chair, has steadily receded from the duties which
he solemnly swore to perform. He has violated
the oath he took to support the constitution and
defend the flag; he has conspired with our ene-
mies; and when we remonstrated with him, he assumed the character of dictator. My children, our
country is in danger. This vile traitor has seized
the treasury and corrupted the army. To-day, I,
your patron, am an exile; driven from Caracas
by Don Jorge!"

His voice had gradually risen until it rang out a clarion note. He was bareheaded, and his white hair seemed to rise and surround his fine old head like a halo. Men and horses were as silent and immovable as statues; but when he paused for a moment at the end of that last sentence, which he knew his faithful followers would accept as indictment and proof of foulest treason, a roar went up, the like of which was never heard before in "El Hato de Santa Barbara." They cheered wildly for their patron, and consigned the President and all his family, friends and followers, to the deepest, darkest, and most dismal dungeons in the nether world.

A semblance of quiet having been restored, Don Ramon continued : —

"I thank you, my children, for this expression of loyalty. I knew I could trust my brave llaneros. Venezuela, in this her hour of need, looks to you, to the gallant llaneros of the Apure, to extricate her from the toils in which Don Jorge, the base traitor, has bound her. I and my friends go to visit the other hatos of the Apure and La Portugesa; but I will return in a couple of weeks to lead you to Caracas. We will teach those despicable traitors that, in the llanos, Venezuela has brave sons who will not stand idly by and see her good name defiled, nor her banner trailed in the mire."

Once more sombreros waved, garrochas rattled

wildly, and a hundred and fifty lusty throats endorsed the speaker's words. They cheered for Don Ramon; for his companions; for Venezuela; the flag and the llanos.

Don Ramon, with his hand on his heart, bowed low. He bowed over and over again. A grim smile overspread his features as he turned to his co-conspirators and asked their opinion of his llaneros. And so a revolution was born.

CHAPTER XI

WHILE the visitors returned to the house, the men gathered in knots, eagerly discussing the prospect of war. They were eager to follow their beloved leader, as they had followed him before, into battle, and the cause was a matter of indifference to them. Don Ramon had said that he wanted them, and his quarrel was theirs. Had not Don Jorge exiled their beloved patron from the city? They would not be content until they saw, each one for himself, Don Ramon with his foot on Don Jorge's neck. The possibility that Don Ramon might be wrong, never occurred to them.

During the next two weeks excitement ran high at the ranch. The vaqueros were like children

impatient for a holiday. The prospect of taking part
in a bloody revolution — of slaughtering a number
of their own countrymen and looting their homes —
elated these pastoral gentlemen to the seventh
heaven. How much nobler to kill men than to drive
cows! They told tales of former wars in which
they, or their relatives, had followed the banner of
that persistent old rebel Don Ramon, and indulged
in brilliant flights of fancy about the deeds they
would do. Saddles and stirrups were put in order,
and garrochas and machetes overhauled and sharpened. New horses were caught and broken, and
the evenings rang with improvised songs, reciting
the heroic deeds of Don Ramon and many other
turbulent spirits whose fame was familiar.

Was a cow to be killed, the butcher would call
to his companions to observe what he would do to
Don Jorge. When a vaquero brought a wild bull
to his knees, he would cry out gleefully: "Asi! asi!
Voy a hacer al traidor, Don Jorge, caramba!"

Tom became inflamed with the universal enthusiasm and shouted: "Viva Don Ramon y Venezuela! Muera Don Jorge el traidor!" as lustily as
any. The vaqueros looked forward eagerly to the
possession of firearms, which alone would have been
a sufficient inducement for them to take up arms.
Their garrochas and machetes — murderous weapons
in the hands of such experts — dwindled into insig-

nificance, in their estimation, in comparison with a gun — any kind of gun that would go off with a bang.

A number of fine, fat steers were rounded up as provision for the army. Everything being in readiness, the eventful day was awaited with impatience. Every morning surmises would be offered that "Mi Señor" will arrive to-day. Scouts went out daily to meet the advancing column, only to return at evening, dusty and disappointed.

At last, on a bright forenoon, with the trade-wind gently rustling the long grass of the llano, a strange horseman came galloping up to the ranch, swinging his sombrero and calling on the followers of Don Ramon to mount.

With a wild hurrah the men sprang into their saddles, the corral was opened and the cattle turned out. Now the head of the advancing patriot army appeared, with Don Ramon leading, mounted on his veteran war-horse, "Bolivar," a magnificent coal-black charger, which was his inseparable companion, and as uncompromising a rebel as himself. Don Ramon's immediate retinue consisted of the friends who had contributed men and animals, as well as their own services, to his cause. As they were still in their own country, they had no advance guard. Immediately following the general and his staff came fifteen hundred llaneros, riding in "open order," or rather regardless of any order at all. They were driving a large herd of cattle and spare horses. Don Ramon ordered the Santa Barbara contingent to fall in at once, as he desired to get part of the cattle across the river before night, if possible.

The new recruits were greeted enthusiastically by the main body. Aguardiente was served, and amid much boisterous patriotism success to the adventure and confusion to the enemy were drunk. The cattle joined the herd, and Tom found himself surrounded by the wildest and most motley throng it had ever been his fortune to meet. They were bold and fearless as eagles ; careless and simple as children; and their devotion to their leaders was fervid and unquestioning. With such backing, what might not an unscrupulous politician accomplish? The cattle bellowed in protest. The bulls pawed the turf in accompaniment to their rumblings, and raised such a cloud of dust that breathing became difficult. Some of them were continually breaking away and making a dash for liberty. Then would ensue a wild scurrying on the part of the vaqueros to bring the truants back.

Sometimes it would be necessary to lasso the leader; then, while one dragged, another followed prodding with a garrocha, until, alternately hanging back and rushing ahead, he would be returned, snort-

ing and shaking his shaggy head angrily, to the herd.
The llaneros kept up a continual singsong to amuse
and quiet the cattle; they told them in improvised
doggerel that they were the pick of the flock, and
should consider themselves highly honored in having
been chosen to feed the patriot army of " Nuestro
Señor, Don Ramon."

Two hours before sundown they reached the river.
Here they had quite a contract on their hands.
Many of the cattle and horses had never seen the
river before, and those who had, protested against the
passage; but the vaqueros knew how to handle
them. Half a dozen men driving a squad of madri-
neros — tame oxen — rode into the river, beating the
water and shouting to drive away the crocodiles.
The others, seeing it could be done, submitted under
the impulse of abundant prodding, shouting, and tail-
twisting. The vaqueros swam their horses on either
side, encouraged and helped them, and finally got the
entire herd across before sundown. Half a dozen
beeves, two horses, and one man were lost at the
ford, and Tom had a toe bitten off by caribes; for,
like the rest, he was barefoot, having learned to ride
vaquero fashion, with only the big toe in the stirrup.

They went into camp on a convenient mata. This
military operation consisted simply in killing beef
enough for supper and searing it at open fires. They
had neither tents nor hammocks. After supper sen-

tries were posted to watch the cattle; aguardiente
was served, and the first night on the trail of "El
maldito traidor, Don Jorge," was passed in singing,
dancing, and bragging until near morning. Then
these doughty warriors, wrapped in their ponchos,
dreamed of the glory they were to win on many well-
fought fields.

Tom and Santiago were detailed for sentry duty in
the first watch. As the cattle were feeding, they
were kept pretty busy galloping after stragglers; but
there was plenty of help. The sentries had received
their share of aguardiente, and, as the Santa Barbara
crowd had not been all day in the saddle, they rather
had the best of it; for the others caroused until re-
lieving time, and were then obliged to stand watch
the rest of the night. The army was up, had breakfast, and was gone, before daylight. Early hours
prevail on the llanos, as the middle of the day
being too hot to work is devoted to sleep. It was
impossible to march fast on account of the cattle.
The way was rough, there were creeks and rivers to
ford, bogs to wade through, and long stretches of
stony ground that made travelling difficult and slow.
With such a lively company, however, the time
passed pleasantly. The most difficult part of the
journey was the crossing of the great swamp of
Camaguan. It was absolutely necessary to cross in
one day, as there was no possibility of encamping in

the swamp. A twelve-hour halt was made to give the animals a good rest, and then at three o'clock in the morning they started.

It was a trying ordeal. The cattle were continually becoming mired, requiring to be pulled out by the men and horses, who were but little better off themselves. There was no lying over in the middle of the day here. Many animals had to be abandoned, many more strayed away, and no one could be spared to go after them; so that, when the army at last struggled out of this slough of despond at eleven o'clock at night, they would have become an easy prey to the enemy. Men and horses were jaded, and the cattle could have been herded by a three-year-old boy. As they were too tired to feed, another day was lost here. On the morning of the second day, bright and early, camp was broken, and a start made for Calabozo, where it was known that the firearms were stored.

At the "Mision de Abajo," by order of Don Ramon, a brief halt was made while all hands cleaned up for their entrance into the city. A guard was left to watch the cattle, while the rest were formed in procession, four abreast, and admonished to retain the formation. Before reaching the city, a deputation was met who had come to escort General Ramon and his retainers to the public square. Here the llaneros were given a reception fit for a conquering army. Calabozo did itself credit. Don Ramon and his centaurs were hailed as patriots, deliverers, and what not; aguardiente flowed in rivers; and the bright smiles and sparkling eyes of the lovely Calabozanas fired every patriotic heart. The llaneros were in clover : nothing was good enough for them; now they knew, if they never had known before, what a fine lot of fellows they were.

General Ramon, fearing the enervating effects of so much coddling, marched them off, with many backward glances of vain regret, and camped them on a beautiful meadow on the Guarico. Here they remained for two days, holding open levee and entertaining the crowds who came out from the city to admire and praise. Tom was so well pleased at once more beholding clean streets and blocks of houses, that he felt severely the privation of being so soon driven forth again; but he was too enthusiastic a partisan, and too much a lover of discipline, to complain. On the morning of the third day they were marched to church — an unprecedented event, with most of them — to partake in the celebration of mass. From church they returned to the great plaza, and were presented with their arms by Don Enrique Robledo, the Governor of the province. Don Enrique made them a speech, which fired their patriotism still more, and then the guns and ammunition were distributed. There were long

Kentucky rifles, United States army muskets, double-barrelled shot-guns, highly prized, and a few blunderbusses and old Queen Anne flint-locks. In addition to these there were some three hundred brass-mounted horse-pistols, and a few — very few — Colt's revolvers. The ammunition was as varied as the guns. There were bags of bird shot, buck-shot, rifle bullets, musket balls, and a lot of sheet lead and old lead pipe for the home manufacture of slugs.

The ammunition, like the guns, was distributed promiscuously; the result being that a man armed with a squirrel gun would receive a bag of Daniel Boone bullets, a quarter or half an inch larger than the bore of his weapon. Another fellow with a blunderbuss, that would hold paving stones, had nothing to put in it but a lot of bird shot. Such little drawbacks as misfit ammunition, however, could not dampen the ardor of the patriots. So long as it was lead, they would get along. A little judicious pounding on a wayside rock would reduce an overgrown bullet to the desired gauge. As it might not be convenient at all times — say in the heat of battle — to manufacture ammunition, the vaqueros, who were men of many resources, pounded out their slugs beforehand. If the fellow with the blunderbuss and bird shot could not knock an angle off a granite fort, he could throw

dust in the eyes of a good many traitors at a single
discharge, and make as much noise as the next
one, which after all was the main thing. So they
took their miscellaneous arms, and were proud and
happy.

Tom, with commendable faith in Uncle Sam,
chose a United States musket, and traded ammunition until he got some that fairly fitted. By his
advice Santiago did the same; so between them
they made quite a powerful battery.

During this important proceeding, the distribu-
tion of arms, they were the centre of an admiring
circle of the wealth and beauty of Calabozo. They
were admired, ogled, and flattered, and when all
had been supplied, the good priest, Padre Antonio,
blessed their weapons. Then, indeed, they knew
themselves to be invincible. Amid waving ban-
ners, a rattling discharge of small arms, and the
huzzas of the multitude, they marched forth — a
gallant band of heroes — to battle for what they considered right. No man can do more. They picked up
their cattle and turned their faces resolutely toward
Caracas — the home of the arch traitor, Don Jorge.

During the next week, they picked up many
recruits — both men and animals. As they were
now approaching the enemy's country, Don Ramon
halted for three days and drilled them. The vaqueros did not take kindly to military manœuvres;

they saw no sense in it. They preferred to whoop and yell, gallop about and fire off their guns. But the old general was a strict disciplinarian, and the only man they feared. They were his "children," his "sons," his "llaneros"; but for disobedience of orders he would have them shot — therefore they loved him.

At the end of three days they could tumble into some kind of order, perform a few simple evolutions, and hold their fire until told to let it go.

On resuming the line of march, two hundred picked men rode a mile ahead to beat up the enemy. Tom Benton and Santiago Nuñez were members of this advance guard. The remainder were divided in two squads, which marched on either side of the cattle, enclosing them in a living corral, as it would be too heavy marching on the ground the cattle had trodden. A small party was detailed as whippers-in to bring up the rear. The fellows to leeward needed to be thoroughly seasoned vaqueros; for none but a thoroughbred could stand the dust, odor, and flies which fell to their lot.

The llanos were now behind them, and they had arrived in a country where opinions differed. The inhabitants no longer flocked to the rebel standard as they had done. The cattle suffered from the novelty of hill climbing; therefore their progress was slower than ever. News of their arrival

now travelled ahead of them, and five days after
leaving their training quarters, the advance had
a brush with a squad of national cavalry.

When the vaqueros saw the cavalry, they
charged, yelling and firing their guns. By the
time they were in range, their guns were empty;
but undaunted, they continued to charge with
garrochas and machetes. The cavalry fired a volley at close range, emptied half a dozen saddles,
wheeled and took the back track. The vaqueros,
who were better horsemen and better mounted,
overtook and killed a score of them. It was no
part of their plan to take prisoners. Extinction
was the motto in these wars. An injured cavalry-
man was dragged to the presence of General Ramon,
who questioned him concerning the movements of
the enemy. He answered with curses and revilings,
and was cut down.

It was learned that Don Jorge was fortified within
the city and had no intention of coming out to give
battle. This information was false. The cavalry
scouts, whom they were continually meeting, kept
Don Jorge posted in regard to their movements.
Don Ramon threw out scouts ahead of the advance
guard. These reported only small bodies of the
enemy in sight, and, as they were continually driven
back, the vaqueros became greatly elated, believing they were going to have it all their own way.

One day, at sundown, they reached a small land-locked valley within five miles of Caracas. Don Ramon went into camp here, intending to leave his cattle and take the city by storm early next morning. Sentinels were posted at the various passes and on the summits of the surrounding hills, while the men were ordered to be ready for instant service.

Don Jorge's scouts had kept track of these proceedings, and every rebel sentinel was covered by a couple of government soldiers with orders to *quiet* him, at the setting of the moon. So well were these orders fulfilled that, for an entire hour, the rebel camp slept unguarded.

A single rocket rose hissing in the clear night air, and simultaneously a deadly volley was poured into the sleeping camp from all sides. Not an enemy was to be seen. Amid the cries and groans of the wounded, the vaqueros sprang to arms. "We have been betrayed!" was heard above the general din, as they fired a futile volley in all directions. General Ramon was everywhere. He was in his element; this was war! He told his men to reserve their fire until they could learn the position of the enemy, and ordered them to take shelter behind the cattle; but the cattle were stampeded and were rushing madly about the close valley, seeking an outlet. They trampled the wounded, and wounded others. As the fire came from all sides, there was no shelter; and as

N

the vaqueros were unable to reload their unfamiliar weapons in the darkness and confusion, many threw them away.

With the ready decision of a veteran, Don Ramon called on his men to follow him to Caracas. Nobly they responded: with cheers and yells, with cries of " A Caracas! A Caracas, muchachos!" they followed their gallant leader in a charge on the pass leading to the city.

Don Jorge, knowing the desperate valor of the llaneros, had foreseen that such would probably be their course. To receive them he stationed a corps of sharpshooters, picked riflemen, on each side of the narrow pass, hidden behind trees and rocks. The llaneros were permitted to enter, until a thousand men were in the trap. A single word rang out sharply on the night air, " Fuego!" and the pass became a deadly crater. From all sides blazed forth a murderous crossfire. With many others, gallant old General Ramon bit the dust. He died as he would have wished — with the music of battle in his ears and a bullet in his heart. The vaqueros, armed only with garrochas and machetes, their highly prized guns thrown away, turned with yells of rage and defiance to climb the perpendicular walls of the pass in search of their tormentors. They were brained with rifle butts, sabred, bayoneted, and tumbled back — clutching wildly at the air — upon their fellows.

These, undaunted by their fate, continued to ascend. The remainder of the government troops descended into the valley from all sides, keeping up a continuous fusillade. The vaqueros, unable to reply with their useless guns, followed, true to their leader, into that deadly defile — the Caracas pass. The stampeded cattle, driven by the soldiers, followed, trampling the wounded and charging madly upon the others. For more than four hours the slaughter continued. The sun rose and poured his blistering rays into the ditch, piled six and eight deep with the dying and dead. The victors, though wearied with monotonous slaughter, maintained a desultory fire, and a moving head or arm among the mass attracted attention and a bullet.

Where was Tom Benton all this time? He and Santiago after canvassing the prospects of the morrow, and deciding that the government troops, shut up in the city, would receive a very unpleasant surprise in the morning, lay down and slept soundly. Tom's last thoughts were a hazy wondering as to why he was here, mixed up in the wars of a people in whose concerns he had no interest. Then he fell asleep, to be aroused by the initial volley fired upon the sleeping camp. He sprang to his feet, dazed by this new experience.

Santiago still slept. Tom, like the others, had discharged his piece. He stooped to shake his friend; but he saw by the dim starlight that it was useless. The top of Santiago's head was shot off, and he had not heard the volley that killed him. Filled with horror and rage, at what seemed like a cowardly murder, Tom sprang eagerly after Don Ramon, who was calling his "children," his "sons," to follow him, reloading as he ran. He tipped the powder horn into the muzzle of his gun, and a handful of grass, gathered as he ran, wadded it home. There were five fingers in her without the ball. A bullet and four buck-shot and she was loaded for bear. He saw Don Ramon throw up his hands and fall over backward. Somebody hit him on the shoulder, leaving a sensation as though he had been branded. He was a partisan before; now he was an avenger. By the glare of the discharge he saw above a rock a head wearing a government uniform cap. He raised his gun; his left arm was dead, yet it did its duty and supported the barrel of his piece. There came another volley, and again he saw the head. The black eyes were looking straight into his — along a shining rifle barrel. Tom fired. His overloaded gun kicked like a mule, nearly dislocating his shoulder and throwing him down. As he fell, he saw the soldier's rifle drop, his cap fly off, and the upper half of his head disappear, as though it had never been. Santiago was avenged!

Tom scrambled to his feet. The boys were charging up the bank. He seized a lance from the hand of a dead vaquero and he too rushed up the bank after them. The comrade of the soldier whom Tom killed had fired at him, and, seeing him fall, supposed his shot had taken effect. He was therefore surprised to see Tom climbing up the bank, lance in hand. He had no time to reload. Tom did not see him. The soldier reversed his piece and brought the butt down on Tom's bare head. It was a blow to brain an ox, but a loose stone rolling under Tom's foot saved him from the full force of it. He saw a blaze of light, as if the sun had fallen at his feet, and tumbled over into the shambles. Other bodies fell on him and he was partly buried.

CHAPTER XII

By ten o'clock the rebel forces were annihilated, and the victors desired to return to town and receive the ovation that was their due. A detail was sent to round up the cattle and drive them in, and an attempt was made to drive them through the pass, but the decent brutes refused to desecrate the last resting-place of heroes.

The sudden cessation of the noise tended to restore Tom Benton to his senses. While still in a dreamy, half-conscious state, he was rudely awakened by a sharp gripping at his scalp and the settling of a heavy weight upon his head. He opened his eyes to see a vulture in the very act of pecking them out. He tried to cry out, but his tongue and the roof of his mouth were as dry as a powder-house. A sign of life, however, was sufficient to frighten off the filthy bird, which languidly hopped a yard away and resumed its horrid feast. As Tom glanced down the pass, the sight sickened him. Carrion crows, vultures, buzzards, and millions of flies swarmed and gorged themselves on what, but a few hours before, had been a magnificent body of brave men.

Tom was pinned down by a ghastly load of rapidly decaying human bodies. If the birds deserted him, not so the flies, for they remained on his face, and in his mouth and nostrils. He was lame, sore, and benumbed; but by sheer strength of will he wriggled himself out. There was a bullet-hole in his left shoulder, his right was bruised and lame from the recoil of his gun, and his head ached and buzzed dizzily. His scalp was torn, and his body and legs were bruised by the impact of the bodies that had fallen on him. The sun blazed fiercely down in the pass, and he was so faint from hunger, thirst, and loss of blood that he could hardly drag his battered body about. He must get out of there. He must find water or die. The thought that there might be others yet alive in that fearful Golgotha restrained him from immediate flight; for he was not one to desert a shipmate in distress.

As he stumbled weakly about over the heap of slain, the carrion birds barely hopped out of his way. He tried to identify some of the dead, but the tropical sun had already done its work. He also failed to find any who needed his assistance. He had not inspected a quarter of the pass; but his feeble body refused to obey his will. He must now look out for himself, so he crawled off, half delirious, into the bush in search of water. How long he staggered about through the thick under-brush, he never knew. At length he stumbled upon a clear, cool spring, the first and finest he had seen since leaving the "Mision de Abajo." Down he went, on all fours, in his haste falling in and nearly drowning himself. He soiled the water sadly, but what of that? He drank, and drank, until he was nearly bursting; yet his thirst was not quenched. He tore up his rags and washed and soaked his wounds, finding the cool water extremely grateful to the fevered flesh. Then he drank again — more yet. He drank until the pure, sweet water tasted bitter, and still his mouth was dry. He wetted a piece of his shirt and laid it on his sore head, and placed another upon his wounded shoulder. It fell off, and it was a trouble to hold it there; yet it felt so good! He sat down and leaned against a tree, placing the wet rag between it and his shoulder. Ah, that was fine! There was a breath of air, which, evaporating the water from his scanty rags, conveyed a sense of luxurious coolness. The myriad voices of the forest soothed him, and he slept. Regardless of wild animals, reptiles, insects, or stragglers from the enemy, Tom Benton, the sole survivor of Ramon's rebellion, slept.

Sir John Laidlaw was one of those adventurous Englishmen who, not content to live quietly at home shooting over their well-kept preserves and attending to the multifarious duties which, as English gentlemen, devolve upon them, go gallivanting all over the world clad in inconvenient costumes, and impressing their obtrusive British individuality on all with whom they come in contact.

Sir John had been two years "doing" South America. Having ascended the mighty Amazon and crossed the Andes, he had tramped to the southern part of Chile, recrossed the Andes, and was now working his way from Montevideo northward. Being possessed — as all Britons appear to be — of unlimited means, he had money and supplies waiting for him at all the principal cities on his route. Consequently he presented the strange sight of a thoroughly equipped sportsman in the dense wilderness of a South American forest — with dogs, guns, camp equipage, and help galore. Although his habit of allowing nobody to precede him frequently got him into tight places, with true British obstinacy he persisted in it. It was due to this habit that, on the afternoon of the massacre in the Caracas pass, he suddenly planted his heavily shod foot on Tom Benton's sore leg.

"Ouch!" roared Tom, on being so rudely awakened.

"Bless my soul! What have we here?" asked Sir John, recoiling in surprise.

Tom, looking like a ragged spirit of the woods in hard luck, and much surprised at the welcome sound of his mother tongue, scrambled clumsily to his feet, and stared at the gentleman rudely.

"Say that again, mister, please," he cried; "I ain't heard a word of English for so long, I'd almost forgot there was such a language."

"You're an Englishman!" exclaimed Sir John, holding out his hand with an air of frank pleasure.

"Not exactly," replied Tom, grasping the proffered hand, and wringing it heartily; "but I'm just as good, I guess. I'm an American!"

"Every bit, my lad, every bit! But what brings you out here in the bush all alone? Why, you're hurt!" he added in a tone of concern, as he caught sight of a patch of blood on Tom's neck.

"Oh, that's nothing," replied Tom; "it's only a scratch. I'd take as many more gladly for the pleasure of meeting with a civilized person once more."

By this time Sir John's retinue, consisting of half a dozen men, came up. He ordered them to pitch his tent at once near the spring. In a remarkably short time they cleared a space with their machetes, and set up a roomy tent. A fire crackled, and the welcome smell of boiling coffee greeted the noses of the hungry men. Sir John produced a medicine-chest, and dressed the wound in Tom's shoulder, which proved to be merely a crease. Then he clipped the hair from the cut in his head, washed it carefully, and sewed it up with silk, their tongues running constantly all the time.

Sir John knew nothing of the rebellion in which Tom had taken part. He had been in "the bush," as he called it. "It's strange," said he, "that these South American republics can't keep order. I see no other way but that England will have to step in and take charge of things. It's a shame, the way they neglect their natural opportunities. They've got some of the most magnificent country on the globe, and they let it lie waste. Can you tell me how far we are from La Guayra?"

"No, I haven't the least idea. I did hear last night that we were within five miles of Caracas," replied Tom.

"Oh, then it's not far. Caracas is only ten or fifteen miles from La Guayra, and I'll not be sorry to get there. I've been two years in the country; and while I must say I've enjoyed every minute of it, I wish to go home. Are you going to stay in the country, my lad?"

"No, sirree; I am not! I want to get away to sea again. I'm only wasting my time here."

" By the way, I haven't asked your name. I am Sir John Laidlaw, of Laidlaw Manor, Kent."

"My name is Thomas Benton; I belong in Portland, Maine." They shook hands again, and each expressed his pleasure at making the acquaintance of the other.

"Then, as you do not intend to remain in the country, if you have no other plans, I should be pleased if you would accompany me as far as La Guayra, at least. We shall be company for each other, and I am sick and tired of these natives. I shall stop a couple of days at Caracas, or perhaps only one, and then go on to the coast."

"I should like to first-rate, Sir John, but you see how I am fixed. I have only what I stand in, and that's about ready to drop off. Besides, I hardly think it would be safe for me to go to Caracas; I'm a rebel, you know," added Tom, laughing.

"Oh, that's all right! I have plenty for two, or for half a dozen, for that matter, and can get more at La Guayra; so, if you'll come, I shall be more than pleased, and as for any one bothering you in Caracas, I'd like to see them try it while you're with me. I'd have an English regiment quartered on the town inside of ten days."

Tom thanked Sir John heartily for his kindness, which he admitted he never expected to be able to repay, and, like a sensible fellow, accepted the good things which the gods had thoughtfully provided.

Next morning they rose bright and early. Tom rigged himself like a regulation Englishman from Sir John's kit, and, after a hearty breakfast, they proceeded to Caracas. Sir John wished to have a look at the pass where the rebels had been ambushed the day before; but as they were to leeward of it, they found it impossible to approach it nearer than half a mile.

Before nine o'clock they stood looking down into the beautiful valley of Chacao. The handsome little city of Caracas nestled in the level bottom, and surrounded by rugged mountains looked as much out of place as though it had been transported from some distant country by one of the magicians of old. Nearly opposite from where they were standing, those two grand peaks — " Naiguata " and " Cerro de Avila," forming the " Silla " or Saddle of Caracas — towered aloft like sentinels. As they approached the city, their attention was attracted by many ruins, still standing, and piles of débris — sad reminders of the great earthquake of 1812, when twelve thousand of the inhabitants were buried under their ruined city. "Why," Tom wondered, "did they rebuild on such a fatal site ?"

When they entered, they found the streets full of soldiers and intensely patriotic citizens, who were making the air ring with vivas for Don Jorge and all manner of anathemas for the accursed rebels, which went against Tom's grain. The entrance of Sir John and his party created quite a little stir. A half-drunken, gold-laced officer swaggered up to them, and, assuming an air of extreme ferocity, shouted as a challenge: "Viva la Republica! Mueran los perros traidores!"

His manner was so insolent that it roused Sir John's ire. The swarthy little desperado stood squarely in front of them, blocking their way. Sir John seized him by the neck and thrust him to one side, saying, "Come, Johnny, get out o' the way!" in English.

Like a flash the officer whipped out his sword, and, ripping out a string of vile epithets, sprang at them. At the very first onset Sir John's valiant retainers took to their heels, leaving him and Tom to take care of themselves. Fortunately, they each had guns. A crowd of cursing, raving fanatics quickly collected. Sir John and Tom backed slowly into a corner, and, with their backs to the wall, kept their assailants at bay. No one resorted to gunpowder, so it became a case of club swinging as opposed to sword play.

The officer, reënforced by a couple of his comrades, pressed them hotly, while the crowd cheered. Sir John, although he spoke the language fluently, jibed at them in English. He called them "Garlic-eating monkeys," and assured them that, when through amusing himself, he would wipe them off the face of the earth, and make their nigger government pay him for his trouble. In spite of his boasting, however, their position was becoming momentarily more unpleasant, for they could hardly ward off the lightning-like blows of their wiry and tireless assailants.

"When I say 'Go,' charge the beggars, Tom!" said Sir John, without taking his eyes off them or relaxing his efforts for an instant.

"All right, sir," replied Tom, "whenever you say the word; though I should like to lay out this red-nosed one."

"Never mind the red-nosed one, lad; we've got to get out of here; they keep coming thicker and faster."

The next moment, with a great clattering of hoofs, a squad of mounted men came galloping round the corner, and charged directly into the crowd, scattering it in all directions. Their leader demanded to know what the fuss was about; but before Sir John could reply, the little scamp who was the cause of it all stepped boldly to the front, and, addressing the officer as "General," informed him that these two rebel spies had entered the city in broad daylight and cheered for Don Ramon.

The absurdity of the charge forced Sir John to laugh, angry as he was. His levity ruffled the dignity of the "General," who gave the order to his followers, "Al Calabozo!" Our two friends were seized forthwith, their hands were tied behind them, and they were thrown across a couple of troopers' horses. The squad proceeded at a trot to the other end of the city, where the prisoners were thrown into the calaboose — a square, stone building containing but one room, utterly destitute of furniture, with the ground for its floor, and one small, heavily barred window ten feet above it. The rawhide thongs with which their wrists were bound, cut and chafed their flesh painfully. They had both received slight wounds during the fracas, and were dying of thirst. Sir John stamped up and down the dirt floor and raved.

"Oh, but you'll pay dearly for this outrage!" he cried. "I'll bankrupt your confounded banana plantation for you! Wait till I get out of here! I'd give every penny I own for half an hour of the Gordon Highlanders or the Enniskillen Rifles! This will be an expensive job for you, Don Jorge!" Thus he ran on until, wearied out, he sat down on the ground and gritted his teeth in impotent rage.

"What do you suppose they will do with us, Sir John?"

"I know very well what they'll do with us.

They'll release us, salute the British flag, and pay a thundering big indemnity. That's what they'll do. I am sorry to have got you into this trouble, Tom; but I'll see you through it, my lad, and you shall not lose anything by it, either."

"Oh, that's all right, Sir John; I'm very much obliged to you. If you had not found me and taken me in tow, I should probably have been killed out there in the woods before this: either by a jaguar, or a party of their scouts hunting stragglers. I don't mind this. I only wish they would take off these bracelets and give us some water; my mouth is as dry as Julius Cæsar's powder horn."

"Have you a knife, Tom?"

"No, sir."

"I have, but it's in my jacket pocket; if I could get at it, I'd soon have these darbies off."

"Couldn't I get it out of your pocket?"

"May be; it's in the right-hand pocket. See if you can reach it."

Tom backed alongside, and after considerable fumbling managed to reach the knife, which was a clasp one, with a very stiff spring. Their hands were partially benumbed by the thongs, so it took half an hour or more to get it open. After that, they quickly cut each other loose and rubbed a little life into their hands and arms. A rapid inspection of the jail convinced them that it was

o

built to keep people *in*, as the window was heavily
barred, while the door was a massive iron grating
opening into a dark passage, and the walls were
heavy blocks of hewn granite set in cement. Sir
John said that if he could get word to the British
Minister, that door would come open mighty lively.
"Yes, indeed," said Tom, "or if I could reach the
American Minister, either."

Sir John gave him a rapid glance, then, looking
away again, said : —

"I wouldn't advise you to say anything about
America, Tom. It isn't a pleasant thing to say; but
during my two years in South America I have had
considerable business with consuls and ministers,
and I have met a good many English and Americans. The result of my observations is that, while
the Queen always protects her subjects, Uncle Sam
sometimes lets his whistle. I have known a number
of cases where American citizens have been compelled to apply to the British Consul for protection,
and have got it, after having been denied by their
own. You leave this to me. I'll appeal to the British
Minister on behalf of both of us, and we'll be taken
care of."

This was a bitter pill for Tom Benton, a patriotic
young American, to swallow, but he knew it was true.
It was a tradition among seamen, so he acknowledged
the corn, and thanked Sir John for this additional

favor. Toward evening the doors were flung open with much unnecessary noise, and a negro entered bearing two calabashes. Through the open door they saw two soldiers. Sir John demanded to be taken before the British Minister. The soldiers cursed him and turned away. One of the calabashes contained about a quart of tepid water, the other a filthy looking mess of boiled black beans. After a miserable, sleepless night, passed in rolling about on the hard dirt floor and scratching, they received a breakfast which was the counterpart of their supper.

About ten o'clock the doors were again thrown open and they were marched, at the head of a hooting, jeering mob, to the military headquarters, where they were shoved into a small hot room and locked up for four hours more. Again their door was slammed open, and four soldiers, armed with rifles and bayonets, entered. They ranged themselves on each side of and behind the prisoners, and escorted them through a narrow corridor, an open courtyard, and another corridor to a large hall. Here half a dozen gold-laced officers were sitting as a court-martial.

Among the crowd that lined the wall, they recognized the little devil who had caused them all this trouble, and three of Sir John's servants. The court was called to order immediately on the arrival of the prisoners, by a pompous old villain in a fiercely cocked hat. He laid his sword with a great flourish

and clatter on the table, and called in stentorian
tones, as though he was drilling an awkward squad,
"Attencion!" Profound silence ensued. After
waiting a sufficient time to allow the sense of his
importance to soak into the minds of the audience,
he stated that it was a fact well known to the court
that the prisoners, with many other foreigners, had
taken part in the recent rebellion of Don Ramon, and
had fought in the battle of the pass. The prisoners
(he added) were captured the day before with arms
in their hands and in open hostility. What had they
to say why sentence of death should not be passed
upon them for their treasonable and seditious act?

Sir John replied that, on behalf of himself and
companion, he denied the charge, and also the ju-
risdiction of the court. As British subjects, they
demanded to see her Majesty's representative. Ignor-
ing this demand, the judge called Sir John's three
servants, cautioned them in regard to their testimony,
and asked the fellow who had been the steward of
the expedition if he knew the prisoners.

"I do, señor. I know them well."

"Who are they?"

"Two Englishmen, señor."

"What do you know of them?"

"I was at work on the tobacco plantation of my
patron, Don Hernandez Acevedo, when I heard the
firing. I started to see if I could be of any assist-

ance to the army of the republic and came upon these two, skulking in the woods. The younger one was wounded in the head. The other was dressing his wound. They stopped me and said they would impress me into the patriot army, as they called it —" "Oh, you infernal liar!" cried Tom, as he sprang upon the scoundrel and seized him by the throat. Sir John leaped to his side, and threw the villain and jumped on him before the guards dragged them away. The soldiers attempted to beat them with their belts, which they slipped off for the purpose. Both Sir John and Tom were sturdy exponents of the noble art of self-defence, and the Venezuelan soldiers were slim, light-waisted little fellows, so they went down before the good Anglo-Saxon fists like ninepins.

"Set 'em up in the other alley, Tom!" shouted Sir John, as he gleefully sent them to grass in windrows.

"Ay, ay, sir," replied Tom, "as soon as I get my pile finished." Three soldiers were piled on top of the lying witness. A half dozen had appeared from somewhere, and were keeping our two friends from becoming mildewed. The group of hangers-on yelled, and the judge pounded on the table for order. Sir John and Tom each seized a gun, and, as they wielded them like flails, the soldiers — keeping well together — backed toward the door.

Our friends were so busy amusing the soldiers that they were unaware of a movement going on behind them. The judge mustered his party of officers and charged on their rear.

They were seized from behind and thrown on their backs on the stone floor. The soldiers now fell upon them and beat and kicked them unmercifully, and having taken the fight out of them, again tied their hands behind their backs. This little diversion having subsided, the court proceeded with the trial. It was soon seen that all the witnesses, except the original complainant, had cleared out during the mêlée. However, a scarcity of witnesses could not interfere with the progress of the wheels of justice. The little viper was sworn, and said that while taking his regular morning walk he had come upon the defendants at the head of a small party of rebels. They were scouting in the outskirts of the city. They attempted to capture him; but though outnumbered ten to one, he cornered these two and detained them until the arrival of the police.

During the recital of this fairy tale both Sir John and Tom continually interrupted with, " Liar, braggart, coward," etc., being rewarded for each of these epithets by a blow in the mouth from the fists of their guards. Their lips and noses were swollen and bleeding; but their pluck was undaunted. When the scoundrel completed his testimony, the court complimented him on his valor in capturing, single handed, two such desperate *hereticos.*

The evidence being all in, the court lighted cigarettes, consulted a few moments, and took a viva voce ballot, with the natural result—conviction. The presiding officer carefully adjusted his cocked hat to the angle of supreme dignity, assumed a solemn demeanor, hemmed portentously and said:—

"The court finds the prisoners guilty as charged. Have you anything to say why sentence should not be passed upon you?"

"I have!" replied Sir John; "but I would not waste my breath saying it to such a gang of sheep-stealers—"

"Silence, dog!!! The sentence of the court is that you be taken to the rear of the barracks at sunrise, to-morrow morning, and there, with your faces to the wall, be shot to death. To the calaboose with 'em!"

Realizing the gravity of their situation, and their impotence, they were stunned. They followed their guards passively, but their spirits recovered rapidly when they emerged from the gloomy "Palace of Justice" into the bright sunlight of a perfect day. To render conversation impossible, Sir John was led ten paces in advance; but his fertile brain was busy thinking out a way of salvation. To be shot at sunrise! Once inside the calaboose all hope would

be gone. Whatever was to be done, must be done
before they arrived there; for escape was not to be
thought of. If he could only get word to the British
Minister, he would be saved. Ay, but there was the
rub. No native would carry such a message, they
were too anxious for the execution of the hated
Gringos. Desperate cases require desperate reme-
dies. Cupidity might induce some among the crowd,
who were jeering at the "Ingleses," to take a message.
They were nearly there; he could see the corner
of the dingy calaboose over the heads of the crowd.
There was no more time to think. Once inside that
door, they would be to all intents and purposes dead.

Having come peacefully thus far, the guards had
slightly relaxed their vigilance, when suddenly, in
carefully selected Spanish, Sir John shouted at the
top of his voice: —

"I am an English gentleman, to be shot at sunrise! One thousand pounds to the person who tells
the British Minister!"

That was as concise as he could think it, and it
was none too concise either; for the last word left
his lips in a muffled gurgle, as the alarmed guards
throttled and threw him down. While one sat on
his breast, strangling him with both hands, another
tore the manta from a woman's head and gagged
him; while Tom's guard, taking their cue from their
fellows, performed the same kindly office for him.

CHAPTER XIII

ONCE on board the *Albatross*, Mr. Druse, by his
suave and genial manner, put his guests completely
at their ease, making them feel that they were con-
ferring rather than receiving a favor by accepting
his invitation.

Mrs. Druse, an invalid of the languid type,
greeted them affably, and the son, a bright lad of
seventeen, seconded his father's welcome with frank
heartiness. This boy, Robert, who was expected
to succeed his father in business, travelled with him
continually. He was a fine, manly, handsome young
fellow, who believed his father to be the greatest
man in the world, and was ambitious to equal him.
He had relinquished a college course to acquire
the broader and more complete education gained
by mingling with men. He was perfectly demo-
cratic in manner, and did not despise girls, not
even his own sister nor her chum, though neither
of them was ravishingly beautiful.

The mate, Mr. Swinburne, — a geordie tar, — made the young people a set of grummets, with which they pitched quoits on deck. They had a swing, played chess and checkers, sang and danced in the moonlight, and listened to the wonderful tales told by the negro cook of hair-raising adventures at sea, and worse ones yet of West Indian Hoodoo and Obé. They romped from one end of the old barkey to the other, and enjoyed themselves famously; while their elders read novels or smoked, according to their several tastes. The weather, with the exception of the first week, was uniformly fine, the vessel was provisioned sumptuously, and all went smoothly.

Although Mr. Druse had chartered the *Albatross* for the purpose of giving his daughter an outing, his business training would not allow him to waste an opportunity, so he had her loaded with merchandise, which he purposed to sell or trade, and return with a cargo of the valuable products of the tropics. In pursuance with this idea he put in at Kingston, Jamaica, where he had many friends, and remained there nearly two weeks, visiting army, navy, and government officials. The party made numerous excursions to the interior, where they were entertained by the families of wealthy planters, who were proud to do honor to their distinguished countryman and his friends, and the little state of Maine girl danced with aristocratic, gold-laced English officers, who unanimously voted her "awfully jolly," laughed heartily at the queer antics of the black pickaninnies, ate strange and luscious fruit, and enjoyed herself every minute.

Reluctantly, they left the hospitable island, and returning through the Windward passage, coasted all the way round the Windward group. Here, wafted gently along by the balmy trade-wind, — a breeze that never knows a squall,— they watched a glorious panorama. Daily, almost hourly, those beautiful emerald gems, set in the sparkling blue Caribbean Sea, rose from the horizon one after another, and passed in stately review, each seeming to excel in beauty those which had preceded it. Oh, what a summer outing that was! It was an episode from which all others should hereafter date — to be remembered and gloried in while life should last.

They dropped anchor for a day and a night in Port au Spain, Trinidad. Here they saw representatives of nearly all the nations of the earth, admired the rich tropical vegetation, and sampled more fruit, and then sailed round the island to "La Brea," the lake of natural pitch. The girls did not admire this particularly, but Mr. Druse prophetically foresaw the great commercial possibilities which have since been developed. On leaving here they shaped their course directly for La Guayra — La Guayra the hot! They thought they would surely roast before the mules were ready to take them up the mountain out of that frying-pan. The girls cast rueful glances at their dainty feminine gear, which had been so bravely starched, and was so rapidly becoming limp, while Robert put his collar in his pocket, fanned himself with his hat, and wondered how in the world they stood it.

At last the mules were ready, and, with much giggling and frantic clutching at starched skirts, they got under way. When they were fairly started, the heat lost its oppressiveness, and as they travelled the old road up the nearly perpendicular face of La Silla, it seemed as if the air grew cooler and the view finer at every step. The grand old mountain rose abruptly from the sea which glistened in the sun like a great silver plate, three thousand feet below. The passage of the dilapidated old drawbridge at the "Salto" was a nerve-testing feat for the girls. Nellie knew she should fall and be killed, but Kitty laughed at her fears, while Robert rode at her side holding her on and encouraging her, and Mr. Druse concentrated his wife's attention on the old tower, " Torre quemada," until the flimsy structure was passed. The beauties of the tropical plants and flowers called forth continued exclamations of delight from the girls, and kept Robert busy supplying specimens. They dined at La Venta, passing a very pleasant hour in the perfect climate which prevails at that altitude.

From here, until the end of their journey, there was no end to the natural beauties of this wonderland; every turn in the road disclosing new and beautiful views, strange birds or animals, and combinations of color and perfume in the wild flowers that almost wearied the senses.

It was late in the afternoon, when, tired and travel-stained but happy, they arrived at the plantation. Tired as they were, they could not deny themselves the pleasure of inspecting this, one of the most beautiful of orchards. The cacao trees, with their large glossy leaves, laden with the rich chocolate-colored, cucumber-shaped pods, looked cool and inviting under the shade of the great erythrinas, whose heads blazed with fiery blossoms as though they had gathered the sun's heat all to themselves, that their delicate charges might thrive in the cool moist air below.

While Kitty Blake was enjoying herself with a merry party at the cacao plantation of "La Assuncion," Tom Benton was driving cattle and scouting with the enemy's cavalry but a few miles away, en route to the deadly pass outside Caracas. In this land of prolific natural wealth, however, the railroad and telegraph were almost unknown, and people knew only what they saw.

After a week's rest, Mr. Druse proposed a call on the English Minister. So on a bright pleasant morning the entire party, accompanied by half a dozen servants, cantered gayly through the mountains to Caracas.

Mr. Arthur Lindsay, the minister, was a man of fifty, who had passed his whole life in her Majesty's diplomatic service. As he had arrived at no higher position than minister to a small South American republic, it is to be inferred that he was not considered a diplomat of high order. The fact was, that he had friends in the right quarter; otherwise he would have been relegated to the scrap pile long ago, for he was more of a *man* than a diplomat. Was a fellow-Briton suffering injustice, Mr. Lindsay would insist that the wrong be righted, regardless of the effect on the concert of Europe. Although he had never made any very serious breaks, it was considered advisable to send him to a country whose demands for an apology might be considered with sufficient deliberation to allow them to die a natural death.

Being a gentleman of ample means, freehanded and jovial, he was well and favorably known to visitors at his rather out-of-the-way post. He was an ardent sportsman; and as his whole life had been passed in courts and offices, he had learned, from the few glimpses which he obtained of it, to love the sea as few landsmen do. Therefore, when he found himself in a post so near it, and received a broad hint that he would not be disturbed for years, he had a handsome schooner yacht built in England and sent out to him. He became expert in handling the *Flora*, and passed much of his time cruising up and down the coast, exploring every island, creek, and bay. He also delighted to surround himself with congenial company; but, with a few exceptions, he did not care for the society of the native Venezuelans, so he pressed into service such strangers as came his way. He had purchased two large adjoining houses in the aristocratic quarter, and had thrown them into one; and it was safe to say that when Mr. Lindsay had no European guests, there were none to be had.

He had not intruded on the Druse family party; but he sent them his compliments and expressed the hope that they would honor him with a visit before returning. He was therefore delighted when, after a brisk morning ride, the merry group clattered up to his door; and as the mountain air had sharpened their appetites, they did full justice to the luncheon served in the park-like garden.

Frank Lindsay, nephew and adopted son of the minister, a young man of twenty, formed a valuable addition to the party of young people. He piloted them on their riding excursions, and pointed out the various objects of interest while the elders reclined in the cool garden. Kitty, the fearless, enjoyed galloping about the lovely valley, as she enjoyed boat sailing or any other healthy exercise. Robert and Nellie, too, found romping about in the exhilarating atmosphere of the high altitude most enjoyable. Mr. Druse had much of interest concerning the resources of the country to talk about with Mr. Lindsay, while Mr. Hayward was an interested listener, and the elderly ladies declared that merely to exist in such a climate, and amid such surroundings, was blissful.

Two days before the battle in the pass, Mr. Lindsay proposed that his guests should join him in a yacht cruise to Lake Maracaibo, promising them an enjoyable time. He had a friend on the lake, who, he assured them, would be delighted to see them, and would entertain them royally. They accepted of course; and a messenger was dispatched to La Guayra to notify the captain of the *Flora* that the party would be on board at sunrise, in order to avoid, as far as possible, the torrid heat of the port.

Just before they were ready to start, Kitty was seized with a slight illness from over-exposure to the sun. Mrs. Hayward became alarmed at once, and decided that she must remain at home. Mr. Lindsay assured her that it was nothing, and that she would recover much sooner on the yacht than if left behind; but Kitty refused to go, much as she wished it, for she knew Mrs. Hayward would not enjoy the trip under the circumstances. He then proposed to put off the start until the invalid should recover, but Mrs. Hayward in her turn refused to listen to a postponement, and sent them off while she remained to nurse her darling. Frank elected to stay also, to entertain the invalid. As they passed the time indoors for the next two days, they heard nothing of the murderous battle that was fought on that bloody Monday within five miles of the pleasant garden where they passed the time with music, reading, and games.

On the day when Sir John and Tom received their sentence, Kitty felt so much better that she expressed a wish for a ride. Mrs. Hayward demurred, as old ladies will, but finally surrendered to coaxing, only stipulating that she and Frank should not be away more than an hour. They were gone more than two; for Frank forgot his watch, and the time flew rapidly as, with merry laughter, they challenged each other to trials of speed and feats of horsemanship. When quite sure they had been out their full hour, they turned their horses' heads toward home, and rode slowly, to breathe their tired animals.

Soon after entering the city, and turning a corner, they came upon a scene of great turmoil. There was a crowd a block away, toward which people were running from all directions.

"I wonder what is going on here?" said Kitty as, touching her horse lightly with the whip, she cantered in the direction of the excitement.

P

"I wouldn't go there, Miss Blake," said Frank, spurring up alongside of her. "It's probably a street row, and they are apt to be rude to Europeans, especially to ladies."

"I'm not a European; I'm an American," replied Kitty, smiling archly in the troubled face of her escort. "Hey! Get out of the way and let's see what is going on here!" she added to the crowd of natives under her horse's nose. They were now within twenty feet of where Tom was plodding along in the grip of his two guards, and could see his shoulders and the wound in the back of his head. Ten paces ahead of him, they observed another little storm centre.

"Oh, come away, Miss Blake, do!" urged Frank. "It's only a couple of drunken natives being taken to the calaboose."

As they turned their horses' heads, there came from the little storm centre ahead a ringing shout, — the deep, clear tones and mispronounced Spanish words proving the owner's assertion that he was an Englishman. They were so close that they heard it distinctly, and Frank understood.

"*I am an English gentleman, to be shot at sunrise! One thousand pounds to the person who tells the British Minister!*"

Frank Lindsay was a quick-witted young man, who had heard stories of the high-handed proceedings of these hot-headed, hardly civilized Spanish-Americans. He knew they would commit almost any outrage for the gratification of the moment, apologizing for it afterwards if compelled to. He understood that here was a case right under his nose, and he knew what he had to do. He must get Mr. Lindsay there before sunrise to-morrow, and he had not the remotest idea where he was. Grasping Kitty's rein, he cried : —

"Come on, Miss Blake; ride for dear life!" Kitty, who had not understood a word of Sir John's statement, was greatly frightened by Frank's words and manner. She dashed wildly after him for a hundred yards or so, then, seeing they were not pursued, she reined up.

"What in the world is the matter?" she asked. "I don't see any occasion for such terrible haste."

"Didn't you hear what he said?" asked Frank, slackening his pace for a moment. "Oh, excuse me, I forgot that you do not understand Spanish. That is an English gentleman whom they have condemned to be shot at sunrise to-morrow morning. I must find Uncle Arthur, and get him here before that time to save him."

"And I have delayed you! Oh, I'm so sorry! Come on!" and she lashed her pet saddle-horse unmercifully, for a man's life was at stake. Frank had no occasion now to complain of want of speed.

Kitty led him a race that made even the natives, born horsemen, look after them in surprise. Mrs. Hayward, who had been on the anxious seat for the last hour, had her nerves entirely wrecked by a clatter of hoofs like a charge of cavalry. Frank assisted Kitty to alight. A servant arrived, to whom he rapidly gave his orders, and in less time than it takes to write it he was on his way to La Guayra on a fresh horse, followed by old Enrique, the groom, leading two others.

Kitty told Mrs. Hayward of the adventure, whereupon that old lady became much alarmed. There was not a soul on the premises with whom they could now converse, and after nightfall would-be winners of the thousand pounds began to arrive, swaggering by the house and watching from the corners of their eyes for others on the same errand. Finding the coast clear, they asked to see " El Señor Inglese." When told he had gone on an indefinite cruise, their faces would drop ; and, on gaining an offing from the house, they would raise their clinched hands to high heaven and curse their luck ; not doubting that the true meaning of the answer was " too late."

As the night advanced, the callers became more frequent, and the majordomo wondered at the sudden popularity of his patron with the native element. Several well-to-do persons came on the same

errand ; he offered to convey their messages to " Mi
Señor" on his return, but his kind offer was invariably declined.

Frank had been thinking rapidly ever since he
heard Sir John's appeal, trying to foresee all possible emergencies, and prepare for them. He dashed
down the La Guayra road at a breakneck pace, followed by old Enrique, audibly cursing such harum-
scarum young Ingleses, and wondering if they would
reach the bottom of the almost perpendicular road
alive.

CHAPTER XIV

FRANK was acting on the supposition that the *Flora* was now homeward bound; but of this he had no assurance. If she was, and he could get his uncle to Caracas before the Englishman was executed, he knew Mr. Lindsay would save him—otherwise he must die. He reached La Guayra at sundown and observed that the wind—a head one for the yacht—was quite light. At Tarbell's ship-chandlery he bought two lanterns—one white and one red—and a box of matches. He had the lanterns trimmed and lighted, and gave them to Enrique. He told him to ride west along the coast at a trot, and to hang the white light from his horse's neck, the red one from the neck of the rear led horse, so that they would be visible from the sea, and be sure to keep them alight. If he saw the *Flora*, or a red and green light hoisted and lowered several times, he was to stop and wave his lantern until his signal was answered by a red light swung in a vertical circle, and then remain where he was until Mr. Lindsay's arrival.

If he saw nothing, he was to continue westward until, by the dip of the southern cross, he knew that it was after midnight; then he could return. Frank promised him a thousand dollars if he got Mr. Lindsay to La Guayra before two o'clock, and five hundred if he got him there later. Elated with the prospect of earning such unheard-of wealth, Enrique set his signals and started at once. Frank told Mr. Tarbell that he wanted the fastest boat there was in the port, and one smart young fellow to go with him.

"What's the matter wi' my *liza Jane?*" asked the ex-skipper.

"Is she fast?"

"Fast? Ay, that she is, the devil a faster this side o' Deal beach."

"Let me have her then as quick as possible. And get a good man and send him out on Enrique's trail in half an hour with two more of the fastest horses you can get. Then have a pair of fast mules here, and another at La Venta. Instruct the men in charge of all these animals that they are to be delivered to Uncle Arthur and to no one else. Be sure to spare no expense — it's a case of life and death."

"Gosh! I sh'd think 'twas," remarked the ship-chandler as he gazed after Frank, who went off at a dead run with the young fellow who was to take him out in the *Eliza Jane*.

They were soon afloat in the clipper sloop, her huge mainsail swung off to a quartering wind. The white spray dashed from her bow, as even in that light breeze she skimmed along five or six knots an hour. Frank promised his skipper five hundred dollars if he put him aboard the *Flora* before eleven o'clock. The man, a native fisherman, said it would be difficult, as there was no moon; but he would try. Frank was worried at his inability to see Enrique's signals, and mentally berated the old rascal for having misunderstood his orders; but on rounding a low point, he saw them. Now where was the *Flora?* Anchored comfortably in front of Mr. Larkin's house on the lake, as likely as not. He hoped not, for then all his efforts would go for nothing and the poor English gentleman would be killed. As no time limit had been set for the excursion, it was only in the bare hope that the yacht might be on her way home that he had started to intercept her.

How his uncle would save the Englishman, he didn't know; but that he would do it if he arrived in time, he was sure. It was only by intercepting her on one of her tacks, that they could see her at all, even supposing her to be on the way — about one chance in a thousand or less. Should they cross her course fifteen minutes too soon or too late, they would go flying down the wind farther from her every minute. He wished now that he had left word at La Guayra, in case she gave them the slip and arrived during his absence. The thought tormented him. She might have passed them and be lying at anchor there now. He had a mind to return and see, but decided not to go as yet.

They strained their eyes and fancied they saw schooner yachts, ships, lights, and Lord knows what, every few minutes. Enrique's signals were in plain sight at any rate, and helped to keep his spirits up. The boat drew ahead of a point of land, and shut them off at last; then there was nothing to see. The breeze strengthened as the night advanced, and the *Eliza Jane* fairly flew, which was another source of anxiety, for he would be very likely to miss her in the dark. He proposed that they shorten sail; but the fisherman disapproved. "I don't think," he said, "that she can have beaten up this far yet."

Frank looked at him in surprise. "Why don't you?" he asked.

The fisherman shrugged his shoulders and replied in that irritating, senseless way they have, "Quien sabe." A second later he cried, "Sail, ho!"

He rushed the tiller to leeward, Frank rounded in the sheet, and they came-to alongside an old

Jamaica brig bound for La Guayra, whose negro captain had fallen to leeward of his port. A row of woolly heads appeared at the rail, all jabbering in concert, and asking how far it was to La Guayra. In a burst of ill-natured disappointment, Frank replied, "Forty miles." He struck a match and looked at his watch — ten thirty-five. They sailed on in silence for another hour or more. Frank was forward, holding on to the forestay, and looking vacantly ahead, having about decided that he had come on a fool's errand.

A squall was brewing. Large black clouds obscured the stars, making the search more hopeless than ever. He sought Enrique's signal to leeward before he remembered that they must have passed the horses long ago. A warning cry from aft caused him to turn just in time to see what looked in the darkness like the sharp bow of a great ship. It rose on the sea and came down like a giant axe. There was a crashing of wood as the *Eliza Jane* was cut fairly in two, amidships, and excited shouts and dancing lights on board the larger vessel, and then Frank found himself overboard, clutching unavailingly at her smooth black sides as she glided by.

The crew of the *Flora* — for it was she who had dealt this unkind blow — threw her head into the wind, and lowered a boat as quickly as her excitable native crew could do it. As they had cut the sloop fairly in two, Frank and his skipper were on different sides of her. Frank struck out instinctively, but he hardly swam a dozen strokes when he collided with a hard substance, which cut his head, and caused him to see innumerable stars. Though believing himself badly hurt, he retained his senses by a strong exercise of will power, and, knowing it must be some of the wreckage, he sought to mount it. The mainmast remaining in the forward part of the sloop had capsized it, throwing Frank out. He climbed onto the short bowsprit, feeling dizzy and bewildered. His head swam, his nerveless fingers relaxed their hold, and he went off backwards. The jib, which had a boom lashed to its foot, formed a floating hammock, into which he fell, and as the water washed over it he was in imminent danger of drowning.

The fisherman, retaining his hold on the tiller, was not knocked overboard. So, as soon as he regained his wits, he shouted lustily for help, with the result that he was soon rescued, and told of the young Inglese with whom he was in search of the *Flora*. The boat's crew rowed a couple of times round the wreckage, shouting and swinging their lanterns, and, having satisfied themselves there was no living person about, they started to return. By good luck they ran into the mainsail and capsized, and, before they got clear again, one of the men tumbled into the jib and found Frank's apparently lifeless body washing about in it. They returned as quickly as possible, hooked their boat on, and hoisted her up.

When Frank's body was recognized, he was tenderly carried to a berth in the cabin amid profound exclamations of sorrow. For the bright, hearty, genial young man had endeared himself to the entire party. Restoratives were applied, and when signs of life appeared, the steward, who was acting surgeon, prescribed an opiate. While he was under the influence of the drug, the steward, with an eye to the dramatic, dressed his wound, swathing his head in yards of ghostly white bandages. Great was the curiosity of the entire party to know why Frank was cruising about in that sloop instead of entertaining his guests at home. The fisherman only knew he had expressed great anxiety to find the *Flora;* then they knew there was trouble of some kind, and orders were issued to make all possible haste to get back to La Guayra.

The fisherman wondered if he had won his reward; but he need not have been uneasy.

Both he and Enrique received more than had been promised them; and Mr. Tarbell wished he had a whole fleet of sloops to dispose of at the rate he got for the *Eliza Jane.*

Suddenly, like a ghost, Frank appeared among

the anxious party in the cabin. He was pale and a bit unsteady on his legs, but chock full of business.

"What time is it, Uncle Arthur?" he asked.

"Why, Frank, what a start you have given us all," replied Mr. Lindsay, as he led the young fellow affectionately to a large easy chair. "Now then, young man," he continued, "give an account of yourself. What were you doing out here in that smack?"

As rapidly as he could, Frank outlined the story, while they listened in silence. Then he repeated his question.

"One thirty A.M." said Mr. Druse.

"Oh, then, I'm afraid we're too late! I told Enrique he might return with the horses as soon as he saw by the southern cross that it was after midnight."

"That's all right," interjected Robert; "the stars have all been obscured since eleven o'clock. Wait, I'll see if the watch have seen anything of his peculiar signal."

He returned in a moment, and reported that the watch had seen and been puzzled by the signal on the last in-shore tack.

"Good!" exclaimed Frank, "the old fellow's desire to win the reward will be our salvation. We'll make it yet, uncle; there are four hours and more between now and sunrise. Anybody can go from La Guayra to Caracas in three hours; and by killing the mules we can cut that time down a good bit. If the scoundrels will only hold their fire till sunrise, we'll give them a run for their money."

When they learned that Enrique was to leeward, the schooner was kept away a couple of points, and the officer of the deck instructed how to signal the land craft. An overwhelming majority decided that Frank had done his share, and was in no condition to undertake the race on shore. He opposed this verdict until his uncle was obliged to tell him that in his present condition he would be more of a hindrance than a help. Unwillingly he submitted and allowed Robert Druse to ride with his uncle on the return journey. By the time this was settled, Enrique had been signalled, the schooner was brought to, and Mr. Lindsay and Robert were rowed rapidly ashore.

They vaulted into the saddles and were off like the wind, Enrique shouting unheeded advice after them, concerning the road. As they galloped along side by side, Mr. Lindsay said : —

"Don't spare your horse, Robert! If that man is executed, and these horses remain alive, I shall always feel like a murderer." He instructed the young man what to do in case of accident to himself, as they plied whip and spur, tearing along in the darkness through an utterly strange country. The next step might precipitate them into anything, but they took no heed of that. The breaking clouds gave them fitful glimpses of the stars, and, aided by the instinct of their horses, they shaped a general course for La Guayra. The horses stumbled frequently, but avoided a fall. Suddenly, with an almost human shriek of agony, Mr. Lindsay's horse fell on its knees, pitching him over its head. A sharp stone, standing upright like a chisel, had stripped the flesh from the poor brute's leg from fetlock to knee.

By great good luck, Mr. Lindsay was pitched into a clump of bushes. He was badly scratched, and his clothing nearly torn off. Extricating himself quickly, he cried : —

" Your horse, Robert ! Let me have your horse ! "

Robert, having reined in, dismounted at once; but before Mr. Lindsay could remount, the peon arrived leading the relay. Thankfully they mounted the fresh horses and were off again with undiminished speed. They arrived at La Guayra without further mishap. Mr. Lindsay looked at his watch before mounting the mule. "Three forty; we've got to gain an hour, Robert! I fear it will be impossible. Thank God, Frank has a relay at La Venta. Come on!"

There was a clatter of hoofs as two frightened

mules sped up the face of the Silla.   They were
only asked to live until they reached La Venta;
for even if they died there, their lives would have
been a success.   Fire flew from their hoofs as they
sprang like chamois up the rocky slope.   Robert fell
in behind, as Mr. Lindsay, being familiar with the road,
could take better advantage of it, riding alone.   They
changed to fresh animals at La Venta, and continued
their upward flight.

As they rode out upon the level land above the
city, the rosy glow of the tropical dawn, so soon to be
followed by the rising sun, was upon it, and the sound
of fife and drum was wafted to them on the pure
morning air.

Without slackening the breakneck pace Mr. Lindsay turned to Robert and said : —

" Do you see that long low building over there ? "

" Yes, sir."

" That is the barracks, where the execution will
probably take place.   I am going there, and you
go to the house and get the ensign — no — that is
upstairs — you won't have time.   Kick open my desk,
and you will find a Union Jack in the right-hand
pigeon hole.   Bring it to me at the barracks."

Without another word they parted, each going his
own way.

When Sir John and Tom were thoroughly gagged,
their escorts dragged them to their feet, and, amid

more jeering and cursing from the crowd, they were kicked and cuffed to the calaboose, and pushed so roughly in that, being pinioned, they fell heavily on their faces. It was heart-breaking treatment; but the English gentleman, descended from a long line of world conquerors, and the Yankee boy, descended from the men who conquered the Englishman's ancestors at Yorktown, were not yet conquered themselves.

They rolled over on their backs, and rendering each other such service as they were able, with teeth and fingers, they not only removed the gags, but also the thongs which bound their hands. Utterly broken down and worn out in body, they sat on the damp ground, leaning their aching backs against the wall, and tried to cheer each other with helpful talk. As they were to die at sunrise, neither food nor water was wasted on them. At last their tongues became too parched to talk, so they sat silent in the darkness, and as the night dragged its weary length along, their heads fell forward on their breasts and they slept.

Tom dreamed he was a boy again on board the *Columbia.* His father's voice rang in his ears, but the familiar tones gradually changed to those of Bully Blake. Before he fully realized that he was being thrown out of the Portland office, he was sitting beside Kitty in the stern sheets of the *Sprite.*

And so his tired brain wove tangled fancies in his sleep, flitting from one subject to another, until, with a bang, the door was flung open. The flickering rays of a lantern dimly illuminated the dark hole, and there was a clanking of arms as the two forlorn prisoners blinked owlishly at the file of soldiers who had come thus early to drag them forth to a dog's death.

Neither spoke — not even to each other. Slowly, painfully, benumbed by their bruises and cramped position, they stumbled to their feet at the command of the officer of the guard. They were quickly pinioned and hustled out into the sweet morning air, fragrant with the scent of the thousands of tropical flowers which bloom continually in this land so favored by nature, so cursed by man.

The guards formed about them; the fife and drum struck up a merry lilt; a sharp word of command rent the air like a bayonet thrust; and they were off. The barracks were nearly a mile from the jail, and in order that the early risers might view the spectacle, and as many as possible be induced to attend the execution, the officers in charge took a roundabout route. The prisoners, who from apathy had refrained from speaking to each other, were now separated, so that speech between them was impossible. What the thoughts of Sir John were on this occasion, I do not know; but Tom Benton has often told me, that though he tried to remember appropriate things, he could think of nothing but the expression on Mulligan's face as he threw his sea-boot at him just before the *Spofford* capsized.

Their long march, tiresome to them with their empty, fainting stomachs, came to an end at last. They doubled the end of the barracks, and were placed with their backs to a whitewashed wall. There were no coffins to be seen, — were they indeed to be thrown to the buzzards? Tom glanced sideways at Sir John, who stood two paces to his right. The Englishman's face showed pale under its tan, but there was a frown on his brow and a defiant glitter in his eye that helped Tom wonderfully. The soldiers were busy deploying about the yard. Sir John seized the opportunity to speak : —

" How is it with you, Tom ? "

" Pretty tough, Sir John."

" It is indeed, my lad. I am sorry I brought you to this, but a man can die but once. Don't let them see you flinch — keep a stiff upper lip, my boy ! "

" I'll not let on, Sir John ; never fear ! "

" That's right, my lad."

So they stood, these two comrades of such recent acquaintanceship, each with unlimited faith in the other, waiting for an unmerited death. But they made no sign, for they were of the breed from which the heroes of Bunker Hill and Balaklava sprang.

A firing squad of ten men was drawn up in front of them. The officer in charge of the execution sat motionless on his horse a few paces to the right. A subaltern put the firing party through the loading drill. The sun was not yet risen, but a brilliant golden halo in the east showed that the time was nearly up.

Tom took in the entire scene with a hasty glance. What a view on which to close one's eyes forever! The filthy barrack yard, a gaping crowd of pitiless natives, and a squad of undersized, swarthy boy-soldiers. Here and thus was to end the career on which he had started so full of hope and ambition.

The man on horseback spoke a few words, two soldiers left the ranks, and advancing, took the prisoners by the shoulders and turned their faces to the wall. Tom submitted passively; but Sir John, watching his chance, bobbed his head sideways, giving the soldier a butt that floored him. Amid the laughter of the crowd he rose, and kicked the prisoner until dragged away.

The sun's edge, like the rim of a great golden disk, showed red above the horizon, his level rays touching with a finger of fire the accoutrements of the soldiers and the gaudy uniform of the officer. The crowd turned their faces to it and murmured impatiently. Like the crack of a rifle came the order, jerked out with military curtness : —

"Ready!"

There was a faint sound as of the distant clatter of hoofs. The awe-silenced crowd involuntarily inclined their heads toward it.

"Take aim!"

The clattering hoofs were at the end of the barracks. A voice — a foreign voice — shouted: "Hold on! Hold on! Don't fire!"

The crowd turned in the direction of the voice. The soldiers shifted their weight to the other foot. The firing party unconsciously lowered the muzzles of their guns. The subaltern and the officer in charge, knowing that the execution of foreigners, one of whom had declared himself to be an English gentleman, was not exactly *en règle*, hesitated, craning their necks.

Round the corner came a hatless, tattered, gray-haired man and a youth, mounted on mules that were nearly spent. The man's face and hands were so disfigured by scratches and dried blood that his own mother would not have known him. As they turned the corner, the youth handed the old man a red, white, and blue parcel. With a jerk he opened it out. It was the Saint George's cross, the British Union Jack. His mule, in turning, stumbled, planted its fore-feet straight ahead, wavered from side to side, and as it fell, exhausted, the old gentleman, with an agility of which a vaquero need not have

been ashamed, leaped lightly to the ground.   He
rushed in front of the firing squad, and spread the
Jack over the shoulders of the prisoners, then, turning to the soldiers with blazing eyes, he shook his
fist at them, and roared in good Anglo-Saxon : —

" Fire on that, you yellow curs, if you dare ! "

CHAPTER XV

Now there has been instilled into the most be-
nighted nations of the earth a wholesome respect for
British bunting, knowing it to be backed by British
guns.

At the sound of that ringing defiance, the two
prisoners whirled round and confronted their de-
liverer, while Mr. Lindsay peremptorily ordered the
officer to release them. As a haughty demeanor con-
veys the idea of authority to the Castilian mind, the
officer reluctantly obeyed. Mutual introductions followed, and there being no conveyance at hand, Mr.
Lindsay invited them to walk home with him.
" And," he added, " we had better get on; force is
trumps in this country. I have overawed this party;
but should Don Jorge hear of it before you arrive at
the Legation, he might dare to recapture you."

Mr. Lindsay took Sir John's arm, and Robert
assisted Tom. Once within the precincts of the
official residence, they knew they were safe, and

there they proceeded to bathe and refit. As Sir John's henchmen had taken his entire outfit when they deserted, he and Tom were obliged to accept the generous offer of their kind hosts, who clothed them from their own wardrobes. While the gentlemen, redolent of arnica and decorated with plasters, were breakfasting, the yachting party arrived full of anxiety as to the success of the relief expedition.

Feeling diffident about showing themselves to the ladies in their highly ornamented condition, the rescued ones did not appear, but word was sent that the most flattering success had attended Mr. Lindsay's efforts, and as nobody had slept much during the night, a siesta was then taken until noon.

At one o'clock the parties directly interested gathered in Mr. Lindsay's office to sign the official report. He handed printed forms to Sir John and Tom, with the request that they should fill them out. When Tom found that he would be required to sign an affidavit, stating that he was a British subject, he declined, whereupon Mr. Lindsay told him that he was unable to extend the protection of his flag to others than the subjects of Great Britain. Tom said he knew that, and asked the gentleman for the address of the American Minister. Mr. Lindsay gave him the address, but asked him to remain over night, or indefinitely, as his guest; adding that he could call on the American Minister at his leisure. Tom felt, however, that he had already received more favors at the hands of the genial Englishman than he would ever be able to repay; so he preferred to go where he had an undoubted right to assistance.

Mr. Druse had entered the office and was reading a paper at the window. While Tom and the minister were talking, Nellie came to the open door and said:—

"Kitty and I are going for a little walk with Robert and Mr. Frank, papa."

"Very well, my dear, but I wouldn't go too far from the house; you know we are not regarded very favorably by the Venezuelans just at present. Gentlemen, this is my daughter."

The men rose and acknowledged the introduction respectfully, while Nellie flushed and bowed. A moment later, hearing the gate click, Tom looked out and saw the backs of the two young couples. He recognized Nellie, and looked earnestly at her friend who bore the familiar name of Kitty.

Mr. Lindsay repeated his pressing invitation to Tom to make his home at the Legation during his stay in Caracas, and Sir John and Mr. Druse urged him to hurry with his business so as to get back in time for dinner, and under no circumstances to allow himself to be cajoled into staying at the American Minister's. With a cordial handshake all round, and kind wishes ringing in his ears, Tom left the hospitable house, the name of Kitty bringing back vividly to his mind his playmate of long ago.

Mr. Jonas Spellman, the American Minister, was a politician of a certain candle power. His personal efforts during the last Presidential campaign had contributed largely to the success of his party, not only in his own state, but elsewhere; and although republics may be ungrateful, the political parties who control their affairs dare not entirely ignore that grandest of all the virtues — gratitude. So it came about that after the new administration had become thoroughly warm in its seat, certain of Mr. Spellman's fellow-townsmen who had never given him credit for any particularly strong points, were thrown into a state of mind on learning that he had been appointed Minister Plenipotentiary to the Republic of Venezuela. Mr. Spellman, having read that fortune knocks once at every man's door, decided that this was his summons, and at once bent all his energies to the task of making the administration of his present office redound to his future credit. Having reviewed the record of his predecessor, he decided that it had been distinguished by a lavish expenditure of public money, and as the motto of the present administration was retrenchment, he elected to shine as an economist.

When Tom Benton, keeping his weather eye sharply peeled for native soldiers, entered the minister's office, he found that diplomat seated with his heels on his desk, in an apartment which contained not another article of furniture. Had he been properly costumed, he would have made an excellent model for a picture of Uncle Sam, and he was industriously chewing plug tobacco, whereby he provided himself with ammunition for the discomfiture of a colony of red ants just outside the window.

"Is the minister in?" inquired Tom, glancing about the bare room.

"Yes."

"I should like to see him if I can."

"Well, sir, you see him right here.   I'm the man."

Tom told him he was an American citizen in distress, and would like a little assistance to get home. Mr. Spellman asked for his "protection."

"My protection?" exclaimed Tom, who was becoming nettled by his indifference. "It was in my chest when the *Jane Spofford* capsized ; I don't know where it is now.   A man doesn't carry his protection round in his pocket when he's on watch."

"So much the worse for you, my boy," replied the minister, cynically. "If you had protection papers to prove your right to the assistance of my government, I'd have to give it to you ; as it is, I don't."

"I'll swear that I'm a native born citizen, and so were my parents and grandparents for I don't know how many generations back," replied Tom, indignantly.

"I don't doubt it; if that was all that was wanted, I could get men to swear every dollar out of the treasury."

"I should think you could tell by my looks and talk that I am an American."

"No; by your talk I should take you to be a Bluenose; and by your looks I should say you might be one o' the rebels that I hear tried to take the town the other day."

"I was in that party; and but for the interference of Mr. Lindsay I should have been shot this morning."

"Oho — a filibuster, hey? I thought perhaps you'd let it out after a while. Shipwrecked sailors are not very plentiful, as a rule, up here in the mountains."

His sneering manner was very galling, but Tom remembered that he had not even a rag of clothing of his own. He wished to return those lent him by Robert Druse, and to be provided with subsistence until he could get out of the country; so he restrained his anger, and stated his position fully. Mr. Spellman listened with a bored expression, as though it was a very old story indeed, and then said : —

"If Mr. Lindsay sees fit to run up an expense account against his government, and to take the risk of raising an international complication, that's his business; I'm not here for that purpose. If you fellows stayed at home and attended to your crops instead of coming out here and stirring up these hot-headed natives to rebel against their government, you'd be better off. You wouldn't get yourselves into these scrapes; and when you do, you needn't come to me to pull you out of them, for I won't do it."

Tom was boiling with rage now. He shook his fist under the nose of the imperturbable minister, and roared : —

" I don't want any protection from you — I wouldn't accept it now if you offered it. I've protected myself so far, and I can do so till I get back to the States. And when I do get there I'll write a letter to Washington about the way you treat American citizens who are stranded out here!"

"That's your privilege, my boy," replied Mr. Spellman, nonchalantly.

Tom was ashamed to return to the British Legation. The boorish manner in which he had been treated by Mr. Spellman was such a contrast to Mr. Lindsay's that he felt somehow disgraced by it. Nor could he return Robert Druse's clothes; and although he felt sure it was not expected, he would have liked to be able to. His poverty made him sensitive. He would have to tell of his failure to obtain assistance from the American Minister; then, knowing him to be destitute, what would they think was his object in accepting an invitation which was probably only tendered out of politeness? He was away from them now; he had no claim on any one there, and he would stay away. There wasn't one chance in a million that he would ever see any of them again, for he would get out of the country as quickly as possible.

It was now evening. He knew approximately the direction in which the La Guayra road lay; and so, after more than a year of hard work in one of the most productive countries under the sun, he started, with an empty pocket and a heart filled with bitterness, to put the first of many thousands of miles between himself and the playmate of his boyhood. Had she only known of his presence in the mountain capital, with what exquisite pleasure would she have sought him out and told him of the little fortune awaiting him in the bank at home.

He had no difficulty in finding the road. He travelled steadily on until he was far enough from the city to feel safe from the military; then he sat down on a mossy log, took his head between his hands, and cogitated. After indulging in all the unpleasant thoughts that came to him, wondering why ill luck pursued him so relentlessly, and almost giving up in despair, he rose and shook himself. The evening in that high altitude was becoming chilly. "Pshaw!" he exclaimed aloud, "I'm getting to be worse than an old woman. It's hardly twelve hours since I escaped being shot, and now I'm whining!" He started down the road. Feeling faint, he had no hesitation in plucking a "hand" of bananas. Surely the country owed him that much! When part of the way down the mountain he left the road, sought a convenient place, and passed the night in comparative comfort. In the morning he broke his fast as before, and continued on to the port.

There were several vessels in the port, among them two American schooners and a brigantine. He walked about the place for an hour or so, and the heat becoming oppressive, he strolled down to the landing, found a shady place among the piles of merchandise, and sat down to enjoy the light breath of air that barely rippled the water. Toward noon a boat put off from the outer schooner, and, with the long, easy stroke of the merchant service, pulled up to the landing. There were but two oarsmen in her, hale, sunburned fellows, with perspiration streaming down their hairy breasts and bare arms. The captain, a typical Yankee skipper, sat in the stern sheets and gave the necessary orders for bringing the boat alongside. He stepped ashore, and telling the men not to leave her, started off up the street.

Tom started after him. "Good morning, captain!" said he, as soon as he arrived within easy hailing distance. The captain — a little, wiry, hungry-looking man — turned quickly and regarding him with a look of mingled curiosity and suspicion, said: "Hey?"

"Good morning, sir!" replied Tom with affected cheerfulness. "You are the captain of that schooner out there, are you not?"

"Yes," he replied shortly.

"I suppose you are bound to the States, sir? I'm stranded here and would like to get home."

"Do you belong in the States?"

"Yes, sir."

"Whereabouts?"

"Portland, sir."

"What vessel have you run away from?"

"I haven't run away from any, sir. I was wrecked, and came here overland."

"I ain't heerd o' no wrecks round here lately, an' I don't like the looks o' ye; ye look as if ye'd been on a long spree ashore; ye're all cut up. I don't b'leeve ye've ever been to sea. Where'd ye get them parson's togs?"

"The togs were given me by an English gentle-man, and I've been to sea all my life, as long as I can remember."

"Sho! Ye don't say! how many sheaves in a lower dead-eye?"

Tom had to laugh at the familiar old chestnut. The captain relaxed a bit too, and said: "I'm going up here to finish a little business, and I'll be back in half an hour. If you are around then, I'll see," and with that he shambled off.

Tom's first impulse was to return to the landing and pump the boat's crew, but, remembering the captain's evidently suspicious nature, he decided not to, but hung about the place where he had spoken to the captain. In the course of an hour he saw him returning. The captain pretended not to see him and was going right by, but Tom hailed him again.

"Oh, it's you, is it? Thought you'd 'a' been drunk long 'fore this."

"I don't get drunk, sir," Tom replied indignantly.

"Don't, hey? Where's your dunnage?"

"On my back, sir — all I have."

"Well, come on if you want to go with me; I'm going aboard and going to sail right away." Tom followed his new commander into the boat with alacrity.

"Nelson," said the captain to the burly Swede who had the stroke, "let this man take your oar."

Tom had eaten nothing but a few bananas since the day before, but he was so elated at feeling a white man's boat bounding under him once more, and at the sound of a genuine Yankee voice, twang and all, that he swung the sixteen-foot ash vigorously, so that the bowman puffed and sweated worse than he had done coming ashore. Captain Tompkins was satisfied long before he got alongside that Tom had "been there before," in spite of his funny-looking togs.

The *Gracie* was a smart two hundred and fifty ton Boston schooner. That much Tom learned by a glance at her heavily laden hull and stern, as the boat rounded to at the starboard gangway. The moment the captain's foot touched the deck he ordered the mate to heave short. As her crew consisted of but four men, including Tom, it was a killing job to get her under way; but when with both gaff topsails and flying jib on her she gathered way and pointed her jib-boom out of La Guayra, Tom Benton felt profoundly thankful. He looked back at the land, shook his fist at it, and said : —

"Thank God I'm through driving bulls and revolutionizing there."

When the last sheet was belayed, and not before, Captain Tompkins called for a man to relieve him at the wheel. Tom, according to his invariable custom, jumped at the word. The other three found no fault with that; for now that the sail was on her, they could go to dinner, schooner fashion. Telling Tom to keep a sharp lookout, the captain and mate went below to dinner, also schooner fashion.

Tom was dreadfully hungry. The hard work and familiar salt air put an edge on his appetite that not even the llanos could equal. Three-quarters of an hour later the captain and mate returned to the deck, smoking and discussing the prospects of a fast run home. Seeing Tom still at the wheel, the captain exclaimed: "What? Ain't you relieved yet?" The mate, taking the cue, roared out: "Relieve the wheel here, one o' ye."

Presently a man came shambling along the lee gangway, and as he took the wheel Captain Tompkins asked: "What's the matter with you fellers forrard there? Don't you think anybody wants any dinner but yerselves?"

It was the Swede whose oar Tom had taken. He muttered something about having a smoke; but the captain told him it was time enough to smoke after all hands had dined. Tom was not in the most angelic temper when he entered the forecastle where the other two "Souwegians" lay in their bunks smoking. The only food visible was a piece of cold boiled yam, about the size of a small potato. An empty pan on the deck indicated by a few fragments of bone and gristle that it had once contained beef. A smaller one bore evidence of having been filled with bread pudding.

"Pretty well cleaned out, hey?" said Tom, with affected cheerfulness. "I'll have to see what the doctor has left in the galley." Gathering up the dishes, he presented himself at the galley door. The negro cook informed him that he had no more food. Aft he went, and exhibiting his piece of yam, told the captain his trouble.

"Go to the galley," said the captain; "the cook will give you something to eat."

"I have been there, sir, and he says he has nothing."

"Wha-a-t! Cook, come aft here! Why don't you give this man something to eat?"

"I sen' all de dinner to de forecastle, sah, an' dey done et it up."

"What did ye do that for? Don't ye know enough to save dinner for the man at the wheel? I swanny, I'm ashamed on ye; an American nigger to let a lot o' Dutch sailors get ahead o' him like that. You go down an' eat whatever you find on the cabin table, young man, an' never mind sparin' any for the cook; he can look out for himself or go hungry. Be hanged if I'll see the man that's done more work than all three o' them hogs together, cheated out o' his dinner."

When Tom finished, he went forward, where he found the other two still smoking. "I had dinner in the cabin," said he, by way of starting a conversation. Nobody made any reply. "Where are we bound for, shipmates?" he asked, with persistent pleasantness.

Restrained by that sense of superiority which men in employment feel over one less fortunate, they silently puffed away at their pipes. Feeling that he had received about all of this silent contempt that his case called for, Tom reached into the bunk of the bigger of the two, and seizing him by the collar, gave him the bull-tail twist. Out came the great lubber, floundering over his chest, his pipe and tinware flying in different directions as he sprawled on deck. Tom jerked him to his feet, slapped his face a couple of times, and said : —

" *You* I'm talking to, Johannus; a little hard of hearing, ain't ye?"

The fellow steadied himself by the bunkboard, glared savagely, and said: "Say, don' you do dat agin. You hear?"

"All right, Dutch; don't ask me to then. Be as civil as you can, and you'll get along better. You fellows mustn't think that because I made a pier-head jump of it, am flying light for dunnage, and have a little bark knocked off in spots, that I'm as green as I look. I asked you where we were bound; now pipe up before the earthquake comes round again."

" Boston, ven you vant ter know."

"Thanks ! If I hadn't wanted to know, I shouldn't have asked; now how comes it that there are only four of us forrard? Are three men a full crew for this hooker?"

"Course not! Didn't Yacopson git drunk ven he vas ashore an' fall overboard an' git de Yaller Yack an' die in de hospital?"

This statement enlightened Tom with regard to Captain Tompkins' generosity in giving him a passage home. He was getting the service of a man for his keep; and thereby assuring his insurance.

Having satisfied the scruples of his shipmates, Tom had no further trouble with them, and they acknowledged the supremacy which intelligence and grit invariably acquire over loutish natures like theirs. Tom replaced the defunct "Yacopson" in the starboard watch. As the captain stood his own watch, they two, with the democracy which obtains on small vessels, became quite well acquainted before the Boston pilot boarded her. The inquisitive Yankee skipper never tired of hearing Tom tell of his strange adventures in Venezuela. He would lie at full length on top of the cabin and ask questions while Tom was at the wheel. Sometimes, in order to hear the finish of an adventure, he would take her himself at four bells, and steer until the story was ended.

He remembered having heard of the *Jane Spofford* insurance case; it had been somewhat celebrated in the courts. He had not heard, or had forgotten, what the verdict was; but he rather guessed that all hands would be interested in Tom's account. He advised him to "see" both parties before telling his story. Tom would not argue with his superior, but he decided that a straightforward course was good enough for him.

He walked ashore in Boston, as he had come aboard in La Guayra, except that his clothes were considerably the worse for wear. After two or three refusals, he found a boarding-house, where the landlord advised him to be present when the *Gracie's* crew were paid, and strike "Old Tompkins" for some money. He did so, and when Captain Tompkins saw him bringing up the rear of the file, he asked him what he was doing there.

"Why," said Tom, assuming as brazen a front as possible, "I know I wasn't regularly shipped; but you were short-handed, and I really took Jacobson's place. I wouldn't ask you for anything, captain, although I feel that I have earned as much as any of the crew on the passage home; but you know how I'm fixed. I've only got the duds I stand in and not one cent of money."

The captain looked at him severely while he was making this long statement. His brow was wrinkled and his lips were pursed. "Did I agree to pay you any wages?" he asked, when Tom finished.

"No, sir; not a cent."

"You was glad enough out there in La Guayra to get a passage home, warn't ye?"

"I was; yes, sir."

"Then I don't see how I owe ye anything."

"I don't claim that you do, sir — at least, not legally."

"Oh, then, if I was to give you anything, you'd take it as charity, hey?"

"Well, no, sir; not exactly that. I consider I have earned it, even though I have not a legal right to it."

"Now, there you just stated the case exactly. I don't owe ye nothin', an' ye don't want no charity. A man ain't compelled to pay what he don't owe, an' I shan't give you nothin'. If you can collect it, go ahead."

Tom could have kicked himself with a hearty good will for giving the old skinflint the opportunity to humiliate him so publicly!

Next day he went to the office of Mr. Jabez Cartwright, owner of the *Jane Spofford*.

CHAPTER XVI

MR. JABEZ CARTWRIGHT — TOM FINDS GENEROSITY
STILL A MYTH — THE "BARRACOOTA" — CAPTAIN
HENRY BRADFORD — A FRIEND AT LAST — LUCK
TURNS FOR THE BETTER — OFF FOR MADRAS

THE clerk looked Tom over suspiciously, and
asked him if he wished to see Mr. Cartwright
personally. "As I don't know any other way,"
said Tom, "I guess I do." His flippancy increased
the clerk's unfavorable opinion. He dallied until
the porter returned from sweeping the sidewalk,
and then, half doubtingly, requested Tom to be
seated while he entered the private office.

"Mr. Cartwright told me to ask you your business with him," said he, returning a moment
later.

"I was second mate of the *Jane Spofford* —"
Here the door of the sanctum, which the clerk had
left ajar, was suddenly opened from within, and a
peculiar figure appeared.

Mr. Jabez Cartwright, the successful merchant
and wealthy ship-owner, the man whose word was
as good as a government bond, but who had never

been guilty of a charitable or even generous act, was at that time in his seventy-eighth year. He was a short, bow-legged, round-shouldered, pot-bellied little man, with a very large square head. His snow-white hair was still thick and stood straight out in all directions, further increasing in appearance the abnormal size of his head. His face was seamed with fine wrinkles; and a pair of expressionless, beady black eyes, looked at you unwinkingly like a rat. The grotesqueness of his appearance was heightened by a gleaming set of false teeth of such a poor fit that his lips failed to meet over them. He also had a very prominent nose, which was bright blue at the tip, shading off into purple, vermilion, carnation, and pink.

His favorite attitude was leaning with his left elbow on the desk, caressing this prominent organ with his hand. He would stroke it gently its entire length, lingering lovingly a moment at the extremity, and then repeat the caress. Various reasons had been assigned by the irreverent clerks for this habit on the part of their employer. Some held that the thing pained him, and he stroked it to soothe it; others, that being sensitive, he tried to keep his deformity covered as much as possible. As he could easily have had it painted a less gaudy hue, this theory had few adherents.

Beckoning to Tom with his free hand, Mr. Cartwright called him in. When the door was closed and they were seated, he commenced polishing his horn, while the little black eyes seemed to look right through Tom's head.

"You were second mate of the *Spofford?*"

"Yes sir."

"Last voyage?"

"Yes, sir."

"Who was the captain?"

"Captain Josiah Beebe."

He produced a paper from his desk, and, keeping his eyes fixed on it, asked Tom to repeat the names of as many of the crew as he could remember. He repeated them all except the cook, steward, and carpenter; who were known only by their titles. The old gentleman checked them off on his list as Tom called them out.

"Now what is your name, please?"

"Thomas Benton, sir."

"Correct. Now, Mr. Benton, where and under what circumstances did you leave the *Spofford?*"

While Tom related the story of the loss of the ship, Mr. Cartwright carefully and industriously rubbed his nose.

"I presume," said he at the conclusion, "that you have no objection to making an affidavit to that effect?"

"None whatever, sir."

"Very well, then; you be here to-morrow at ten o'clock, and it shall be attended to."

" All right, sir," replied Tom, and bowed himself out.

Mr. Cartwright touched a call-bell, and a boy entered. "Jones," said he. The boy silently withdrew, and Jones appeared. "Follow that young man who just went out, and let me know if he has any communication with the underwriters."

"Ay, ay, sir." Jones left, and on the repetition of the signal the boy had " Davidson " fired at him.

Davidson was a big enough man to take a seat in the presence without waiting for an invitation. Mr. Cartwright told him of the return of the second mate of the *Spofford*, and dictated Tom's story to him verbatim. Mr. Davidson drew up the affidavit, and suggested that it would have been a good idea to detain the young man until his signature had been obtained. On learning that Jones was watching him, however, he seemed satisfied.

The next day Tom met the two gentlemen at the appointed time.

"I have had your report reduced to writing, Mr. Benton," said Mr. Cartwright, when they were seated and the door closed. " The notary will read it to you, and if you find it correct you can sign it."

In a rapid, droning tone, Mr. Davidson read the document. To Tom's surprise it was correct in every detail. Three gray-headed clerks signed after him as witnesses.

"May I speak to you privately, Mr. Cartwright?" asked Tom.

"You may consider me alone now."

"I lost everything I had in the *Spofford*, and worked my passage home from La Guayra. I am, in fact, actually destitute."

Mr. Cartwright rubbed his nose slowly, meditatively. "Well, sir?" he asked, as Tom, suddenly realizing that he was almost begging again, stopped for very shame.

"I thought — perhaps — in consideration of my bringing you news of your ship, you might — might help me in some way."

"In your affidavit you state that the *Spofford* capsized on the twenty-ninth day out. You received a month's advance, did you not?"

"Yes, sir."

"Then in strict justice you owe me a day's pay. It would hardly pay to sue for it, even if you had any effects, though in that case I should probably do it from principle. I fail to see how you have any claim on me."

"Isn't my affidavit worth anything to you?"

"I am not sure that we shall use it at all; but if I needed your evidence I could have you sent to the House of Detention, and when the time came you would have to testify under oath. I have put myself out, and spared you this annoyance, by allowing you to make this affidavit. If you are out of employment, I may be able to find a place for you. Are you competent to sail as mate?"

"Yes, sir, or master. I was educated by my father, and brought his vessel home from the West Indies after he died. I was only fifteen at that time."

"Hm-m-m-m! Willis!"

"Yes, sir?"

"See if Henry has a mate yet; if not, tell him not to employ any until he hears from me."

"Yes, sir."

"If you will call at this time to-morrow, Mr. Benton, I may be able to do something for you."

Tom thanked him — he hardly knew why — and returned to his boarding-house.

The boarding-master greeted him with: "Sa-ay, young feller, you don't want ter go strayin' round. I've been lookin' for ye for the last two hours — might ha knowed ye'd turn up at dinner-time — I got a ship fer ye!"

Tom replied that he believed he had found a berth himself.

"B'leeve, hey? B'leeve nothin'! B'leeve is all right, only it don't pay board bills. There ain't no *b'leeve* about this ship; an' you got ter go in her.

You owe me enough now — board and bar bill — to eat up all yer advance."

" Bar bill ? "

"Yes, *bar bill.* That's United States, ain't it ? Do you think I furnish free whiskey ? "

" I don't know, nor care anything about your whiskey ; but I pay no bar bill ! Mind that ! "

"All right, me fine buck, I'll see whether you'll rob me or not. I'll attend to your case. You'll pay yer bar bill all right."

Knowing the futility of arguing with the shark, Tom walked away ; but he decided to keep his weather eye lifting. He would have locked his sleeping-room, but it was a public dormitory, open at all hours. Sometime during the night, he was awakened by a sensation of cold, and of being jolted about. He soon discovered that he was on a truck-load of seaman's baggage, and being driven through the street. He had been drugged ! The boarding-master was seated beside the driver, both silently puffing at very inferior cigars. Not having been tied, he had little difficulty in wriggling himself to the rear of the load. From there he dropped quietly to the ground, the wagon rumbling noisily away over the cobblestones. He was in his stocking feet, hat-less and coatless. With all the speed that was in him he dodged around the first corner — plump into a fat policeman, who was leisurely patrolling his beat, absorbed in contemplating his own grandeur.

"Ah ha! young feller! Glad to see ye! Come along!" said the officer, grabbing him by the collar. The policeman was old and stout, Tom was young and slim; he had an engagement for ten o'clock; and it was already becoming daylight. In answer to the officer's questions, he told the truth; only to be answered with: "Likely yarn! I know ye! Ye are one o' them Long Wharf gang! I'll get more of 'em yet! Been layin' fer you fellers for a month!"

As they turned a corner, Tom saw the boarding-master coming toward them at a trot. His escape had been discovered. A happy thought struck him. The officer said he had been "laying for the gang." Imitating the slang of the guttersnipes, Tom exclaimed: "H—l! Dere's Muggsey himself."

Having distracted the officer's attention, he "gave him the toe," broke the grip on his collar, and darted back in the direction from which he came. "Muggsey," attracted by the scuffle, ran up in time to be arrested by the indignant officer on regaining his feet. "Muggsey" received the benefit of the policeman's experience with Tom, and was safely locked up; while that agile young man made his way to a neighboring boarding-house whose owner was a rabid opponent of his former host. Here he told as much as was necessary of the night's adventure and was received like a returned prodigal. He was clothed, breakfasted, offered whiskey, and promised the best ship in port.

Ten o'clock found him again at Mr. Cartwright's office. A letter was handed him by the boy, addressed to "Captain Henry Bradford, Bark *Barracoota*, Long Wharf." He boarded the *Barracoota* and inquired for the captain. A boy who was sweeping the deck told him "the ole man" was below. He knocked on the after-companion slide several times, and, receiving no answer, pushed it back, descended the stairs, and knocked at the door. Still no answer. As the door was not latched, he pushed it ajar and looked in. Everything was at sixes and sevens. The lamp was burning on the table, there were empty glasses, surrounded by swarms of flies, and articles of clothing all about. He rapped again on the inside of the door.

"Is Captain Bradford aboard?" he asked in a loud voice.

"Yes, Captain Bradford is aboard, but he ain't got any money. Wait till next voyage," came in muffled tones from somewhere.

"I have a letter from Mr. Cartwright, sir," replied Tom.

"All right; leave it there and clear out."

Tom laid the letter on the table and going on deck, took a survey of the bark. She was an old but

s

stanch vessel of four or five hundred tons register. A thousand details told the practical seaman that she had been neglected. Although recently returned, her rigging had not been rattled nor tarred for an indefinite time. Stays and rigging were slack, and her paint was nearly all gone, while the deck looked more like a barn floor than a ship's deck. While noting these shabby details, a deep voice from the companion said : —

"Hey! Who are you? What do you want? Get out o' here before I throw you overboard. Come, git!"

Not a whit rattled by this warlike declaration, Tom stepped up to the handsome, but dissipated-looking young giant who was glaring at him from the companion.

"Is this Captain Bradford?" he asked politely.

"Yes, this is Captain Bradford. You didn't suppose it was Commodore Perry, did you?"

"I just left a letter on the cabin table for you, sir."

"Oh, was it you left that letter? Well where is — what's his name?"

"Thomas Benton, sir?"

"Yes; I believe that's it."

"That is my name, sir."

"The deuce it is? Are you sent down here to go as mate with me?"

"I believe there was an understanding of that sort, sir, though I'm not sure."

Captain Bradford looked at him a moment in blank surprise; then he started off across the deck, swinging his arms and exclaiming: —

"Well, I swear! Well, I'll be hanged! I wonder what he'll send me next? He's getting worse and worse." Returning to where Tom still stood, and glaring at him fiercely, he asked: "Say, bub, what Sunday School grab-bag did old Jabe pull you out of?"

Tom could not help laughing. He knew it was his youthful appearance to which the captain objected, and he liked the bluff, open manner in which he expressed his opinion.

"I know my appearance is against me," said he, " and I look like neither mate nor cook. But I have been at sea as long as I can remember, and have sailed before the stick in some of the hottest old wagons in the Western Ocean. The reason I appear in this jury rig is because I have been in rather tough luck lately. I was second mate of the *Jane Spofford* —"

"The devil you were! What has become of the old ship?"

"The last I saw of her, she was floating bottom up about three hundred miles northeast of Trinidad."

"Capsized, hey? What was the matter? Squall catch her with everything set, halliards hitched on the pins, and so forth?"

"No, sir — oh, no.   Nothing of that kind at all — "

"Well, don't let's stand here talking.   Come down below.   Boy!   Tell the cook to get breakfast along as soon as he can — breakfast for two."

"I have breakfasted, thank you, captain," said Tom, remembering the rigid economy on shipboard in regard to provisions.

"Never mind; you can eat a bite with me.   Now what will you try for a bracer?   I generally take a drop of Medford first thing in the morning to freshen the old nip.   The blamed stuff smells like bilge water, so if I'm able to keep it down, I know I'm in pretty good shape.   But take whatever you like. Here's some Martel that never saw a custom-house officer — "

"Thanks, captain.   I'm a strict teetotaler."

"Good again!   I sometimes drink more than I ought to, in fact, but I approve of teetotal mates. Well, if I must go it alone, why, here's to a better acquaintance."

He took a stiff horn of rum and molasses, making a horrible face over it; then they sat down to breakfast.   While eating, Tom gave his new commander a short account of the loss of the *Spofford*, and of his adventures since.

Captain Bradford was the only child of Mr. Jabez Cartwright's only sister, and had been an orphan since his tenth year.   Mr. Cartwright took charge of him at his mother's death, intending to give him a first-class education, and train him as a business man under his own eye, and as he had no other near relative, it was presumed that young Henry would become his heir. The handsome, generous boy became a universal favorite; but, not being sufficiently strong-minded to resist the evil influences of his flatterers, he frittered away both his own time and his uncle's money; he neglected his studies, and devoted his time to idle pleasures. The taste for liquor, acquired in the company of his jolly companions, eventually mastered him. Mr. Cartwright, hearing so many adverse reports, set a watch upon him, and when convinced that the habit had obtained a hold on the boy, he sent him to sea. Henry was not one to resist; if his uncle had ordered him to learn blacksmithing, he would have tried it cheerfully. He was not vicious; he was simply easy.

When the ship returned, the captain had nothing but good to say of him. He was smart — no one had ever doubted that; he made friends of all with whom he came in contact, and the entire crew — mates and all — swore by him. He liked the change and excitement of sea life, and as it kept him away from liquor, his uncle decided to let him make it his calling. Not desiring to punish the young man for a mere constitutional weakness, he put him in

command of the old *Barracoota*, gave him a veteran
mate to take care of him, and let him go.

While in port young Henry enjoyed himself after
his own heart, leaving the mate to play captain; but
when the pilot boarded her he resumed command.
As he never carried any liquor to sea, this plan
worked very well. The mate kept Mr. Cartwright
posted, and the old gentleman's opinion of his nephew
gradually changed for the better. Henry knew nothing of this, and though he esteemed his benefactor,
he acquired a habit of grumbling to his cronies, and
accusing the old gentleman of meanness. At last
he became dissatisfied with the old bark. He never
mentioned the matter to his uncle, but he thought
he should have been given one of the fine new ships
which slid from the ways in Mr. Cartwright's yard
every year.

His uncle would have been proud to see the young
man on the quarterdeck of the finest ship that flew
his house flag from her main truck; but he hardly
dared to trust him yet.

On the return of the *Barracoota* from her last
voyage the command of a ship which was a finer
vessel had fallen to Henry's mate, — another source
of disappointment to him. Mr. Cartwright had been
sorely puzzled to find a suitable mate to send with his
nephew, but when Tom told of bringing his father's
ship home from the West Indies he remembered the

circumstance, and also the name. He decided that Tom Benton was just the man he wanted; so he sent him to Henry that he might escape from leading-strings, and prove his worthiness of confidence.

By the time they finished breakfast the two young men had decided to like each other — an opinion that never changed.

Tom entered upon his duties at once. Captain Bradford pressed a temporary loan upon him for his immediate wants, and before they sailed he saw that Tom was equipped with everything needful to his station.

Tom Benton now entered upon the first period of prosperity he had known since his father's death. He sailed as mate of the *Barracoota* for three years. Under his care she became a very different looking vessel from what she was when he first saw her. Without relaxing the formalities necessary to the maintenance of discipline, he and Captain Bradford became like brothers, confiding their ambitions and disappointments to each other. Though Captain Bradford had never become deeply attached to any woman, alleging that he loved them all too well to discriminate in favor of any particular one, he sympathized with Tom's unfaltering regard for the sweetheart of his boyhood, as it was the one tie that bound him to the human race, and kept him from becoming an utter barbarian. He encouraged

his young mate with the assurance that now he was
in the way to fulfil his promise to Kitty Blake.

"Uncle Jabe will give ships to everybody but me,"
he added; "see what a fine one he gave old Merritt
after sailing with me only two years. The old man
don't say much, Tom, but you can bet he's got his
eye on you, and knows exactly what you are worth,
to a cent, and when he gets good and ready, you'll
get your ship."

Uncle Jabe also had his eye on Captain Henry.
Once or twice he almost had his mind made up to
promote him. Then he would hear of a new es-
capade, and, slowly stroking his bejewelled nose,
he would say: "I guess I'll let him make one more
voyage in the *Barracoota*. It won't hurt him; he
knows her, and there's plenty of time." And so the
comfortable old bark would sail again, in charge of
the two friends.

Sin is progressive. Henry Bradford the school-
boy, shudderingly took a sip from a wine-glass; but
there came a time when his name was mentioned
in consular reports and diplomatic correspondence.
A party of Christian dogs — jolly dogs, no doubt —
were discovered within the sacred precincts adjoining the harem of the Grand Turk in Constantinople.
When discovered, they soundly drubbed the watch
and fled. It was at one of those delicate crises in
European politics, when the dignity and honor of

his Sublime Highness was a matter of deep concern to the old lady in Threadneedle Street. Consequently, such a violation of international courtesy could not be overlooked. The name of Henry Bradford was, I am sorry to say, mixed up in the disgraceful business.

When Mr. Cartwright heard of this scandalous report, he ordered his nephew to appear before him. Although the captain vehemently denied any complicity in the scrape, his uncle refused to believe him. "You were there. It's just like you!" he said, and ordered him off to Madras.

"Take any paying freight you can get out there, and keep away from the States until you are compelled to return for repairs; while I endeavor to settle this disgraceful affair," were his orders.

CHAPTER XVII

WHEN Tom Benton failed to return to the English Minister's for dinner, it was supposed that Mr. Spellman had detained him as his own guest. Sir John was introduced to the ladies at table, and the story of how he came so near being shot was briefly told, calling forth such exclamations as "Oh my!" and "I should have thought you would have been frightened to death!" Kitty told Nellie when they retired that evening, that all the time she was listening to the tale of Sir John's providential rescue, she was thinking of Tom Benton, and imagining him in such a strait with no one to help. She succeeded in working herself into a very uncomfortable state of mind over this purely imaginary case, but Nellie told her she was foolish to think of such a thing, reminding her that sailors never went so far inland; always staying near the sea and their ships.

Sir John, having complied with all the necessary legal forms to perfect his claim for damages, bestrode a mule and rode off, leaving the matter entirely in Mr. Lindsay's hands for settlement. As the gallant Englishman was too bashful to be much of a lady's man, he was hardly missed. Mr. Lindsay, with the assistance of his astute nephew, conducted the affair so successfully that, at the end of four years, a very satisfactory indemnity was awarded; and the British Lion, who had raised his head and cast a glance of impatient inquiry across the Atlantic, lowered his muzzle between his paws and dozed again.

Mr. Druse, having concluded his business, and remembering several other irons which he had in the fire, asked the girls how much longer they wished to stay. They would have remained indefinitely, but school would open shortly, and they desired to be on hand, so with many regrets and backward glances, they bade good-bye to the friends they had made, and turned their backs on the beautiful land where they had passed such a delightful vacation. They reëmbarked on board the *Albatross*, which awaited them with sails loose and anchor atrip. Frank Lindsay bestowed an unnecessary pressure on

the hand of Nellie Druse, which was not to be wondered at; for in Caracas, home faces were scarce,
and few were as fair as hers. Kitty saw the quick
glance that passed between them, and awoke to the
fact that Nellie had matured wonderfully since starting on this trip. As the *Albatross*, swinging steadily
along with the trade wind, lulled the inseparables to
sleep that night, Nellie, under cover of the kindly
darkness, said : —

"Don't you think Mr. Frank Lindsay is rather
nice, Kitty ?"

"Very nice, dear," Kitty responded, as she imprinted a sympathetic kiss upon the fair brow.
Thus was born, and immaturely died, Nellie Druse's
first love-affair.

Again the *Albatross* threaded the Windward passage and crossed the Bahama banks, where her passengers enjoyed every waking moment. They spent
hours gazing down at the strange objects to be seen
through the crystal clear water, and admired the
lovely islets, which, like miniature Edens, succeeded
each other before their delighted eyes. Finally they
passed under the frowning walls of Morro Castle,
and dropped anchor in the picturesque harbor of
Havana, "The Queen City of the Antilles." This
stop was made to enable Mr. Druse to see personally
a gentleman with whom he had transacted business
for thirty years, but whom he had never met. All

hands scurried ashore to make the most of the very limited time at their disposal. They drank the incomparable coffee which is to be obtained at any of the cafés fronting the Plaza, the ladies bought guava jelly, and the gentlemen cigars. They took one of the queer-looking carriages, and drove about for a couple of hours, paying their respects to the tomb of Columbus, as all good Americans should. They were careful to return aboard in time to get out of the harbor before sundown, as otherwise, according to the ancient custom prevailing so near the land of universal liberty, they would have been detained until the next day.

The girls were disposed to grumble as they cast longing glances back at the bright-hued houses. They had hardly seen Havana at all, and would have liked to stay a week; but their time was limited. They now dipped into the Gulf Stream, that grandest and most wonderful of all the great ocean rivers, and with a fair wind and under blue skies, they bade a regretful adieu to the land of eternal summer, the garden of the world, the ever-blooming tropics.

Off Hatteras, they received the usual salutation which Boreas deems a fitting welcome to all who approach our coast. A nor'wester struck the *Albatross* butt end first, blowing some of her old fine weather canvas to ribbons, and scaring the girls half to death; for they thought they were surely to be wrecked. They marvelled at the hardihood of the steward, an ungodly old sea-dog, who laughed in their faces when they timidly asked if he thought there was much danger. But long before the gale blew itself out Kitty recovered some of the daring spirit that had nearly been educated out of her.

Hanging to a backstay, she watched gleefully the big combers that rose towering far above the rail. On they came with a rush which it seemed that not even Gibraltar could withstand, but the old *Albatross* would lift her head saucily and glide over them without an effort. Sometimes, to be sure, the old girl would fail to calculate just right, and then the sea would hit her a thump that made her stand still and shudder, while every timber in her trembled. The sailors grabbed the nearest rope or pin, and bent their oilskin-clad shoulders to receive it. Over it would come in tons; looking a clear crystalline green above the rail, and tumbling in a cataract across the deck to leeward, each obstruction to its course, such as hatches, pumps, harness, casks, etc., coming into prominence as the centre of a mimic cascade.

Nellie never mustered courage to come on deck during the gale; all that Kitty could persuade her to do was to crawl quaking up the steps, and peep for one terrified moment to leeward.

The gale blew them a hundred miles off shore,

and then blew itself out, to be followed by a fine whole-sail breeze from the southward and westward, which took them right into New York harbor.

Mr. Druse secured accommodations for the entire party at the Astor House. New York was not the city then that it is to-day; but it was the metropolis of that time, and to most of our party a very wonderful place. Though Nellie Druse had been in London, she admired the American city as much as Kitty. They had a week to spare, and they employed it fully, visiting all the most interesting places about the city, and filling in odd hours with that never-failing source of delight to the feminine mind, be it young or old, shopping. Not necessarily buying, just shopping — pawing over the beautiful things in the big stores of the day, to their hearts' content. They refurnished their own wardrobes, and bought presents galore for teachers and schoolmates.

At last, the day that always comes too soon, the day to say good-bye, arrived. There was weeping and wiping of red noses. The old ladies bade adieu to their darlings, as if they were about to enter an African jungle unarmed, and the girls made all the fuss necessary on such a solemn occasion. The gentlemen, including young Robert, stood apart and chatted, pretending to be unaware of the wet spell so near. The conductor shouted with official importance: " All aboard ! " and the fireman set the bell ringing. There was a flutter in the dovecote, during which young Robert brazenly kissed both girls — who took no notice — and then a rush for the cars, as, in a more peremptory tone, the conductor repeated his warning, and a craning of necks by those on the platform, in their efforts to see their friends within. When they succeeded, a pantomime of nods and grins followed. Sometimes the struggle of the imprisoned ones to raise a window was successful; then the farewell addresses were repeated as long as they were able to hear each other. When the last petticoat disappeared up the car step, the conductor waved his hand in a lordly manner to the watching fireman, who said, " All right!" to the engineer, and rang the bell again. The engineer took a final glance down the yard at switches and signals, and carefully, so as not to slip the big driving-wheels or jerk the train, worked his throttle open. A jet of white steam, whose vicious hissing proclaimed the pressure in the great boiler, blew horizontally far out from the open cylinder cocks, slowly the wheels began to revolve, and the Montreal express was off. Nine cars — the last three sleepers, the sleepers of those days, very primitive compared with the wheeled palaces of to-day, — sagged back heavily on the engine.

But the engineer and fireman understood their duties; better yet, they understood each other. No word passed between them on the wildly rolling engine. The time was short, the train was heavy, and the best efforts of all concerned would be needed to get it to its destination on time. It would go a little slow up the long hills, and time would be lost, but the brow of the hill passed, a listener in the train would have noticed that the long, heavy "cha-a, cha-a" of the iron horse gradually shortened and quickened until, as she gathered headway, it would become "tucker tucker tucker," soon to be blended into a faint whirr, and then lost altogether, which meant that she was then flying down grade, literally on the wings of the wind, regaining as much as possible of the lost time.

The girls watched the monotonous scenery from the car window until it wearied them. The brown and dreary view could not charm eyes which had so recently feasted on the royal luxuriance of the tropics. They talked, tried to read, listened to the mournful shriek of the whistle as they passed road-crossings or flew by way-stations, and wished their journey over. Evening came on; the car lamps were lighted, and the outer world obliterated entirely. Now, indeed, the time hung heavily. They reviewed the pleasures of their vacation, and finally settled down into mutual adulations of Tom Benton and Frank Lindsay.

Each praised the other's choice; for, though Nellie

T

had never seen Tom, Kitty's approval was sufficient recommendation for her. At last they were enjoying themselves, having hit upon a topic that was rich in possibilities. The heavy rolling of the car proved they were going at a rapid gait. They were enjoying the ride now, as they sat with their arms about each other's waists, and peeped fearlessly into their own rose-colored future.

There was a crash, the lights went out, the two friends were violently separated, and the darkness was filled with the most dreadful shrieks.

A broken flange on a wheel, a rotten tie, or a loose fish-plate, — something, — had derailed the train, and thrown it down a fifteen-foot bank. The engine broke loose from its train, and went on ; the engineer, with the presence of mind for which locomotive engineers are famous, seeing his train piling itself in the ditch, never closed his throttle, but ran to the next station, nine miles away, and telegraphed the news to his superintendent. He received orders over the wire to procure all the medical assistance possible; to gather a force of laborers — all that could be obtained — with crowbars, axes, tackle, chains, and lanterns, and return to the wreck.

So readily did the people respond, and so well did the railroad men perform their part, that in less than forty minutes a half-dozen fairly well equipped physicians were on the spot, and dozens of willing hands were chopping, prying, and tearing the wreckage asunder in the noble work of relief. Forty minutes is not much; but it is a long time to lie in helpless agony, pinned under a railroad wreck. During these forty minutes many willing hands had been at work; otherwise the relief party might have been too late, for the fire from lamps and car stoves would have got in its deadly work.

Fortunately the conductor had worked on that section of the road years ago, on construction, and knew of an abandoned well near the track. Fire buckets were fished out from among the wreckage, bell cord was unrove, and, under the conductor's instructions, the uninjured passengers formed a bucket brigade. Wherever a curling tongue of smoke made its appearance, it was drowned out at once, but they were unable to respond to the piteous cries for assistance that rose all about them. The urgent danger of fire must first be attended to. The welcome whistle of the returning engine, loaded with men and implements, renewed their courage, and as the rear sleeper had remained on the track, the doctors took charge of it and converted it into a field hospital.

Now, indeed, there was help at hand. Car windows and doors were smashed, roofs torn off, and the injured taken, as soon as extricated, to the hospital car. It was a heart-rending sight. We can stand

with a semblance of equanimity the sight of a
mangled man, but we do not like our mothers,
wives, or sweethearts to be thus injured.

Kitty had lost consciousness at once. Nellie was
thrown against the roof of the overturned car, and
held there by a mass of broken seats, where she
screamed in unreasoning fear for some time, and
then fainted. After clearing away some of the débris, the wreckers found Kitty, and she was taken at
once to the hospital car. Several other victims
were removed, and thinking the cars were empty,
the workers were about to leave when one of them,
holding his lantern high overhead, looked directly
into Nellie's face. In removing a broken seat from
her ankle, they hurt her so badly that she regained
her senses.

"Oh, Kitty!" she cried. "Where is Kitty?"
As they carried her tenderly out, she kept calling for
Kitty. "I want my Kitty! Where is my Kitty?"

"Yes, yes! We'll get your kitty for you, little
one," said the conductor, soothingly, supposing her
to be calling in her delirium for a household pet.

When Nellie arrived at the hospital car, the
dreadful sights caused her to faint again. Finding
her only hurt to be a fracture of the left leg, the
doctors set it, and rightly guessing from her delicate
appearance that she was suffering from shock,
they ordered her taken to the relief train, with

instructions to send her home as soon as she was able to make her destination known.

Kitty's injuries were much more serious, — concussion of the brain, and possibly a fractured skull. A case for the Albany hospital. In the hurry and confusion at the moment, she was handed over, still unconscious to a farmer, Mr. Ephraim Stagg, who had just notified one of the doctors that his house was at the disposal of the medical men and their patients. The gentlemen thanked him hurriedly and turned away to attend a newly arrived case.

Mr. Stagg and his maiden sister, Miss Melinda, lived on a rather unproductive farm a little way back from the railroad. They were of the ordinary poor farmer class to whom the opportunity of making a dollar was an event. They were good hearted enough; but too poor to be able to afford the virtue of generosity, therefore Ephraim's offer to the doctor was not dictated by pure sympathy. People who could travel must have money, and would be able to pay for entertainment. A cow which had met its death on the railroad a year previously had, besides the loss of herself, plunged them into expensive litigation with the company. The suit was still pending and they needed money. For these various reasons Ephraim's heart palpitated with pleasure when he saw what a richly dressed young girl had been confided to his care by the railroad men.

On his arrival home, Miss Melinda—a bud of
forty-seven springs — was considerably flustered.
She hastily prepared her best spare room, and Kitty
was undressed and laid on the soft, sweet corn-husk
bed. Early in the morning, as soon as the family
doctor returned from his voluntary service at the
wreck, he was summoned to the Stagg cottage. He
prescribed perfect rest and quiet, saying she was
a strong, healthy young woman, and would undoubtedly get well. Kitty remained under the
humble roof of the Staggs for nearly three months.
She recovered entirely from the physical effects of
the accident, but her mind was extremely hazy, and
her memory almost entirely gone. She was also
no longer the robust Kitty of former days, but was
frail and weak. To their credit be it said, the lonely
elderly couple became attached to the gentle girl and
hoped no one would ever claim her.

At last Nellie was sent on to Albany, where
a representative of the company telegraphed Miss
Lavinia Randolph of the predicament of her pupil.
"Would she come or send some one at the company's
expense?"

Miss Lavinia would not think of sending any one
on such an important and delicate mission, but came
herself. The meeting between teacher and pupil
was most affecting, and when Nellie sobbed out the
story of Kitty's disappearance, Miss Randolph be-

came nearly distracted. She appealed at once to the railroad officials; the superintendent, however, declared that the wreck was all cleared up, and everybody accounted for. He suggested that Kitty had probably escaped uninjured and had been taken away by friends. This explanation was of course rejected, both by Miss Randolph and Nellie, as Kitty had no friends on the train or in the state.

There was absolutely no information to be obtained in Albany, so they returned as soon as possible to Montreal, where Nellie was subjected to most careful and tender nursing, with the result that she was soon entirely recovered.

When the *Albatross* arrived in Portland, a long telegram told her passengers of the wreck and of the unaccountable disappearance of Kitty. Mr. Druse chartered a special train, and the entire party went to Montreal to get the story from Nellie's own lips. They learned so little there, that they proceeded to Albany. The railroad officials were closely questioned, but were unable to throw any light upon the subject. Detectives were placed upon the case, who scoured the country far and near, and even visited Ephraim Stagg's dilapidated cottage half-way up the mountain side. As they were working on the theory that the young lady had been abducted for the purpose of extorting a reward, they asked no questions; and, as Kitty timidly avoided all strangers, they failed to find her. As a last resort, Mr. Hayward offered a large reward for information that would lead to her recovery; but as the Staggs never saw a newspaper, they knew nothing of it.

At last, worn out and heartbroken, the Haywards returned to Portland, and Mr. Druse, after cautioning Miss Randolph never to lose sight of his ewe lamb for a moment, returned to the endless business of piling sovereigns one upon another. Disastrous indeed had been the aftermath of the pleasant vacation.

Kitty's mental faculties gradually improved as her bodily strength increased; but they were oddly distorted. Her entire past life had escaped her memory, or appeared in such a fragmentary manner that she was unable to gather it into a coherent whole. She answered readily to the name of Sarah, bestowed upon her by her new friends. She knew it was not hers, but in the maze of her troubled brain she was unable to disentangle her own name, so she accepted it with a sense of weariness, as being good enough.

There was one subject that stood out bright and clear to her dimmed mind, and that was that she must find Tom Benton and return to him twelve thousand dollars, of which, in some way that she failed to remember, she had robbed him. This strange notion she kept to herself. As the Staggs had never seen her in perfect health, they now supposed her to have fully recovered and, as they dreaded the day of parting, they never mentioned the subject, supposing she would notify them when ready to go. Miss Melinda, with almost reverent care, cleaned and repaired Kitty's clothing. She had never seen such rich fabrics and dainty articles of apparel in her life. She laid the soft velvets to her wrinkled cheek, and passed her rough hands caressingly over the rich silks which rustled deliciously under them, but caught on her toil-worn fingers as though they were burrs.

Sometimes, to please her friend, Kitty would dress herself, and by the crinkly glass in the little parlor, arrange her hair as she had always worn it. These occasions were a rare treat to Miss Melinda, giving her a clear insight into many things which she had never been able to understand. There were twenty-seven dollars and some change in the little pocket-book, and this she insisted that Kitty should keep in her own room.

There was to be a great awakening at the Methodist Church on the other side of the mountain. A professional exhorter had arrived who was to arouse the whole countryside. ·His fame, with exaggerated accounts of the multitudes of souls he had been instrumental in saving, had travelled before him, so that, when the great day arrived on which he was to open on the enemy's works in Ashton, the people flocked for miles around. If the Staggs were ignorant, they were devoutly pious. The advent of this powerfully gifted man was an epoch in their quiet lives, and they would no more have thought of missing the meeting, than declining the summons of the last trump. They were grieved to note an utter absence of enthusiasm in Sarah, but she said she did not care to go, and they would not force her to do so.

No sooner had the bony sorrel horse and rickety shay disappeared round the corner of the unpainted barn, than Sarah carefully dressed herself in her own clothes. She wrote a note thanking her friends for all they had done for her and begging them to forgive this act of apparent ingratitude, telling them she was going on an errand of justice and promised to return when it should be completed. Then she covered the fire with ashes so that it might keep till their return, and remembering that they did not expect to get back until after dark, she lit the lamp. She enclosed a ten-dollar bill in the note and placed it conspicuously near the lighted lamp. Closing the door carefully, and taking a farewell glance round the humble but pleasant home, she started on her five-mile walk over the spur of the mountain to the railroad station of which she had heard, but which she had never seen. It was a weary road, and she was not accustomed to long walks; but fortifying herself with the thought that she was going to find Tom and return his money, she persevered, holding up her skirts and picking her way that she might not present a bedraggled appearance.

She arrived at last, footsore and weary, with a bursting headache and on the point of collapse, but thankful. As she had an hour to wait for a New York train, she crossed the track to a small hotel and sensibly strengthened herself with a hearty meal.

CHAPTER XVIII

AFTER an uneventful passage Captain Bradford
arrived at Madras with the old *Barracoota*, left Tom
in charge, and took up his residence in Blacktown,
where, as he was handsome, brilliant, and free-handed,
the young Yankee skipper became a valuable acquisi-
tion to the somewhat jaded English colony. Tom
notified the captain when the cargo was out, and
received orders to keep the crew busy until he heard
from him again. Nearly a month elapsed, and Tom
began to worry, for he feared his friend was over-
doing it, and would get himself into further trouble.
The butcher's boat came off regularly, keeping them
well supplied with fresh provisions, and all hands
were fat and hearty. About six weeks after their
arrival the *Oriental*, of the same line, dropped anchor

within a quarter of a mile of the *Barracoota*. Tom boarded her at once, and learned from Captain Jermyn that Mr. Cartwright had died, cutting off his nephew, Captain Bradford, with a dollar. Tom was deeply grieved, for he liked his large-hearted captain, though he deprecated his wild course. He gave Captain Jermyn as little information as possible, and, telling him that Captain Bradford was staying on shore, gave him his address. Next morning Captain Bradford came off bright and early. He was excited and angry. Calling Tom into the cabin, he closed the door, and, turning to him with flashing eyes, he said:—

"What do you think of that, Tom? What do you think of the miserly old skinflint? He has cut me off with a dollar, after deluding me into sailing this old woodpile all these years. If I hadn't expected to get his money, do you suppose I'd have put up with it as long as I have? No, sir! I've eaten more humble pie to please that old villain than any white man ever ought to! Serves me right, too! If I'd stood up to him a little better, I guess he'd have thought more of me. Hang him, I say! This news couldn't have come at a worse time if he'd planned it. But never you mind; I'll land her yet! See if I don't."

Here he ceased pounding on the table and raving long enough to toss off a glass of rum and water. Then, feeling somewhat revived, he continued:—

"I was working a good scheme here, Tom.
There's a lady ashore, a major's widow, Mrs.
Hargrave, who is worth stacks and stacks of ru-
pees; she has indigo and tea plantations, town
houses in all the principal cities, bungalows in all
the most desirable country places, and the Lord
knows what all; and she's a fine woman, too, a
regular English aristocrat.   I've been shining up
to her, and was making splendid progress.   Of
course I let it be known that I was the old man's
heir; and I had just about got ready to pop the
question when in comes Jermyn with this infernal
news.   It will be all over Blacktown in twenty-
four hours, and if I'm not awfully mistaken my
cake is dough.   Hang it all, it's enough to drive
a man to drink.   Hand me that brandy!"

Tom, whose knowledge of women was confined
to his silent worship of a boyish memory, had, perhaps, an exaggerated idea of the sacredness of the
tender passion.   Hearing his captain run on in this
sacrilegious manner, he asked: —

"Do you love the lady, sir?"

"Do I love her?   Hear him!   Why, Tom, I
loved her before, but I worship her now!   Who
could help loving such a woman?   Don't you suppose I'd rather live in a nice airy bungalow on an
Assam tea plantation, with servants to hand you the
brandy and water *pawnee lao*, and brush off the flies,

wear a cork hat and white linen clothes, and have nothing to do but to play gentleman all the year round, than to eat salt horse and fight cockroaches in this old hooker? If she were ninety, I'd love her! But she isn't; she's a fine, well-preserved woman of thirty-five, — not a day over that, — a little stout and red in the face, you know, but that's the climate; you can't expect a woman to live in India twenty years and bury two husbands without showing the effects of wear and tear. It's better than if she were yellow and shrivelled, — most of 'em get that way. Oh, but I forgot to tell you; I've chartered the old ship to her brother-in-law for a six-months coasting voyage. We won't get much stuff here; it will be all aboard this week, and they will go with us as passengers."

"Who, sir?"

"Why, Hargrave and his sister-in-law. She wants to see some property she bought awhile ago in Trincomalee, so she takes this opportunity. I let her have the passage cheap, and being a shrewd business woman, that appealed to her. I hope to land her before the voyage is up. Once I get her away from that Scotch colonel who is always hanging round her, I think — I hope, at least — I'll be all right. Hargrave and I are great chums; that's one point in my favor — I've cultivated him!"

Tom was far from pleased with this news. Passengers — especially lady passengers — are not regarded favorably as a rule by sailors, nor was he pleased with the flippant manner in which Captain Bradford spoke of the woman whom he was so desirous of marrying.

Five days later, having received all the cargo they were to get in Madras, and the passengers and baggage being safely stowed below, they sailed for Pondicherry. Tom was introduced to the passengers at dinner, and found Mr. Ernest Hargrave, a portly gentleman of fifty, very much to his liking. The widow, he at once decided, had not understated her age. She was undeniably stout, also quite red in the face, but, in spite of these physical drawbacks, she proved on better acquaintance to be not only ladylike, but extremely good company. She was not a bit fussy nor troublesome, but jolly and companionable, and possessed of rare tact which prevented her from ever being in the way. Tom was glad to see that, in spite of Captain Bradford's frivolous manner when speaking of her in Madras, he was deeply in love with her and appreciated her superiority. They remained but one day in Pondicherry. From there they went to Negapatam, where, without anchoring, they discharged what little cargo they had for the agent, took in a few bales of jute, and proceeded to Trincomalee.

Here both Mr. and Mrs. Hargrave insisted that Captain Bradford should accompany them ashore on their trip to the interior to inspect the lady's purchase. It is needless to say he was easily persuaded. Tom was again left in charge. Once more the old *Barracoota* swung idly at her anchor for a solid month, and when the explorers returned, there were three days of hard work taking in the cargo Mr. Hargrave had bought up country and brought down with him. From here they made short stops at Batikala, Matma, and Kaltura. As Captain Bradford paid but little attention either to the handling of the ship or the cargo, Tom took his orders from Mr. Hargrave and attended to everything; while the lovers cooed in peace and contentment.

When they arrived in Colombo, it was known that the lady would leave the ship. Mr. Hargrave was too thorough an Anglo-Indian to allow business to interfere with pleasure, and both his sister-in-law and himself had numerous friends in the Cingalese metropolis, the result being that another long rest was taken here; while Captain Bradford enjoyed himself on shore with his friends and their friends and acquaintances.

As Captain Bradford did not confide the result of his courtship to Tom, he had no positive knowledge regarding its success. The captain's behavior was so contradictory that it was impossible to judge by it; sometimes he appeared in the very best of spirits, and again he would be down in the dumps,

Tom, being entirely ignorant of the symptoms of his disease, found it impossible to diagnose his captain's case. He would no sooner decide to venture a congratulatory remark, than the captain would appear on deck with a visage so woebegone that he wondered how he could have deceived himself into believing this poor human wreck a happy and successful lover.

The captain now resumed charge and drove the old ship as though he was competing for an international cup. After diving into all sorts of little holes in the bushes alongshore, their time expired in Batangiri. Mr. Hargrave offered to renew the charter for another six months, but Captain Bradford declined. There were a few tons of cargo in the hold to be delivered in Bombay, so he said he would go there and secure a charter for Europe or the States. As Mr. Hargrave had some business to transact along the coast, they regretfully bade the jovial gentleman adieu and left him behind.

The anchor was no sooner down in Bombay roads, than the captain hailed a dinghy, and, telling Tom he would send a lighter off for the cargo, went ashore. A week later he sent off a shore boat with a note requesting Tom to meet him at the hotel. Wondering what was up, Tom shipped his shore togs, and after giving the second mate instructions to keep a sharp lookout, went ashore.

The dinghy wallah piloted him to the hotel, on the spacious veranda of which he found his captain and Mrs. Hargrave enjoying the cool evening air. He observed that the widow had emerged from her mourning, and was very becomingly dressed in a light costume. When Tom approached, Captain Bradford rose, blushed a bit awkwardly, and taking the lady's hand said : —

"Mrs. Bradford, allow me to introduce Captain Benton, of the *Barracoota*. You have met before, I believe."

It was now Tom's turn to blush. His unexpected promotion, so suddenly announced, together with his desire to acquit himself creditably in congratulating the happy pair, nearly threw him on his beam ends. He righted himself, however, with an effort, and congratulated them heartily. The *ci-devant* widow received his good wishes with evident pleasure, and the captain with an assumed air of indifference which deceived nobody.

They told Tom they had been married less than two hours, and had sent for him to dine with them. During this most enjoyable dinner Captain Bradford told Tom that, as his wife objected to his going to sea again, he should hand the ship over to him. He had obtained a freight for her from Mocha to Liverpool; and he might sail as soon as he could get his ballast in.

Mr. and Mrs. Bradford dined with Captain Benton on board the *Barracoota* two days later, and on leaving the ship they wished him a hearty "*Bon voyage.*" Captain Bradford explained to the crew that he had given the command of the ship to Tom, and, as they could see a hole in a ladder as well as the next man, they gave three rousing cheers for him and his lady. The courtesy was acknowledged by Mrs. Bradford, who bought the entire contents of a bumboat that happened to be alongside, and presented it to them; and amid more cheering and waving of hats the happy pair left the old ship forever. Tom's elation at his promotion was tempered by regret at the loss of his companion. They had sailed together a long time, and though there were many traits in Captain Bradford's character of which Tom did not approve, he had always been a steadfast friend.

The next morning, at four o'clock, the *Barracoota* sailed from Bombay. Tom Benton was now master, but he had not yet accomplished what he promised Kitty Blake that day, so long ago, in Portland. He was master, but he was only a hired man; he did not own a cent's worth in the ship, nor was she the kind of vessel he had in his mind's eye when he said so proudly to Kitty: "I'll not come back until I command as fine a ship as ever your father did."

Now that he was captain it did not seem such a dizzy height as he had once thought it would, and no wonder. As he glanced about the old *Barracoota*, ramshackled and weather-worn, with the evidences of her twenty-five years' combat with the elements registered indelibly on every square inch of her, he knew that she would never astonish the natives of Portland. He knew that crabbed old Rufus Blake would never be overwhelmed by the grandeur of the position occupied by her captain. Besides, he had no assurance that the new owners would confirm his appointment. It might be a repetition of the *Columbia* case; so he resolved not to plume himself too much on his sudden rise. Experience had taught him that his very next voyage might be in the forecastle.

Captain Bradford's marriage recalled Kitty forcibly to his mind. He longed to see her, and wondered where she was now, and if she still remembered him, and if they would ever meet again. And so, dreaming and building castles, alternately hoping and fearing, unconsciously indulging in the same mental flagellations that had so disturbed Captain Bradford's serenity after parting with his lady-love at Colombo, the new captain paced his quarterdeck, and the old *Barracoota*, indifferent as to who commanded her, bobbed serenely through the blue waters of the Indian Ocean.

It was the season of the change of the monsoons, when the weather is entirely unreliable. Tom, feeling the weight of his new responsibilities, remained on deck nearly all the time. He watched the weather closely, but for some time the most he had to contend with were light baffling winds, squalls, and calms. For several days he failed to get an observation on account of the weather, and as the dead reckoning showed her to be making more westing than was desirable, he was not surprised one morning when he discovered land to the westward which he knew to be the island of Socotra.

The weather was detestable. The sky was obscured by low-hanging, heavy black clouds; the wind came in scarcely perceptible whiffs, — usually catching her aback, — and it was terribly hot and sultry. Toward noon Captain Benton observed, away to the southward, a small waterspout. Inside of an hour there were half a dozen of them in sight; none very near, but they helped to increase his anxiety. The ship lay entirely becalmed while the vicious little spouts travelled about, each the centre of its own corkscrew breeze. As he was utterly powerless to get away from them, he could only hope they would miss him, for, even though they failed to board and swamp her, one of them might easily pass so close as to whip the sticks out of her.

They increased in number and drew nearer as the day wore on, until, with the low-hanging cloud roof and these numerous slanting and twisted pillars of

water, the scene took on somewhat the appearance
of a goblin forest. The sea, from the effects of so
many varied forces at work upon it, began to re-
semble the surface of a boiling caldron; tossing the
old ship about in a most disconcerting manner, so
that several of the men, seasoned shellbacks, became
seasick. Sometimes a spout, as if in a spirit of spor-
tive deviltry, would come tearing down toward the
Barracoota until the green veining of the whirling
mass of water was plainly discernible from the deck.
Then, for no apparent reason, it would be suddenly
deflected, just in the nick of time, and go roaring
away to one side; while sails, ropes, and blocks
rattled and flapped thunderously in the tangle of
the contrary air currents.

The most apparent effect of these assaults was that
the ship was being gradually forced over toward the
eastern coast of Socotra.

As the young captain peered anxiously about him,
first at the threatening land, and then at those eccen-
tric shafts of whirling water on whose next movement it was idle to speculate, he wondered what
witch's curse it was that pursued him. In all his
seagoing he had never seen a similar case; the instant he got command, it seemed that the elements
conspired to produce some new and unheard-of combination to deprive him of it. Was this to be the
end of his career as captain? While thus bitterly

ruminating on the ill luck which seemed to pursue him so relentlessly, his attention was drawn to three unusually large spouts away on the starboard quarter. A very short inspection showed them not only to be drawing together, but also nearing the *Barracoota* with terrific speed, and Captain Benton calculated that they would just about meet on her deck. After that his interest in them would cease.

He watched their approach gloomily, his whole soul raging with helpless anger. Tradition says that a cannon-shot will burst a waterspout. It might as well have said a broadside of Koh-i-noors, as far as the *Barracoota* was concerned; she was a marine cart, a peaceful, commerce-carrying wagon, and she had no cannon.

When the spouts arrived within a quarter of a mile of the ship, the sun burst through a rift in the clouds and shone directly on them. It was a magnificent spectacle. They had increased in size, until now they must have measured ten or fifteen feet in their smallest diameters. They were of about equal dimensions, and revolved with such speed that the water seemed drawn out into threads. But it was solid water, no spray; for even at the thinnest part it showed green and clear; while now that they were so close together, the whole surface of the sea about their feet was a leaping, tearing mass of liquid fury impossible to describe.

Captain Tom glanced along the deck. The men were all at the rail, watching, their faces hidden under the overhanging flaps of their sou'westers, so that he was unable to note their expressions. He ordered all hands called, as he would not have them drowned in their bunks. They told him all hands were on deck.

When within a cable's length of the quarter, the three spouts met. Tom grasped a backstay and drew a long breath. They must surely now collapse and swamp the old ship under the weight of falling water. They did nothing of the kind. As the three united, the shock of meeting deflected the single column, so that it passed clear of her stern. There was a shock that nearly threw Captain Benton off his feet, as her stern rose in the air, while she buried her jib-boom and rolled both rails under. The fore and main top-gallant masts went by the board, and as the giant spout crossed her stern she was bombarded with a shower of shells, sand, and live fish, accompanied by a drenching shower of water. Captain Benton had dodged forward of the mizzenmast. She had a pilot house, but as the scuttle was open on account of the heat, the helmsman, cut and bleeding, stood in a pile of sand and squirming fish. The crew nearly all received slight injuries. The sails, old fine-weather canvas, were cut to ribbons, while the spars and after-surfaces of the houses were scraped and battered to pulp by this great natural sand blast.

When it became possible to leave the shelter of the mast, Captain Benton looked anxiously after the great spout, which was now half a mile away on the port quarter, going toward the land. As he watched it, it seemed to sink and dwindle as though some mighty force was drawing it into the depths. It sank, leaned far over, and thrashed and tugged as though fighting with some unseen monster for its life. Then of a sudden it shot up, higher and bigger than before, but no longer composed of clear green water. It was dirty, muddy, and the troubled sea at its base was yellow.

As Captain Tom watched the thing, half dazed with fear and wonder, he perceived that when it shot up in that peculiar manner it became changed in some respects. It no longer revolved so rapidly as at first, and there was a dark object visible in the smallest part, which seemed to project outside the spout itself, something, evidently, which had been torn up from the ocean's bed. Fascinated by the strange sight, he brought the long telescope from the companion to bear on it. Sometimes the object, whatever it was, would slowly descend nearly to the sea-level, then as gracefully rise again in the supporting pillar of water to a height of fifty or sixty feet, as a pith-ball rides on a fountain jet. As nearly as he could make out, it bore a resemblance to a vessel's hull, but he could not be sure. The spout was approaching the land, and, even as he looked, the watery giant bowed its great head, as if in submission to inevitable fate, and plunged upon the rocky point of Socotra. Captain Benton saw land and trees sloughed off by the resistless deluge, until only the rocky skeleton remained. The water raced back in a thousand muddy cascades to its parent ocean, and the great waterspout was gone.

In the mean time, the crew, under the mate's orders, had cleared away the wreckage and were now bending sails. It was an all-night job. Towards morning a light breeze sprung up, the weather cleared, and with a heart full of gratitude Captain Benton once more contemplated the broad wake over the taffrail.

The cargo was ready for him when he arrived, so he was at sea again within a month. He fell into a calm belt at once, and fussed and fumed, for he was ambitious to make a good passage. But it was no use; as usual his luck was against him. Slowly and laboriously the *Barracoota* waded to the southward. Every mile of her way might almost have been sailed in the sweat of her crew, who perspired, ay, and swore as sailors will, at her braces, tacks, and sheets, day and night. One bright hot morning found them rolling lazily in a raging calm off the naked point of Socotra.

With genuine Yankee curiosity, Captain Benton brought his glass to bear on it. Nothing but bare and very uninteresting rocks. There was a light current sweeping the ship slowly to the southward. As he watched listlessly he noticed a queer-looking object coming into view as the bearings gradually changed. A few minutes' inspection assured him that it was the burden the waterspout had borne ashore, and as the ship was quite close in now, he could almost swear it was a wreck. There was not a sign of wind, so he ordered a boat out, and, telling the mate to signal him if the least whiff of air appeared, pulled ashore. As he drew nearer, he saw that it was indeed a vessel's hull, of an entirely different build from anything he had ever seen. The landing was difficult, as the rocks were round and smooth, presenting almost perpendicular faces to the sea, but with the assistance of the boat's crew he finally scrambled up to where the wreck lay wedged between two great rocks.

She was about sixty feet long; her upper works were gone, and her back was broken across the rock. She had been in the water so long, and afterwards so thoroughly kiln-dried by the blazing tropical sun, that she looked more like the wreck of a basket than of a vessel, and the planking was so thoroughly bored by teredos that it resembled honeycomb. Here and there, through the hungry cracks, the spindling remains of bolts were visible; which, when scraped, were found to be copper, or bronze. There was no trace of fastening in the upper works; they hung together from force of habit alone. It was impossible to say which end had been her bow; she was too far gone in decay. Helped by one of the men, Captain Benton tore off enough of the mummified planking to enable him to enter. There was but little to see; a few skeleton-like ribs, bleached to a grayish white, and a trace of what might have been a port-hole for an oar. There was a layer of sand and shells in the bottom where the seams had not opened wide enough to let it drop out; and that was all.

In climbing aboard, a bit of the rotten planking had broken off in his hand. As he stood looking about, he poked idly in the sand with it and encountered a resistance; scratching away the sand with his hands, he uncovered a brick or bar of metal similar to that of which the bolts were made. He decided to take it aboard with him as a souvenir of this queer old vessel which had been so strangely resurrected, and on digging further, he found there were several more of them. Probably it had been a part of her cargo, and, owing to the bottom being preserved in the sand, it had been brought up with her. As all sorts of things come handy on a long voyage, he passed all he could readily find out to the men, who put them in the boat. They were as heavy as lead; so he decided they might have been used by the ancient mariners as ballast. By the time he had handed out sixteen of them, the men in the boat reported the ship making signals, and as Captain Tom was nearly prostrated with the heat, he was glad of an excuse to quit. They returned aboard, hoisted the boat in, threw the copper bars in the boatswain's locker, and, a breeze coming up, soon left Socotra astern.

In spite of his inauspicious start, Tom made a good passage to Liverpool. The *Barracoota* — as her name implied — was built for sailing; and, though she was too old now to stand very hard driving, Tom laced it to her pretty well, with the result that he was complimented by the owners, and his appointment was confirmed.

He went from Liverpool to Cardiff, where he loaded coal for Rio, and from there he took a cargo of coffee to London.

While in Rio, he received a present. The consignee had a handsome young Newfoundland dog, and fearing the effect of the climate on the animal, and being very fond of it, he begged Captain Tom to take it with him. Tom soon became attached to Neptune, who, dog-like, knew that his master was also master of everybody else on board. Neptune was frolicsome and playful as a kitten with the captain, but he despised everybody else. He was obliged to tolerate the mates; but no sailor could approach him without risking a nip from his powerful jaws. One morning, while the watch were washing down, Neptune deliberately attacked an Englishman and tore the man's bare leg severely.

Attracted by his cries and a fierce growling, Captain Benton rushed on deck with his revolver. He would have shot the dog, but Neptune, leaving his victim, rushed to welcome his master with such extravagant signs of affection, that Tom's just wrath at the evil deed was overcome by love for his pet. He told the mate to drown Neptune at eight bells; for it is an unwritten law on board ship that biting dogs must die. Desiring to insure his poor friend a merciful death, he ordered him to be well ballasted.

"A holystone, sir?" suggested the mate.

"Yes, that will do — or, say, Mr. Janeway, there should be some bars of copper in the boatswain's locker."

"Yes, sir."

"Tie half a dozen of them around his neck and drop him off the cathead!"

"Too bad to use so many of them, sir. That copper might come handy some time, and anyway, one would do the job."

"Will you do as I tell you?" shouted the captain, angrily.

" Yes sir, of course."

" Well, then, tie six of 'em to him ; do you hear ? "

" All right, sir."

So there went six bars of the ancient copper.

When the cargo was discharged in London, freights being low, Captain Tom received orders to lay the ship up and wait for better times. He hauled her into an out-of-the-way corner of the Victoria Dock, where wharfage was cheap, and tied her up.

Tom Benton was becoming morose. He had reached the top rung of his ladder, but he was as far away as ever from the accomplishment of the task he had set himself on starting out. He knew that he needed to own the controlling interest in his ship. Ever since he first sailed in the *Barra-coota* he had been saving his money with that object in view ; but he was getting tired. The saving from wages accumulated so slowly, and it takes so much money to pay for the controlling interest in a ship ! Now that she was laid up, he got no pay, but only his keep. He would be an old man by the time he could save enough, even if everything went all right. His ambition was becoming discouraged and his boyish romance a silly memory.

In pursuance of his economical theory, he lived aboard, doing his own cooking. One evening while looking to his shore fasts, the coffee-pot boiled over

in the cabin, boiled dry, and the bottom became un-
soldered. He washed his supper down with " scuttle
butt juice," and, for want of employment, decided
to mend his coffee-pot. A search of the tool chest
brought to light rosin and solder, but no soldering-
iron. After trying ineffectually to utilize an iron
bolt, he remembered that soldering-irons were made
of copper. He was unable to find a copper bolt,
but there were plenty of those old copper bars in
the boatswain's locker. A cold chisel and hammer
were soon found, and, with the crown of the anchor
for an anvil, he chopped a suitable piece from one
of the bars. It was soft even for copper, so he
readily hammered it into the required shape. It
glistened under the hammer as the moon shone on
it, and he reflected that it must be a very pure specimen to have survived such a long immersion in salt
water. How heavy it was! It felt more like lead
than copper.

Leaving the larger piece on the forecastle, he returned to the cabin. He inspected his work by the
light of the cabin lamp — and nearly fainted. In
his hand, roughly hammered into the shape of a tin-
smith's soldering-tool, he held a lump of pure gold!

X

CHAPTER XIX

WHEN the train arrived, Kitty boarded it and took the only vacant seat. Her attention was attracted to an elderly lady who occupied the seat directly in front of her. She was a woman between fifty and sixty years of age, the undeniable richness of whose apparel denoted ample means. She was travelling alone, and, in spite of the exertions of her strong will, betrayed the fact that she was suffering great pain. As she leaned her head against the side of the car, Kitty observed the fine face grow pale and flush again, while the corners of the mouth were drawn, as if in an effort to suppress a cry.

Her distress appealed to Kitty's sympathetic nature, and when she saw the lady make an ineffectual attempt to raise a heavy satchel that lay at her feet, she offered her services.

The sufferer glanced at her with an expression of

gratitude. "If you will kindly hand me my satchel," she said, "I shall be very much obliged."

Kitty raised the satchel to the seat by her side, and, the one ahead having been vacated at the last stop, she deftly turned it and seated herself facing the lady. The latter produced a small key, and took from her bag a medicine phial and a graduated glass. She attempted to drop some of the liquid into the glass, but owing to her nervousness and the motion of the train, was unable to do so.

"If you will allow me," said Kitty, "I think I can do that for you."

"Thank you very much, if you will be so kind. My nerves are rather unsteady."

"How many?" asked Kitty, as she began to count the drops.

"Not more than seven, please — then if you will get about a tablespoonful of water to put in it — I am sorry to trouble you so."

"It is no trouble at all, I assure you. I am only too happy to be of use to you."

The lady drank the medicine eagerly, and laid her head back and closed her eyes. As Kitty watched over the invalid and noted the kindly expression of the weary face, her heart went out to the traveller, who, in spite of her evident wealth, was so dreadfully alone. Presently she raised her head, opened her eyes, and with a smile of great sweetness, said: —

"I hardly know how to thank you. You have rendered me a great service. It is not that I might have died for the want of those few drops — I should not have cared for that; but I was in dreadful pain. My maid left the car for a moment just before we started from Albany, and failed to return in time; and alone I am so helpless."

Her head drooped as she spoke, and before Kitty could reply to her grateful acknowledgment, she was sound asleep. Kitty arranged her wraps so that she would rest comfortably, and remained at her side. The old lady slept soundly for fifteen or twenty minutes, and awoke much refreshed. Being mutually attracted, they then conversed freely, and the lady gave Kitty a short account of herself.

Mrs. Eugenia De Lacey was a native of France, having been born in Bordeaux. She came to America when but eight years of age, landing with her father and mother in New Orleans. Two years later she lost both parents by yellow fever. Left alone, though wealthy, she made her home with friends, and during the winter of her sixteenth year she made the acquaintance of Mr. Maurice De Lacey, a wealthy flour merchant of Rochester, New York. Mr. De Lacey, though ten years her senior, won the affections of the little French girl; they were married and lived happily for forty years.

At his death, two years previously, he left his

widow and only son an immense fortune. This son, Gerald De Lacey, a young man of twenty-three, was the apple of his mother's eye. She wished him to go into political life, and as his own tastes tended in the same direction, the business was sold, and after graduating with honors from Harvard, he entered the law office of the senior senator from his state, where he acquired that practical knowledge of the law, which is the first step toward successful statesmanship.

Shortly after his father's death, while taking an active part in a gubernatorial campaign, Gerald invited the voters of his district to a picnic and barbecue. It was the grandest affair of the kind ever witnessed in the county. Ten four-horse coaches took the party to a grove five miles from town. The day was perfect and all enjoyed themselves to the utmost. Mrs. De Lacey was present, and her heart overflowed with maternal pride as she saw her handsome and talented son the acknowledged leader in a throng where there were many clever men. The deference paid him by gray-haired veterans of the political arena was sweet to her soul, and when, in response to calls for a speech, he mounted a stump and made the woods ring with his eloquence, her cup of happiness was full.

The barbecued ox having been disposed of with many savory accompaniments, and the happy day having come to a close, the merry crew reëmbarked in the coaches, and with the horns blowing, and flags waving, with songs and merry jests, they started for home. Gerald, as the host, drove the leading coach. He was an expert whip, and led the procession royally, while Mrs. De Lacey with a number of elderly ladies had the rear coach principally to themselves.

There was a railroad track to be crossed — an insignificant single-track branch running to a gravel-pit. It was seldom used, but Gerald, whose well-trained mind neglected no details, had cautioned all the drivers not to cross it until satisfied that it was perfectly safe. On the return trip this crossing was at the foot of a very steep hill, and the view of the track was obstructed by a dense growth of trees on either side. Gerald set his foot-brake as soon as his coach started on the descent. Half-way down, the bolt connecting the lever with the brake-rod dropped out, and the heavy coach leaped ahead, nearly taking the horses off their feet. The wheelers, a pair of high-spirited colts of his own breeding, became frightened and jumped forward. Gerald tugged at the reins, and friends on the box helped him; he talked to his horses, trying to quiet them ; but in spite of all he could do they dashed madly down the hill.

The railroad track was seen to be clear; so, steadying them as best he could, and speaking to them soothingly, he kept them squarely in the middle of the road. They were going at a frightful pace, and the stage rocked like a dismantled hulk. The off leader's iron-shod hoof slipped on the steel rail, and he went down. There was a tangle of hoofs, heads, and legs; a snorting and pawing as the wheelers fell on top of him, and a ripping and rending of leather, wood, and iron as the coach topped the struggling pile.

A long string of empty flat cars was being pushed around the curve on its way to the gravel-pit. It wasn't going very fast, — only fifteen miles an hour, — and there was a man on the leading car signalling continually to the engineer. By the time this man saw the stage and plunging horses, the wooded curve obscured his signals from the watchful engineer. With the quick thoughtfulness his training had taught him, he jumped to the ground and ran back, waving his arms and shouting frantically. The front wheels of the stage were squarely on the track, and the approaching cars were seen by its occupants. Those on the outside leaped for their lives and called on Gerald to follow. He might easily have done so, but he knew that those inside were helpless. Vainly he struggled to bring the horses to their feet and back the stage from the track. As relentless as fate the cars came rolling on. The leading car demolished the stage, dismembered the horses, and turned itself at right angles to the track, — others mounted it, and climbed over the pile of wreckage and dead and dying men and horses, mangling them beyond recognition.

When, from the horrified cries that were wafted back to her, Mrs. De Lacey gained an idea of what had happened, she ran to the scene, white and breathless, past the other vehicles. Men tried to detain her; but she turned on them with the ferocity of a tigress. She tore wildly at the wreckage, lacerating her delicate hands until they were raw, but piled-up cars are not to be removed by such means. When she realized the futility of her efforts her mind gave way, and she was carried shrieking to a coach and driven home.

The remains of the brilliant young man, who had given his life in a vain attempt to save his friends, were buried while his mother raved in delirium.

When she came back reluctantly to life and reason, her surroundings were hateful. Everything reminded her of her double affliction. There was nothing to keep her. Maurice was gone, and Gerald was gone; she would go too. Anywhere, to drag out the few remaining years of her loneliness. While in this frame of mind her thoughts returned to the home of her early childhood, — "La Belle France." She had not heard from there since she had cast her lot with her American husband, but there might be some of her name there yet; some member of her family to whom she could be of service — perhaps Suzette, the bright, jolly, sparkling cousin who had been her earliest playmate.

Suzette had said she would marry a soldier, and now Mrs. De Lacey remembered, or thought she did, that years ago when she was prosperous and happy, she had heard somehow that Suzette had married a dashing young lieutenant of dragoons who was immediately ordered to Algiers. She was probably poor and the mother of a large family. Mrs. De Lacey would help them. She would obtain the lieutenant's discharge from the army, and educate the children. She would even adopt the entire family.

With this idea she again became interested in life, only fearing she might not live to accomplish the work. So, before she was fit to travel, she had started; and here she was bound on a three-thousand-miles journey to assist Suzette, who, for all she knew, might have been dead for thirty years.

Kitty was unable to give a very connected account of herself, and was unwilling to tell all she did know; for there was a hazy idea in her muddled brain that she must keep her mission secret. But as Mrs. De Lacey was exhausted with her own story and the emotions which it called up, she paid but little attention to her young companion's tale.

Mrs. De Lacey proposed stopping at the Astor House. The name was somehow familiar to Kitty, so she announced her intention of going to the same hotel, and during the following week these two became strongly attached to each other. Mrs. De Lacey lavished all the love of her broken heart on "Sarah Stagg," and although she had learned but little of the girl's antecedents, she had been told she was an orphan, and was satisfied with the beauty of character and honesty of soul that shone out of her clear brown eyes.

Kitty herself, though as yet incapable of sufficient consecutive thought to know where the twelve thousand dollars were coming from when she should find Tom, realized that her quest must end where she was, for want of funds. So, although her attentions to Mrs. De Lacey occupied her fully, she worried in a foggy way over her own dilemma. The derelict maid arrived in due time and relieved Kitty of the many personal offices she had been performing for the invalid, thus enabling her to devote all her time to the companionship for which she was so eminently fitted. Mrs. De Lacey delayed her departure from the city from day to day for the purpose of remaining in "Sarah's" company as long as possible. She had refrained from asking her destination and was agreeably surprised to learn, during a conversation one evening, that she too was bound Europe-ward.

"Why should we not sail together, dear — unless you are tired of the whims of an old woman? I should really esteem it a great favor," said Mrs. De Lacey, eagerly.

Kitty hesitated. How could she sail? She had but a few dollars left. With quick intuition, the elderly lady guessed the difficulty. Gently, so as not to offend the most delicate sensibility, she proposed that "Sarah" should go as her companion, or rather guest, and after some little fencing between them — as women will — Kitty gratefully accepted the generous offer.

A week later found them both inhaling great draughts of health-giving ozone on the quarterdeck of the old Havre packet ship *Andes*, Captain James Austin, and once recovered from the slight attack of sea-sickness incident to sailing, they both improved in health rapidly. Mrs. De Lacey declared she was really ashamed of her voracious appetite; but the jolly captain assured her that he hoped to see her powers in that line doubled before she left his ship.

As Kitty's bodily health improved, her mental faculties also grew stronger. She began to catch fleeting glimpses of a former existence which she was unable to reconcile with her present surroundings. Mrs. De Lacey frequently noticed that "Sarah" would sit with wrinkled brow, staring vacantly into space, and although this strange conduct fretted her, she decided to say nothing, believing her young companion would confide in her when she should have solved the riddle, whatever it might be.

On the morning before the arrival of the Havre pilot Kitty Blake awoke in full possession of her senses. At first she supposed herself in the car-seat with Nellie; but finding she was on board ship, she was sadly puzzled at the strange dream which she supposed herself to have had, for this was not the *Albatross*. She sat up in her berth and looked through the little round deadlight at the gently rolling seas that flashed along in the bright morning sun, and remembered that she was on board the *Andes*. The more she tried to straighten out her ideas, the worse they became mixed. There was a blank somewhere, a missing link, without which these two separate existences would not run smoothly one into the other. She hastened to Mrs. De Lacey's stateroom, and frightened that good lady nearly out of her senses by declaring that she believed herself insane. A single glance, however, reassured the elderly lady; there was no insanity in her face. Fear, yes, and perplexity, as Kitty sat on the edge of her friend's berth and told what she knew of herself. The older woman listened with absorbing interest. The *something* she had never been able to understand about "Sarah Stagg" was being cleared up.

"I was sitting in the car talking with Nellie," Kitty concluded, "and the next thing I knew I was Sarah Stagg, up in that farm cottage."

Mrs. De Lacey thought a moment, and then asked how long ago this change occurred.

"It was on Friday, the fourth of September. School was to commence on the following Monday."

"In what year, dear?"

"What year?" asked Kitty, in unfeigned amazement. "Why, this year, 18 —."

"I asked what year, my dear, because one or more years might easily have elapsed since you lost your identity. Now that I think of it, Sarah, — or, I should say, Kitty, — I believe I can explain what happened to you. The date is fixed in my mind because it was the day before the barbecue, and I can never forget that. On that day, that unlucky Friday, there was a bad wreck on the Hudson River Railroad, in which several people were killed and many more injured. I think, my child, that you must have been on that train; though how your friends could have lost track of you so completely I cannot imagine."

"I shouldn't wonder if that is it," replied Kitty. "I remember, now that you have told me, there was a crash and the lights went out, or perhaps I became unconscious. But I don't understand, either, how I came to be lost. I should have thought my

friends would have found me long ago, shouldn't
you? And why did those people keep me, do you
suppose?"

She suddenly paled, trembled, and, burying her
face in her hands, burst into a violent fit of weeping.
Mrs. De Lacey soothed her as best she could, and
when the first paroxysm of grief had somewhat
abated, she exclaimed: "Oh, I know now, I know!
Nellie was killed, and the *Albatross* never reached
Portland. Everybody belonging to me is dead, and
I wish I were too."

When she became sufficiently calm, Mrs. De Lacey
endeavored to reassure her. "It doesn't follow at
all," said she, "that your friends are all dead; in
fact, it is very improbable. I think I see how it all
may have happened. Either the wreck may have
caught fire, and it was taken for granted that you
had perished, and that your body was consumed in
the flames, or another body may have been wrongly
identified, and buried as yours."

Kitty's grief burst forth afresh at this view of the
affair.

"Why, what is the matter, my dear? You are
surely not sorry to have escaped such a terrible fate,
are you?" asked Mrs. De Lacey, smiling, and stroking Kitty's glossy hair affectionately with her thin
white hand.

"Oh, no, indeed," replied Kitty between her sobs,

"but when you spoke of such dreadful things, it occurred to me all at once that if they had reason to think that was my fate, it probably was poor Nellie's. She was a weak little thing and always depended on me."

"It might not be, — the very fact that it was not yours gives you reason to hope that she too may have escaped."

Still Kitty wept. "Poor Father and Mother Hayward!" she cried. "How they must feel! They loved me as if I were their own daughter!"

"I am sure they did, my child; they could not help it. But as there is nothing we can do until we arrive, try not to mourn so, but take a more hopeful view of the matter. I feel sure that you will find your friends are all safe and sound. It would be an almost unheard-of case for so many to have met with disasters at the same time. Try and imagine the pleasure with which they will receive the news of your safety. It is a much pleasanter subject for thought; and I feel quite sure that everything will prove to be all right."

A long time passed, and many letters went to and fro across the Atlantic before the story of Kitty's adventure was made plain to all concerned. When Nellie learned that the chum whom she had mourned as dead was alive and well, her joy knew no bounds. She declared it to be stranger than the story books, while good Mrs. Hayward wept and prayed alternately. She wrote her darling a long letter, in which she begged her to return by the first ship; but as Kitty's mind was now relieved of worry, she became interested in her strange surroundings, so she replied that, for the present, she would remain with the kind woman who had so generously befriended her.

Mr. Hayward hunted up the Staggs, and, after expressing his gratitude for their kindness to Kitty, he paid off the mortgage on their stony little farm, and replaced the slaughtered cow with a full-blooded Durham.

Our travellers rested two days in Havre. These were delightful days to Kitty, who never tired of watching the strange outlandish ways of the Frenchmen. Their extreme politeness flattered her, though she knew it was to a great extent superficial, and to have every one, even the newsboys in the streets, politely touch their caps when spoken to, gave her a pleasing sense of importance she had never known before.

When Mrs. De Lacey felt quite recovered from the fatigue of the voyage, they departed for Bordeaux. Inquiry at the office of the chief of police produced the information that but one representative of Mrs. De Lacey's family resided in the place: Monsieur Pierre Fouchet, her cousin, a retired cheese manufacturer. Monsieur Fouchet was a bachelor;

reputed to be very rich, and known to be exceedingly cranky. The day after their arrival the ladies called on him. He was — as an old bachelor should be — a little, weazened creature, clean-shaven, and wearing enormous spectacles, and whose thin gray hair stood out in flimsy wisps from his head, in all directions.

Monsieur Fouchet suspected every one of designs on his pocket-book; consequently he was ever on the defensive. He disliked strangers, and as he believed with his illustrious countryman that "language was given to man the better to enable him to conceal his thoughts," it is safe to say that few gained anything by an interview with the little old miser. When the two ladies called, he received them in a shabby, musty drawing-room which was as dingy as his most unlovely self, and without offering them seats, he inquired their business. Mrs. De Lacey introduced herself as the daughter of his father's brother Robert, adding that the family had emigrated to America many years ago. Her cousin's grimy fingers spread apart to their utmost extent, as he answered with a squeak like a rat behind a wainscot: "I know him not, madame. What have I to do with him? He went to America. *Bien!* I stayed at home. It is late in the day for him to come to me now. I am an old man, and, as you see, very poor. I can do nothing for him. He should have stayed here. Or, having gone to America, he should stay there. What does he suppose? That I shall stay here and work all my days that he may come to me after wasting his time in America! No, it cannot be."

When Mrs. De Lacey was able to break through this torrent of disclaimer, she told him her father had been dead forty years, and that all she asked was news of the family.

He knew nothing of the family; he was not aware that there had been any family. Did he not remember Suzette? "Suzette? Oh, certainly!" He remembered Suzette; she was his sister. Where was she now? He could not say. She married a soldier and went off somewhere, as such people do. Oh, yes; he had seen her several times since then. She had come and told him of her troubles; they all did; but he had troubles of his own; he couldn't be bothered with hers; let her tell them to her husband.

And so he ran on garrulously, his fingers adding their dumb eloquence to the expression that his one desire was to be left alone. After half an hour of this sort of thing, the ladies, tired with standing, and satisfied of the impossibility of obtaining any information from the old man, returned to the hotel. Thoroughly disgusted with the selfishness of her kinsman, Mrs. De Lacey decided to discontinue any further efforts toward looking up her family. If Suzette appeared on the scene, she would assist her; but as for seeking any more of them, she would not, and she proposed that Kitty and herself should travel further, and that Kitty should continue her studies in order to complete her education. This proposition met with immediate and enthusiastic approval on Kitty's part; so they proceeded to carry it out without delay.

CHAPTER XX

STAGGERED by his discovery, Captain Benton sank
into a chair and gazed stupidly at the bit of metal
in his hand. A doubt was in his mind: after all, he
might be mistaken — he probably was. He took it
close to the lamp and examined it carefully; he
scraped a bright place on it and compared it with
his watch-case. It was finer, and much richer in
appearance. The last vestige of doubt was set at
rest; it was undoubtedly gold—gold of remarkable
fineness and purity.

He bethought him of the large piece he had left
on the anchor, a prey to any chance prowler. Hurriedly he darted up the companionway, halted at the
top step, and returned. He hid the piece between
his mattresses, locked the cabin windows, felt the
fastenings of the skylight, glanced feverishly around
to see that all was secure, and, returning to the deck,
locked the door, and put the key in his pocket. He
started to run forward, but checked himself, and
walked decorously, even slowly. There were watch-

men on the other vessels; they might see, and wonder at his haste.

There it lay, glittering richly in the moonlight. He seized it greedily, and dived under the forecastle to the boatswain's locker, where he rummaged among the marline spikes and serving mallets in the dark until he found the other nine. It seemed as if he turned everything in that locker over a dozen times before he found the last one. He feared it had been used for some purpose, or lost; perhaps, out of pique, the mate had used seven instead of six to ballast Neptune — oh, that infernal dog! When he got them all out, he hardly knew how to manage. They were too heavy to be carried aft at one load, and somebody from one of the other vessels, seeing him working so hard, might come and offer to help. He was afraid to leave them lying on deck while he went aft, so he shoved eight of them under the heel of the bowsprit, and, taking one in each hand, carried them below and hid them at the foot of his bunk.

He locked the door again and returned for another load, feeling nervous and feverish. On his way aft his foot struck a ringbolt, and he fell at full length, whereat the two bars flew out of his hands and went clattering along the deck. He picked them up, the sweat pouring from him like rain, and glanced guilt-ily around.

On his last trip forward the watchman on the ship ahead hailed him. "What the deuce are ye up to, cap?" he asked. "I sh'd think she was afire, the way you're racin' about. Ye've got my ol' woman so nervous and worked up she can't go to sleep." And then he stood there and talked for half an hour, until Captain Benton excused himself on the plea of feeling chilly; and with a sense of deep thankfulness he transferred the last of his treasures below.

This was a memorable night in Tom Benton's life. He sat until nearly morning, building castles in the air. Now his brightest dreams would be realized — what a ship he would build! And Kitty Blake! All his plans and hopes, his ambitions and aspirations, brought him back each time to her. How proud she would be, and how glad! In imagination he could hear her say, "I always knew you would succeed, Tom." To be sure, he was obliged to admit that his possession of this wealth was not due to any great achievement of his; it was luck, that was all, just good luck. But then he decided not to find fault with it because his possession of it was not due to any wonderful qualifications of his own; for, after all, he had done what he could. Without friends or assistance he had worked up to the top, and, if this was luck — well, he had had enough of the other kind, too. So having, metaphorically, patted himself on the back, he took a last look at his treasure, went over the door and window fastenings again, loaded his revolvers, and turned in to dream it all over again.

Next morning, after hiding the nine whole bars in a barrel half full of flour, he wrapped the two pieces in a silk handkerchief and took them to his consignee. He frankly told the whole story to his friend; and locking the larger piece in his safe, they took the other to an assayer who promised to report on it the next day. They then made an appointment with a firm of wealthy Jewish brokers, to have a man authorized to act for them at the consignee's office at twelve o'clock on the following day.

Mr. Davis, the consignee, furnished Captain Benton with a trustworthy porter, who carried all the stuff to the office, and at twelve o'clock the three men met, — Captain Benton, Mr. Davis, and Herr Lindeman, the senior partner of the brokerage firm. The Jew was armed with a delicate pair of scales, acid, a powerful magnifying glass, and his checkbook. He carefully scrutinized the assayer's certificate which stated that the sample contained one hundred and thirty pennyweights of gold, twenty-two carats fine.

Herr Lindeman filed a protest against accepting this assay as applicable to the entire lot, claiming that there might not be another bar equally fine. Captain Benton admitted the truth of his objection,

and agreed to defer the transaction until the whole
lot could be assayed; but after the Herr had examined the bars and applied his test, he waived his
protest and announced himself ready to proceed.   It
was found that the bars weighed exactly alike.   This,
the Jew said, was owing to the fact that the molten
metal had been weighed before pouring into the
moulds.   Accepting his bid as a basis, it was found
that the bars were worth two thousand five hundred
dollars each.

Mr. Davis called Tom aside, and advised him not
to be too precipitate in accepting this offer.   While
they were talking, the Jew had been examining the
stamps, of which there were three on each bar.
He had his magnifying glass on them, and, in spite
of his training, betrayed considerable excitement.
He looked up as they returned and asked : —

"Mine frent, vere dit you get dat stamp vat you
haf on dose ingots?"

"It was on them when I got them," replied Tom.

"Is dot poseeble?   Are you sure?" he asked,
displaying, in spite of himself, marked agitation.

"Quite sure.   I have done nothing to them except
to cut this one."

"And vere dit you get dem, if you bleese, captine?"

Tom laughed.   "Oh, they're all right!" said he;
"you needn't be alarmed; I came honestly by them."

"Oh, certainly, certainly! You take mistake, captine. I mean dot not; but I like to know, if you bleese. You see I am much interestet."

As there was no good reason for concealment, Tom gave him a brief account of how they came into his possession. He noticed, as he told of the resurrection of the ancient wreck, that the Jew's eyes sparkled. He was indeed much interested. At the conclusion of the tale, Herr Lindeman nervously stroked his black beard and said : —

"I tank you ferry much for de story, captine. It ees ferry fine; ferry interesting. But, shentlemen, time ees money. I vill now, of you bleese, write you de check; and so, ve feenish our leedle dransactions." And, with a grin that was intended for a smile, he opened his check-book.

But here Captain Benton, mindful of his friend's advice, called a halt. He told the Herr that he had only asked him to bid on the stuff, remarking that it would hardly be considered good business to accept the first offer.

The Jew became intensely alive at this. "Vy, captine! My tear sir!" he exclaimed. "Dit you not figger up de amount yourselluf? Vot is it, dem ingots? Gold, huh? dot's all! For vat shall you hav oder beeple come into de peesness? Vill dey bay you more ash it iss vort? I dink not. I haf shpend two hours on dis peesness alretty, unt shall

it not be feenish? For vy not? I no unnerstan'
you."

And so he ran on, getting more excited, and talking louder and faster until, in sheer desperation, he
raised his own bid five per cent.

Although Captain Benton was no business man,
he was a born Yankee; so, when a Jew offered more
for a thing than it was worth, his instinct taught
him to hold off; and he did. He leaned back, bal-
ancing his chair on its hind legs, and, with both
hands thrust deep into his trousers pockets, gazed
coldly and pitilessly at the tortured son of Abraham.

Herr Lindeman talked and argued; he squirmed
on his seat and perspired, as vainly he raised his
price, a few dollars at a time. Then he jumped it
by hundreds, — by thousands; until at last, almost
grovelling on the floor, he offered fifty thousand dollars for the bullion whose value was only twenty-five.

Amazed, almost fearful for the man's sanity, Captain Benton cried, " I accept."

The Jew sank back in his chair. His face was a
ghastly yellow, and his chin quivered as he mopped
the perspiration from his brow. " Father Abram,
I been a ruint man!" he murmured. "I haf to go
to de poorhouse vonce!" But he quickly recovered,
and, as if fearing Tom might repent, he hastily filled
out and signed a check for the amount. As he
handed it over and clutched his hawk-like claws on

the receipt, he asked Captain Benton if he was satisfied.

"Perfectly," replied Tom.

"Me too," said the Jew; "I mek goot peeseness to-day! I don' care ven I nefer mek no more peeseness. I been plenty reesh now. Shendlemen, haf somedings mit me?"

A splendid lunch was served in the office at Herr Lindeman's expense. He was a generous host; and, after regaling themselves right royally, they lighted Reina Victorias, and blew a fragrant cloud.

"I haf von leedle favor to ask you, captine," said the Jew. "I like dot you mek von affidavit for me, 'bout de vay you fin' dose ingots; vot?"

Tom replied that he would give him the affidavit if in return he would tell them why he had paid such an exorbitant price for the bars. The Herr did not take kindly to the suggestion. "It vas nodding," he "like to haf dem," and so forth, but when Tom declined to furnish the affidavit, or even to testify before witnesses, he surrendered. After binding them to secrecy he said that there existed, in all the large cities of the world, branches of a great Jewish secret society, of which none but the very wealthy were able to pay the exorbitant fees. He denied belonging to the society himself, and was therefore ignorant of its object, but he knew, however, that members were zealous collectors of everything bear-

ing on the history of ancient Judea, and purchased
all articles of this kind that were offered, paying for
them generously.   They sometimes found an important link missing in their historical chain, and in
such cases the faithful throughout the world were
notified, through the synagogues, that, on presenta-
tion of the desired object, accompanied by satisfactory corroborative evidence, a liberal reward would
be forthcoming.

More than four hundred years ago the central
lodge in Vienna had come into possession of a fac-
simile of the seal or stamp with which all the pre-
cious metals belonging to King Solomon had been
marked.   It was the official seal of his royal mint,
or treasure house.   The most exhaustive research
up to the present time had failed to produce any
article bearing the seal, although it was known
that the fortunate discoverer could name his own
price.

"Shentlemen," concluded Herr Lindeman, "I
haf der only tvendy-nine of dem seals in der vorld —
der captine he shpile von mit his voolishness — vot
you tink?   I been all right, huh?"

"I don't know about that," said Captain Benton.
"I am not at all sure that I got them all.   There
may be hundreds of them lying there yet."

Herr Lindeman's jaw dropped and his sallow face
flushed.   "So-o-o?" he asked in a tone of deep

concern. "Vell, vy tit'n you tole me dot before?" Then, recovering himself, he rose hurriedly. "You vill oxcuse me, shentlemen," said he; "peesness is peesness. I vas bleesed to have meet you, captine, unt you too, sir. Good-tay, shentlemen!" And he was off.

Twenty-four hours later, in response to an urgent telegram from "Lindeman & Co., London," their confidential South African agent left Table Bay on a swift steamer for the Arabian Sea. On his return he telegraphed his principals that, owing to a recent typhoon, all traces of the ancient wreck had been washed away.

Being now provided with ample means, Tom wrote to the *Barracoota's* owners, resigning his position and asking to be relieved as soon as possible, as he was anxious to return to the States. Six weeks later the new captain arrived, and, after turning the old vessel over to him, Captain Benton took passage on the first ship to New York. He made no stop there, but took the train to Boston, and from there he went direct to Thomaston and contracted for the building of a two-thousand-ton ship. Her keel was laid within thirty days, and eleven months later, the *Socotra* was launched, as fine a specimen of the shipbuilder's art as ever slid from the ways in the Pine Tree State.

His boyish ambition still swayed him. The time

had arrived when he had as fine a ship of his own
as ever flew the stars and stripes. Now he could
afford to indulge his pride — just once. He took
his new ship under sail round to Portland; ostensibly
to procure stores, but really to show her to the natives — and Kitty Blake.

It was a proud day for Tom Benton, his cheeks
glowed and his heart beat high, when, with a fair
wind, his gallant ship swung around Cape Elizabeth.
How familiar it all looked! He caught himself
watching out unconsciously for the *Sprite*. But it
was seven years since the *Sprite* boarded the *Columbia*, and she had undergone many vicissitudes
since then, being now degraded to the humble but
honest calling of delivering lobsters. As soon as
his ship was anchored, Tom went ashore. Portland
had changed but little. A new building here and
there was all he noticed in the way of improve-
ments. Nearly all the old familiar signs, only a little
older and dingier, met his gaze. He dropped into
a ship chandlery where he had been well known as a
boy, and to his surprise, the leathery-visaged, chin-
whiskered proprietor called him by name at once,
but with as little evidence of interest as though he
had stepped out of the door but five minutes before.
When he learned, however, that Tom was captain
of the big new ship that had just arrived, he began
to solicit business at once. Tom saw many men in

the street whom he knew; but, as he had allowed his beard to grow, few recognized him.

He remained in Portland three days, buying supplies and inquiring in a roundabout bashful way for Kitty Blake. All he could learn was, that old Rufus had died at about the time of his departure, and that his daughter had been taken in charge by Mr. Hayward. There it seemed the information was bound to stop, the Haywards having gone south for Mrs. Hayward's health. Hoping to learn something from their neighbors, he called at the house next door, where a gossipy old lady who answered his ring told him that Captain Blake's daughter had been killed in a railroad accident two years ago.

The sun seemed to go out, as Tom clutched the side of the door for support. Kitty had seemed very real to him since he had been in Portland. He had expected—had hoped—to meet her in the street. And now to hear such a tale as that! A story of violent death in a railway accident. Kitty killed with all the horrible accompaniments which imagination could conjure up! It was horrible. When the old lady observed the effect of her calmly spoken words, she manifested much concern. "Are you a relative, sir?" she asked.

"No," said Tom, controlling his voice with difficulty, "only a friend. But I have been away at sea for the last seven years — we were children together — and — it is so sudden. I cannot realize that she has been dead so long — and by such a death!"

Poor Tom! Having been at sea all his life, he did not know how seldom the dreams of childhood and youth are realized. He hastened his departure after that — his petty triumph had fallen flat. For a few days, the *Socotra* looked almost hateful to him; the decks were dirty and littered with stores; riggers and stevedores overran her and she was much dishevelled.

But Tom Benton was too well inured to disappointments to succumb even to such a crushing blow as this, so he took his ship to New York and laid her on for San Francisco. He made a fair passage out, — a hundred and twenty-seven days, — discharged his cargo, and reloaded for London.

CHAPTER XXI

FOR two years Mrs. De Lacey and Kitty Blake travelled on the continent, visiting all the European capitals and principal cities. They patronized art in Italy, dodged the dogs and porters in the narrow streets of Constantinople, crossed over to Alexandria, and rode the funny little donkeys out to Pompey's Pillar, vainly tried to answer the sphinx's riddle, climbed the great pyramid, drank tea under the surveillance of the Tsar's police in St. Petersburg, and returned to listen to German music in Berlin. In short, they went the rounds. It was a series of never-ending pleasure to the little girl from Maine; for Mrs. De Lacey was determined that Kitty should have all available good things. The old lady renewed her youth in ministering to the enjoyment of her young charge, while Kitty prosecuted her studies faithfully, and, as they travelled slowly, remaining as long as they chose in the different cities, she became fairly proficient in French, German, and Italian — Russian, she decided after a short trial, to let alone. Her musical education received a finishing polish in Germany; so that the once hoydenish Portland lass developed into a handsome, accomplished, and self-reliant young lady.

The style in which they lived and travelled caused it to be noised about that Kitty was an American heiress, and consequently there were no end of French, German, and Italian princelings trailing in her wake. But Kitty was loyal to the memory of her girlhood's playmate, — sturdy Tom Benton, the boy who, wronged by her father, had gone out alone and bravely to carve his own way in the world. Kitty believed in Tom. She knew he would succeed just as she knew the sun would rise on the morrow. Long ago she had confided her little romance to Mrs. De Lacey; and that good soul, remembering her own happy married life, sympathized with her heartily.

Having pretty well completed the circuit of the continent, Kitty desired to return home. Mrs. Hayward wrote saying that her health was failing; and she believed that if Kitty were at home she would be more likely to hear from Tom. This, together with a natural longing for the familiar scenes and language of her own country, combined to make her somewhat homesick. Mrs. De Lacey did not encourage this train of thought. There was nothing to attract her to America, and she entertained a selfish fear that Kitty might become estranged from her when she came again among her own people. Then there was Tom; a somewhat indefinite possibility, to be sure, but still a possibility. Besides, Mrs. De Lacey did not share Kitty's love of the sea; indeed, she disliked it heartily, as she was always seasick. But, observing that Kitty was becoming thin and pale, that she was growing nervous, and losing interest in all things European, she acknowleged with a sigh that, dearly as she loved her charge, she had no right to keep her all to herself.

As Kitty had ceased bothering her kind friend with importunities, she was agreeably surprised when, as they were strolling on the beach at Ostend one morning, Mrs. De Lacey remarked quite abruptly: "To-morrow we take the train for Havre."

"Havre?" questioned Kitty, in surprise. "Why, I thought we were to go to Brussels from here."

"That was my original intention, my dear," replied Mrs. De Lacey, kindly, "but I have changed my plans. We will go to Havre, and from there take ship to New York."

"Oh, I'm so glad!" cried Kitty, eagerly; then, detecting a shade of disappointment on her companion's face, she checked herself, and added: "But you don't wish to return yet, aunty! Don't, I beg of you, change your plans on my account. I should really like to see Brussels — and the Antwerp cathedral with its old paintings," she added dutifully.

Mrs. De Lacey smiled. "You're a dear, good girl, Kitty!" said she, gazing affectionately into the eager brown eyes; "but I realize that it is wrong in me to keep you so long from those other friends who have a prior claim on you. Tom, for instance," she added with a sly twinkle.

So it came about, that a week later, our two friends found themselves the only cabin passengers, on board the *Sutherland*, bound for New York. Captain Nick Tyler was highly pleased at having two such agreeable ladies as shipmates on his passage to the westward; for though he had been married a score of years, and was as gray as old Neptune himself, Captain Nick, like all genuine sailormen, was fond of the ladies, and he assured his two passengers that they could not have chosen a more comfortable craft than his ship.

"Not quite as fast as some of these new ones," said he, "but very comfortable; and safe, ladies, perfectly safe. I've sailed her for twenty-five years and never lost a passenger. I love the old ship, madam," with a profound bow to Mrs. De Lacey, "because it was here in this very cabin that I first saw the lady who afterwards became my wife, and is now the mother of three as fine young men as you'd wish to see. Two of 'em — the two oldest — are mates in this same line, and the other, mate of a big deep-water ship. She occupied the stateroom to which I have assigned you, miss, — " another profound bow, this time to Kitty, — "and I must say, that, until the present time, I have never seen it occupied by so fair a lady."

Verily, Captain Nick was a corker.

All he had said in praise of his ship was true. She was a comfortable craft; but she was also old. She had just come across with a cargo of cotton, and the Galveston cotton jammers had nearly screwed her sides out, while a seaman would have noted that the handles of her pump-brakes were polished by continual use. Captain Tyler proposed docking her on her arrival in New York, and having extensive repairs made, including sister keelsons and other strengthening devices.

They sailed from Havre on a pleasant morning, the ladies taking their last view of the land before going down to dinner. The hourly clanking of the pump was quite noticeable in the cabin. It rather annoyed Mrs. De Lacey, and she asked the captain what it was.

"That is the pump, madam. The watch are just giving it a bit of a jog," he answered nonchalantly.

"Why, I have heard that before," said Kitty. "It

seems to be going about all the time. I hope the ship doesn't leak, captain?"

"Oh, no, my dear young lady, not at all. She barely makes enough water to keep her sweet, I assure you. But I always like to be careful when I have passengers, ladies especially, so I have given orders to have the pump tried hourly."

Before they emerged from the Channel the pumps were *tried* half-hourly. Kitty noticed the increase at once, but would not alarm Mrs. De Lacey by speaking of it. Captain Tyler was very polite, and refrained from alluding to the matter himself, so she did not like to impeach his former statement by asking questions. The weather remained, if not exactly fine, fair for the North Atlantic until they arrived near the Azores, when it began to cloud up, a heavy swell came from the westward, and it looked "dirty." The light kites were doused one after another, and as the wind increased, the old ship groaned and shrieked from the effects of the injuries inflicted on her by the Galveston screwmen, and the pump now "jogged" almost continuously. As the wind increased, Captain Tyler made frequent visits to the cabin. Kitty, who was alert for signs of trouble, noticed that he looked carefully, even anxiously, at the barometer every time he came down, and on his return to the deck she would hear him bellowing orders to the mates which were followed by sounds of flapping canvas, and a great "yo-hoing" by the sailors, which she knew indicated a reduction of sail. The ship was now laboring heavily. Mrs. De Lacey had retired, so occupied with the miseries of sea-sickness that she had no thought for anything else. The gale continued for three days; then there was a twelve-hour interlude, and it piped more furiously than ever. Kitty was becoming frightened. She had listened in vain for a cessation of the pumping during the preceding twenty-four hours. The monotonous "clank-clank, chug-chug" could be heard in the cabin at all hours, even above the howling of the gale and the working of the ship's timbers.

At half-past one in the middle watch Captain Tyler came down. Kitty, unable to sleep, was lying dressed in her berth, having kept her door open for the sake of ventilation. She watched him as he stood with his long oilskin coat glistening wet in the dim light. He steadied himself by the table, and peered from under his sou'wester at the barometer, and she heard him make a startled exclamation as he turned and lurched toward the companion steps.

She leaped lightly from her berth, steadied herself in the doorway as the ship staggered under the blows of the great seas, and called him.

"My dear young lady," said he, in a surprised tone, "what are you doing up and dressed at this time of night? Go to bed, I beg of you."

"I can't sleep, captain. Tell me the truth, — I am a sailor's daughter, — is not the ship in danger? I hear the pump going all the time, and it seems that every time one of those big seas hits her she almost goes to pieces."

He looked over her shoulder instead of straight into her eyes, as usual, and she noticed it. "No danger at all, my dear young lady," he replied; "that is," he added, "not more than usual. Of course there is always some danger at sea. There's a capful of wind just now, but nothing to what I've been through in the old ship, many a time. I keep the pumps going, of course — I explained that to you before. Now please retire. I shall be on deck all night, and you may feel perfectly easy."

"May not I come on deck, too? I should like to see how it looks out there."

"Impossible, my dear young lady; you would be wet through the minute you put your head out, and you couldn't see anything — there's nothing but blackness out there. If you will just lie down in your berth and close your eyes, you will be able to see as much as you could from the royal yard. Now go to bed, do! I must go on deck again."

Far from satisfied with her interview, Kitty returned to her berth; and in spite of the clanking of the pump, and the internal complainings of the overstrained hull, was soon sound asleep.

On deck, Captain Tyler stood hanging on to a weather mizzen topmast backstay. There was a tarpaulin stretched across the weather rigging, — the only speck of canvas she carried, — and under the lee of this he stood. The wind howled like a legion of devils; the big Atlantic combers, their crests illuminated with phosphorescent spray, loomed suddenly and fearfully out of the blackness. They hammered and pounded the poor old ship as if they knew that at last she who had successfully defied their power for nearly half a century was to become their prey. Captain Tyler's mind was racked as it had never been racked before. Veteran as he was, the storm had deceived him. The old-fashioned wooden compass spun round so that he could not be sure how she headed, but the ever-changing direction of the seas had almost convinced him that he was in one of those terrible revolving storms known to seamen as cyclones. His last visit to the barometer, when he was betrayed into using that forcible expletive, had confirmed that fear.

What particularly worried, ay, shamed him, was the fact that he, Old Nick Tyler, was caught in this storm *on the wrong tack*. If she had been on the other tack, she would have drifted out of it, but now her drift would take her through the very centre of this whirling hell of shrieking wind and raging water, and it was too late to wear ship. On passing the central calm, he would have to fight his way through it all over again. The water in the hold was gaining steadily, in spite of the fact that the nearly worn-out crew kept the pump going incessantly. If he had not those passengers — those two helpless, confiding women — on his hands, his mind would be easier.

Suddenly he became aware that the wind was dying out; the crisis was upon them. He must get her headed round before the reverse side of the storm struck her, or she would founder.

Deprived of the restraining force of the wind, she rolled fearfully. He expected his masts to go by the board from the whiplike strains. Rapidly he shouted his orders for sail to be made. To go aloft was about equivalent to committing suicide; but the mates were thoroughbreds, the crew of mongrels feared them worse than they did the elements; so they went; and the much-maligned Yankee mates were vindicated for once. As there was little or no prospect of the sail being furled again, the captain ordered the gaskets cut. The fore-topsail was quickly loosed and set, and the tumbling ship fanned round until the sea was abaft the beam. Then he clewed up his topsail and hauled out his spanker, just in time to catch the first of the wind. The sails lived but a moment, but that was enough. Before they flew, like puffs of steam, away into the lee blackness, her head was up to the wind, and once more the gallant old packet was fighting for her life.

It was a weary, uphill fight — a hopeless contest. The dumbest Scandinavian sailor knew that. They would have liked to stop pumping, seeing how useless it was; but, here again, the "brutal" Yankee mates filled the bill, and the crew continued to pump. The blackness became a little less dense — there was to be daylight. But of what value is daylight to those who are shortly to be drowned?

The seas were now visible before they broke. A gull appeared off the weather quarter, and a few of Mother Carey's chickens fluttered about, dipping their wings in the seething brine astern. It was daylight — gray, miserable daylight, more disheartening than the darkness, for they could now see the hopelessness of their case.

The mate, haggard and bleary from want of sleep, came up from the main deck to report four feet of water in the hold. From sheer force of habit, as his head rose above the rail he glanced to windward, and then, half strangled by the wind blowing down his throat, he shouted: "Sail ho!"

The men heard and understood. They let go the pump-brake to go and look, but a stern "Go on with that pumpin'!" from the third mate, recalled them to their duty. Captain Tyler stepped from behind the tarpaulin, and there, a couple of miles to wind-

ward, under close-reefed topsails, fore-topmast-stay-
sail, and main spencer, he saw a big new American
ship. She was a goodly sight, as she heeled gracefully to the storm, her new cotton sails looking as
bright and clean as those of a yacht. After a hasty
conversation between the captain and mate, the latter
went below, returning shortly with the ensign, which
he hoisted union down.

There was a feeble cheer from the slaves at the pump.

The big fellow showed his colors, the code was
brought into requisition, and Captain Tyler learned
that his neighbor was the *Socotra*, of Thomaston,
Maine; Benton, Master; one hundred and thirty days
out from San Francisco for London.

In reply he gave his own number, and asked the
ship to stand by him. Captain Benton readily consented, and reduced sail. Kitty pushed the companion slide back and looked out. She saw the ship,
admired her, and observed that they were signalling.
She returned to the cabin much easier in her mind.
There was help at hand in case it should be needed.
Presently Captain Tyler came down to breakfast.
He was as polite as ever. He assured the ladies
that the storm would not last much longer, and
hoped they had slept well.

Kitty would not ask him if they were in danger;
she knew he would deny it, and felt sure he would
not let the big ship leave them if they were.

At evening much of the viciousness had gone out of the wind, and the next morning found her with whole topsails on her. The *Socotra* was barely a mile to windward. Signals again fluttered from the peaks of both ships, the burden of whose message was that Captain Tyler would leave his vessel, as she was sinking, and that Captain Benton would lend a hand to take them off. The *Sutherland's* watch below were called, and proceeded to get up yard-arm and stay tackles, while the others pumped.

The stewardess called the ladies, saying it was Captain Tyler's request that they should breakfast as speedily as possible, while she packed their trunks. Kitty understood, but Mrs. De Lacey became nervously inquisitive. When informed that the *Sutherland* was unseaworthy, and that they were to be transferred, she gave way entirely. Kitty talked soothingly to her, and while they were making a feeble attempt at breakfast Captain Tyler came down. He was profuse with apologies. The ship had been strained, and the last storm, the worst he had ever known, had proved too much for her. Were it not for the ladies he should not dream of abandoning her; but a fine, new, and much larger ship having opportunely appeared, he would consider himself derelict in his duty if he exposed them to even a shadow of danger.

"Are you going to leave her yourself, captain?"
asked Kitty, rather pointedly.

"Ahem! Well, yes, my dear young lady. You
see at this season of the year, and on the wrong
side of the Grand Banks, it would hardly be good
judgment to remain on board under the circumstances; though I dare say, if the weather were
not too rough, we might fetch in all right."

He avoided Kitty's suspicious glance while making
this statement, and appeared to feel greatly relieved
when it was over.

After the hurried and uncomfortable breakfast,
the ladies, warmly wrapped, were escorted on deck
by Captain Tyler. The gale had broken, and the
clouds, in great black masses, were drifting away,
displaying patches of sky so brightly blue between the
rifts that even the dull Scandinavian sailors felt its
hopeful augury. The *Socotra*, now within an easy
half-mile to leeward, whither she had run to facili-
tate the transfer, presented a beautiful and cheering
shining sight. Everything was new and bright on
board of her; and as she rolled easily on the great
round-backed swells she presented glimpses of well-
ordered decks that were a fine contrast to those of
the old *Sutherland*, littered with ropes, blocks, and
seamen's dunnage. Signals were again exchanged,
and in a few minutes a great white long-boat rose
from the *Socotra's* forward house and swung gracefully over her side.

"Get a side ladder along here for the ladies!" shouted Captain Tyler. The ladder was suspended from the lee bumpkin and trailed in the sea.

"Do you expect me to go down that thing, sir?" asked Mrs. De Lacey, indignantly.

"My dear madam, it's the best we can do," replied Captain Tyler, deprecatingly. "We'll have a rope's end fast to you, and I doubt not you'll be all right."

"Never, sir! A rope's end, indeed! I don't think you are treating us fairly, Captain Tyler — making a spectacle of your passengers in this manner. I won't submit to it."

By this time the *Socotra's* long-boat was under the *Sutherland's* stern. The third mate, who was in charge of her, was shouting for the passengers to be sent down; but Mrs. De Lacey refused to make a move. In vain both Kitty and the captain explained the necessities of the case to her. At last Kitty said: "I'll go first, aunty. I'm sure it's not half as bad as it looks."

She stepped fearlessly out on the bumpkin, a rope was passed about her waist, and she started down. Before she had descended half a dozen rounds, the sailors in the boat seized her, shouted, "Let go!" and down she went into the bottom of the boat, as on the receding wave it fell fathoms away from the ship. Mrs. De Lacey, who was anxiously watching Kitty's progress, screamed hysterically when she saw her let go the ladder. In a sort of maternal frenzy, she tried to spring after her, and did partly mount the taffrail.

Captain Nick perceived his opportunity. "Quick, men!" said he. "A bowline here!" A seaman deftly slipped a bowline under her, the lee spanker vang was hooked into it, and, before she knew what was going on, she was swayed, kicking and screaming, off her feet. Captain Nick bore her out over the quarter, all the time giving orders to the men at the vang. "Lower — lower away now — steady — whoa, hold on! Lower now — lively — lower — — lower — let go!" The long-boat rose under her, and a sailor grabbed her unceremoniously by the legs and pulled her into it.

She had been shrieking in terror; and when she felt herself falling, she fainted dead away. Kitty took charge of her in the stern sheets; but regardless of all her efforts Mrs. De Lacey remained unconscious until some time after she was snugly tucked away in her berth on board the *Socotra*. The stewardess descended the ladder with only a minimum of feminine squealing (as befitted her position), the ladies' baggage was lowered into the boat, and the six sturdy sailors bent their oilskinned backs to the oars.

Captain Benton had thoughtfully rigged a whip on his lee cro'jack yard-arm, and slung a cabin chair for the hoisting aboard of his fair passengers. Mrs. De Lacey was secured in the chair, hoisted aboard, and carried below by a couple of sailors under the mate's directions. Then Kitty seated herself in it, and swung for a moment dizzily between wind and water.

As the chair rose above the rail, a handsome young man hanging by one hand to the royal backstay, reached out and pulled it inboard. Kitty clutched nervously at the extended arm, and looked Tom Benton squarely in the eyes.

2 A

CHAPTER XXII

THE recognition was instantaneous and mutual;
Kitty's cheeks flushed and her eyes sparkled with
pleasure. Tom's paled and his mouth came open,
as, after swinging her inboard, he stared in stupefied
amazement while she scrambled unassisted from the
chair.

"Oh, Tom!" was Kitty's first surprised exclamation.

"Why, Kitty!" he replied, still more surprised.

Seeing him stand there so awkwardly, without
a word of welcome or an offer of assistance, Kitty's
training came to her aid and she froze at once into
a state of becoming dignity.

"You appear surprised," said she, shaking out her
ruffled plumage with a touch of pique.

"Excuse me," replied Captain Benton, recovering

himself and making a futile offer of the service which was now too late, "it would hardly be strange if I were; I heard such terrible news when I was in Portland a year ago."

"Terrible news?" asked Kitty, paling with apprehension of — she knew not what.

"Yes, Kitty — excuse me — Miss Blake — or am I wrong again?"

"No," said Kitty, the old familiar smile returning. "No, I am still Kitty; or, if you prefer it, Miss Blake."

Tom did not prefer it; but thinking it safer, continued: "Yes, Miss Blake, I took the liberty of inquiring for you when I was in Portland, and I heard — well, in fact, I heard that you had been killed in a railroad accident, a long time before."

"I don't wonder that you were startled, then, on seeing me suddenly hoisted alive and kicking — did I kick? — out of the sea," said Kitty, with a merry laugh, which Tom thought was the sweetest sound he had ever heard. She glanced along the magnificent length of the *Socotra's* snowy deck, and asked in a lower tone, "Are you captain here?"

"Yes," replied Tom, with a flush of honest pride; "captain and sole owner."

"How well you have redeemed your promise! I always knew you would. Allow me to congratulate you, Captain Benton."

Tom grasped the dainty fingers in his strong brown palm, and, encouraged by the frank kindness of her manner, said rather diffidently, "I hope you like my ship."

"I do indeed, captain! She is a beauty! I am afraid poor papa never commanded anything half so fine. But excuse me; aunty will think I have surely been drowned. Will you kindly send some one to conduct me to her, captain?"

"I will show you the way myself, if you please, Miss Blake."

When Tom returned to the deck to receive the rest of his passengers he literally trod on air. He had never seen the sky so blue, nor the sunshine so brilliant. Her name was still "Miss"—how glad he was of that! As he looked along the noble length of his handsome ship, he was better satisfied with himself than he had ever been before. The trials and disappointments of the last eight years were nothing now. He ordered the steward to kill the pig and give all hands fresh meat and plum-duff.

When Kitty told Mrs. De Lacey, the good soul took her in her arms, kissed her affectionately, cried a bit, and said, "I'm so glad, dear."

Tom Benton was an utter stranger to ladies' society. He had not even the remembrance of a mother or a sister to guide him. He had always believed that women—all women—were angels, and that Kitty

Blake was the high admiral of the fleet. Therefore he was humbly bashful in her presence. He had hoped to win her for his wife; but as they became better acquainted, and he found what a very superior young lady she had become, he felt that, in spite of his fine ship, she had left him far astern. He became almost afraid of her. Quick-witted Kitty saw this, and tried to put him at his ease; thereby she again demonstrated her infinite superiority, and poor Tom felt as awkward and out of place as a walrus in a parlor.

The passengers left the ship at Gravesend. Captain Tom accompanied them to town, and attended the ladies to their hotel. He received a cordial hand-grasp from Kitty, and an invitation from Mrs. De Lacey to call often.

"It seems to me," remarked the good lady after Tom had gone, "that Captain Benton is rather diffident; don't you think so, Kitty?"

"Poor Tom! I know what the trouble is, aunty,—he thinks I'm too fine for him. I wish—I wish—I had never—never—gone to school a minute, nor—nor—travelled—nor anything!" And Kitty broke down and wept.

Mrs. De Lacey, who had learned to admire Tom, decided that some one would have to take the bashful young captain in hand and instruct him as to the lay of the land; and she resolved, like the good soul she was, to throw herself heroically into the breach. But we are told that:

"The best laid schemes of mice and men gang aft agley."

In this case the schemes of women were included, for somehow the fates prevented Mrs. De Lacey from carrying out her good intention; and, though Tom called as often as, to his uninstructed mind, etiquette permitted, he made no progress. His love-affair was most disastrously becalmed.

He took long walks to pass the time and ruminate on his unworthiness. One afternoon, as he was strolling moodily down Leadenhall Street, a tall, athletic-built gentleman, sunburned and wholesome-looking, came striding along in the opposite direction. His walk, so different from the short, dodging gait of the city business men, spoke of the free life of the bush, the veldt, and the pampas. He shouldered the opposing pedestrians aside as if they were but the fragile growth of a tropical jungle. Black looks and softly — very softly — muttered anathemas followed him; but he plunged heedlessly on. He nearly ran Tom down, threw him a hasty glance, which deepened into keen scrutiny, and seizing him roughly by the shoulders, exclaimed: —

"By Jove! Tom Benton! Give an account of yourself, will you? Why didn't you come back, hey? Where did you go to?"

"Why, how do you do, Sir John?" cried Tom, in pleased surprise. "Who would ever have thought of seeing you here?"

"Oh, I don't know!" replied Sir John Laidlaw. "I have a right to be here—this is my country, you know. But what stroke of good luck brings you here, just as I was heartily wishing I might find somebody besides these Londoners to talk to?"

As it was the hour for London's tiffin, Sir John carried Tom off to his club, where they compared notes. He listened with interest to Tom's account of himself, and congratulated him heartily on his good luck. As for himself, he had been, as he expressed it, "banging round ever since." His claim against the Venezuelan government had been allowed, and he might collect it if he lived forever. He told Tom he would send him half if he would give him his address, but Tom declined, saying that, having appealed to his own government at the time, he would abide by their decision.

Two days later Sir John dined on board the *Socotra*. After dinner, with the cabin filled with a convenient haze of tobacco smoke, he confessed that he was shortly to be married, and went off in a lover's rhapsody concerning the charms of his betrothed. He wound up with an invitation to visit him at his home in Kent, where he promised to introduce Tom to the lady. "By the way," he added,

"I was first introduced to her that day in Caracas when you skipped out; the whole family were on a visit to Mr. Lindsay. We met at dinner that same day."

Tom demurred to the invitation. He was not posted in the usages of good society, his friend would be sorry he had asked him, and his friend's friends would not care for his company.

"My dear boy!" exclaimed Sir John, "you were never more mistaken in your life. You have the very best of manners, those that proceed from an honest and kind heart. I have often spoken of you to my mother and my sweetheart, and they will both be very much pleased to see you. You must not think that ladies admire those peaches-and-cream skinned puppies — they don't. They associate with them of course, they have to; but Lord bless you, my dear boy, when a fellow like you or me, made in the image of God instead of a hair-dresser's figure, comes near them, they know the difference. And as for my friends not according you a welcome, you will be there as my friend; and you can bet your boots, Tom, that 'where McGregor sits is the head of the table.' I'll expect you next Wednesday, and I won't take no for an answer. Good-bye!"

When, with many misgivings, Tom followed his friend into the handsome drawing-rooms of the ancient mansion in Kent, he found himself surrounded by a company of British aristocrats. There were twenty-five or thirty persons present, stiff, pompous, elderly people, who acknowledged the introduction with an air of condescension that rather overawed the young skipper. There were young fellows whose immaculate-ness made him feel like a woodchopper by contrast, though he had fitted himself out with a brand-new rig from keel to truck, and ordered the tailor to spare no expense.

When Sir John introduced him to some of them, and they glanced casually at him through their eye-glasses, said "Aw!" and turned away, Tom thought he would like to chase them out on a topsail yard-arm on a reefing match, or send them down a royal stay in a bowline with a tar pot. By the time he arrived at the far end of the large room, where Sir John's mother sat in state, surrounded by a little court of the neighboring dowagers, he knew the perspiration was pouring down his face, but dared not use his handkerchief. The lady saw his embarrassment, and with matronly tact received him kindly, inviting him to a seat at her side. But Sir John, who also perceived Tom's distress, and doubted his mother's ability to allay it, asked where "Nellie" was.

"I think you will find her over by the bay window," his mother replied, "with a party of the young people."

Sir John threw Tom the end of his towline again, and they shaped a course for the bay window. Miss Nellie failed to observe their approach ; she and her particular chum, with heads together, were discussing some matter of, no doubt, grave feminine importance.

"Miss Druse," said Sir John, "allow me to present my friend, Captain Benton."

The two girls looked up, and once more Kitty Blake and Tom Benton met very unexpectedly.

There were many things to be explained: how Tom and Sir John came to be acquainted; how Kitty came to know Miss Druse, and how Kitty and Tom came to know each other. When it came out that they all had been at Mr. Lindsay's that day in Caracas, and that Tom had seen Kitty and Nellie as they left the house for their walk, and that Kitty had seen him on his way to the calaboose after being sentenced to death, the story became intensely inter-esting. The relation of one adventure led to another, and Thomas Benton was the man of the day — or rather evening. He sat between the two handsomest girls in the room, — Kitty and Nellie, — and, in answer to their endless questions, told them a tale of ups and downs, and of hard luck, which, almost by an inter-position of Providence, was at last changed to good.

Tom forgot his bashfulness, encouraged by Nellie's sympathy and Kitty's evident pride in him and his doings. When, at a late hour, the party dispersed,

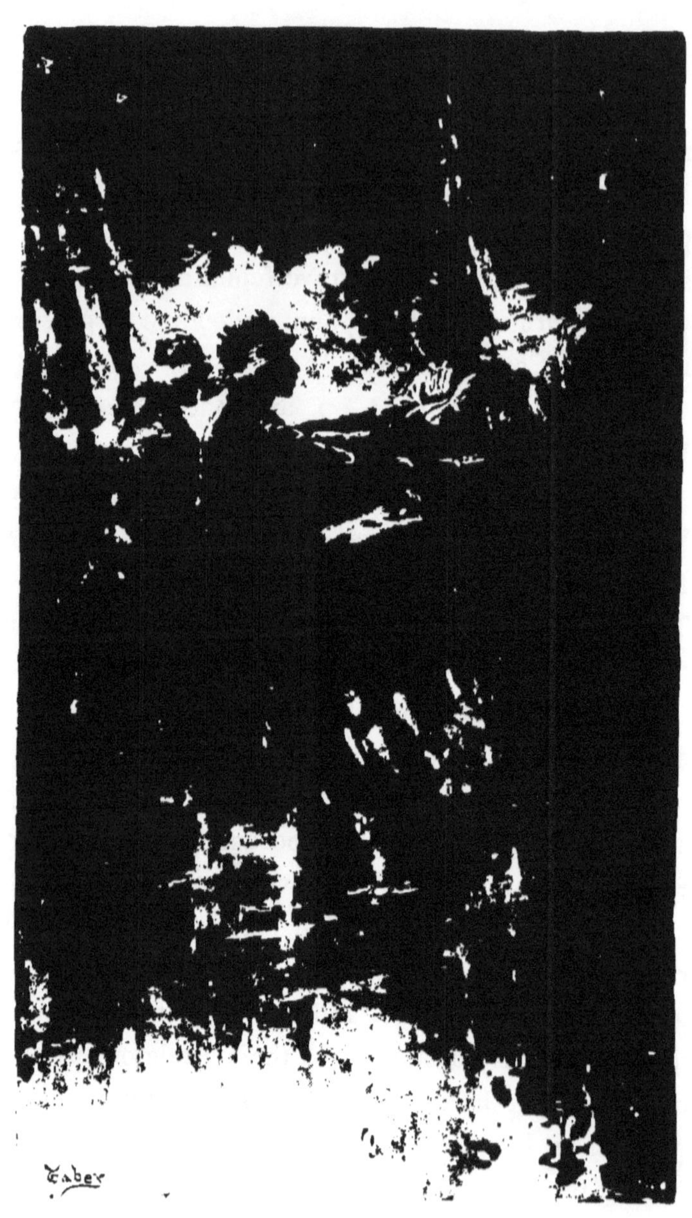

"Looked Tom Benton squarely in the Eyes."

Sir John accompanied him to his room for a smoke
before retiring.

"I say, Tom," said he, as he puffed a concealing
cloud, "aren't you a sly one, though?"

"A sly one, Sir John? I don't think I quite
understand."

"I told you all about my affair the very first chance
I had; and you never said a word, but just let me run
on like a fool."

"I'm sure I don't see anything foolish about it.
I think Miss Druse is a very charming young lady
indeed. I congratulated you before I had seen her,
and now that I have, I repeat it most emphatically.
You are a man to be envied, Sir John."

"Of course, I know that, but how about yourself,
old man? Why did you keep so mum about your
own affair? I rather think you are to be envied
too."

"I really don't know what you are talking about.
My affair? What is my affair?"

"Well, if I must out with it, I'll admit that I had
a little scheme in my mind when I invited you down
here. I'm a great admirer of Nellie's friend, and I
said to myself, it will be a kindness to introduce
Captain Benton. She is an American, and they
would make a fine match; and now I'll be hanged if
you haven't been about the same as engaged to each
other all your lives."

"Miss Druse's friend?"

"Why, yes. Miss Blake. How dreadfully obtuse you pretend to be all at once."

"Excuse me, Sir John, you are entirely mistaken. Miss Blake and I were playmates in childhood, and the closest friends; but she has grown away from me," replied Tom, with an ill-suppressed sigh.

Sir John smoked furiously in silence for some minutes. Then, removing his pipe and slowly knocking out the ashes, he said : —

"Tom, I believe you and I may call ourselves friends, may we not?"

"I am certainly very proud to think so," replied Tom, heartily.

"Very well, then, I am going to exercise the privilege that makes friendship odious — I am going to give you some advice."

"All right, go ahead. I am satisfied beforehand that any advice I get from you will be disinterested, at least."

"Thanks. No bouquets in advance, please! Now, then, I know you are heels over head in love with Miss Blake. I know you are bashful, just as bashful as I was when I proposed to Nellie. And I tell you, Tom, I would rather have gone out unarmed to meet a wounded jaguar that day, than to propose to that little woman, — and she is not so very terrible, either. You see, I had no reason to hope for success, but with you it's altogether different. Miss Blake has waited years for your return, and now that you have returned she's waiting yet."

"Hold on, Sir John! Hold on! There are some things a man doesn't like to hear spoken lightly of."

"Aha! What did I say? It's your confounded bashfulness, or rather the undervaluation you put on yourself, that stands between you and your own happiness. Now don't interrupt me again, please, and I'll prove it to you. You can understand that Nellie tells me a great many things nowadays that she would not have told me a month ago, and being in love ourselves, we are very naturally interested in the love-affairs of our friends. Nellie and Miss Blake were inseparable at school, and long before Nellie ever dreamed of having an affair of her own she listened to, sympathized with, and cried over the story Miss Blake told her of the sailor-boy who had gone away to conquer the world single-handed, and for whose return she hoped as she hoped for nothing else in this world. She was ambitious to study and improve herself solely that she might be the more pleasing in his eyes. Do you know that during her tour of Europe she has been often sought in marriage, and has discouraged her suitors because she was waiting, hoping, and praying for the return of Tom Benton? Do you know that, since you have met again, she has been alternately happy and depressed as you seemed to approach or recede from the important question? I haven't very much grit myself in matters of this kind, but, by the Lord Harry! if I had the assurance of success that you have, I wouldn't delay a minute."

Tom was deeply affected by Sir John's recital. He was obliged to turn his head while listening to the story of Kitty's unfaltering faith in him, and when he felt able to control his voice he asked: —

"Do you think Miss Blake still feels as kindly toward me as she did years ago at school?"

"Why, only to-day Nellie carried me off on a long walk to tell me the latest developments in the case. Womanlike, she only remembered such parts of the story as interested her; but I knew, when she told of the rescue in mid-ocean, that it was you; and I nearly let the cat out of the bag, which would have spoiled all the pleasure of a surprise this evening. Now there you are. I'm off to bed, and if I don't hear a satisfactory report of you inside of twenty-four hours you are not the gallant sailor I take you for. Good-night."

Tom sat and smoked and thought a long time after Sir John left him, and his last thought before he fell asleep was "God bless her, she's a jewel!" He slept the dreamless sleep of perfect health, and rose in the morning to find the sun shining gloriously on the fair English landscape. It was a day for joyous deeds and unalloyed happiness.

Sir John proposed a riding party after breakfast.

"I'm afraid," said Kitty, "that Captain Benton doesn't ride. You know sailors seldom do."

Sir John laughed. "I can assure you," said he, "that you need have no fear of Captain Benton's abilities in that line. Any man who has served two years as a llanero on the Apure need have no fear of an English saddle-horse."

Away they cantered, as merry a party as could have been found among the flower-scented lanes of old England that day. Sir John (sly dog) proposed that Tom and Kitty should take the lead, as, being strangers, they would thus enjoy the pleasures of discovery. They both blushed consciously; but neither objected. Sir John and Nellie gradually dropped astern, and he told her of his conversation with Tom the night before. When they arrived at a crossroad they turned off, unperceived by the couple in advance.

Tom and Kitty talked at first on commonplace topics, addressing each other as, "Captain Benton," and "Miss Blake," but gradually the conversation took a retrospective turn; they spoke of the sails they used to enjoy in the *Sprite*, and of their rendezvous on the island.

"Those were the happiest days I have ever

known," said Tom, "and I wish we could go back to them again."

"So do I," Kitty replied with frank ingenuousness.

Tom cast a furtive glance toward her, and caught her in the same act. "You called me 'Tom' in those days," said he.

"I know it, and you used to call me 'Kitty.'"

"I should like to again — may I?"

"Why, certainly. I see no harm in that."

"Thank you! And call me Tom again — won't you, Kitty?"

"Yes — Tom."

He reined his horse close to hers, and continued in low, earnest tones: —

"Kitty, when I left Portland that time, I told you I would never return until I was captain of as fine a ship as your father ever commanded. Of course I did not realize then the great social distance existing between me, a penniless sailor, and the daughter of wealthy Captain Blake. My highest ideal of success was the position of captain of a fine ship. You were the only friend I had in those days, Kitty; you encouraged me and believed in me. During the years that have passed since then, I have had but one object in view, — to prove to you that your faith in me was not unfounded. During those years of hardship and disappointment I never lost hope of some day — I didn't know how — coming to you, and saying, 'Kitty, I have succeeded.' And when the day came, and I sought you in Portland, and that woman told me you were dead, — had been dead for years, — you may imagine how I felt. I wished that I too had died, rather than come back to this. It seemed that all my exertions had gone for nothing, and my success had no value, now that you were not there to approve it. But I have found you again, dear Kitty; I know how far you are above me socially, but I loved you then, I always have loved you, and I love you now. You know me, you know who and what I am; I want you to be my wife — will you?"

Kitty had been gazing straight ahead between her horse's ears, the color coming and going prettily in her cheeks as Tom, hesitatingly, — and in tremulous tones, awkwardly and bashfully, but with the eloquence of deep feeling, — told his love. When he asked the momentous question, she turned — her eyes brimming — and answered simply : —

"Yes, Tom."

When the four met at dinner, Sir John and Nellie glanced at their friends, and then at each other, knowingly. After dinner, the gentlemen adjourned to the garden for a smoke, and Nellie, assuming a matronly, protective air, passed her arm affectionately about her chum's waist, saying : —

" Let's go up to my room, love."

And so the murder was out!

Tom wrote to his agent in London that he would not be ready to sail for a month yet. Before the month expired, there was a double wedding in the old mansion down in Kent, and Mrs. De Lacey graced the ceremony with her presence and added her wishes for long life and happiness.

When the *Socotra* sailed, Mrs. De Lacey and Kitty resumed their interrupted voyage on board of her.

As Kitty, her arm linked lovingly in Tom's, paced the good ship's quarterdeck, she gloried in her self-made sailor husband. But from her experience in the *Sutherland*, she had acquired a dread of the treacherous, unstable sea, and she begged Tom to quit it. He laughed at her, and defied her to compare his ship with the old worn-out basket in which she had unwittingly taken passage. He declared he felt safer on board the *Socotra* than he did ashore, where he was liable at any time to be run over by a truck. "It has been my best friend — except you, Kitty," said he, "and besides, every cent I have in the world is invested in this ship, and I should not like to hand her over to a stranger."

Then Kitty remembered something she had long since forgotten ; and she told him of the twelve thousand dollars that had lain all these years in the bank awaiting his orders.

Tom took her in his arms and pressed a resounding kiss on her rosy lips. "If ever a man had cause to be proud of his wife," he said, "I am that man! Kitty, you are a jewel! This is the first favor you have asked me, and I promise you faithfully that I will manage — somehow — so that this shall be my very last voyage."

And she was so grateful and so happy that he wondered how he ever had the heart to refuse her even for an instant. What was ambition, a career, a ship, even his peerless *Socotra*, that it should cast even a momentary shadow on her happiness?

When they arrived in New York, Kitty insisted on going with him to hunt up Jerry Hale. They found him farther down the market in a new stall. They patronized him, and Kitty complimented him on the lightness of his butter-cakes. Jerry was nowise astonished when Tom called him by name, for like other celebrities, he was known to more people than he could remember. He was a bit gray and slightly hard of hearing. So, when the lunch was finished, and Tom asked, "Had anybody scraping your ham-rinds lately, Jerry?" he inclined his head and answered, "'Ow's that, sir?" and when Tom told him that he was the boy who, some nine years previously, had scraped the ham-rind that he found in Jerry's swill-tub, the old fellow was so mixed,

between pleasure at the meeting and morti-
fication at the remembrance, that he could only
shake Tom's hand and laugh and blush furiously.
A comparison of notes showed that Jerry's fortunes
had remained about stationary during all this time.
There had been several opportunities, of which he
had been unable to take advantage for the want of
capital.   There was one now: a very successful
restaurant in Catherine Street was for sale, the owner
having recently died; but it would require five or
six hundred dollars to get it; and as far as he was
concerned it might as well be the same number of
thousands, ay, or millions.

Before Tom left New York, Jerry was in the
Catherine Street restaurant; and before another year
rolled round, he paid his indebtedness to Tom and
owned a fine business all clear.

Then there was a flying trip to the Staggs, who
were delighted and flattered by a visit from "Sarah"
and her smart young husband; but Mr. Hayward
had looked after their welfare so thoroughly that
they declared themselves in want of nothing, absolutely nothing.   Kitty insisted on being allowed to
make them a present as a keepsake from herself,
to which they finally agreed; and she sent them
a silver tea-set from Tiffany's, which is the pride
and boast of the neighborhood to this day.

They went to Portland and became the guests of

the Haywards, whose joy at seeing Kitty was un-
bounded. Tom chartered a yacht as much like the
Sprite as he could find, and, with Kitty at the helm,
they renewed their youth by taking long sails on the
beautiful bay. They visited the island where they
had played at keeping house, and one of the most
prized articles in Kitty's cabinet of curiosities is
a broken iron teaspoon which she discovered on the
site of their former hearthstone.

Mindful of his promise, Tom sought a reliable man
as master for the *Socotra*. His search brought him
in contact with the maritime community of his native
city, and as his story became known, the sterling
character of his father was recalled, and the gray-
beards decided that Tom was made of the right kind
of stuff himself.

The manager of the line to which the *Columbia*
belonged saw fit to retire; the directors, looking for
young blood, had their attention attracted to Tom,
and offered him the position. He asked if they
would take the *Socotra* in lieu of stock, and they did;
so it came about that in nine years and four months
from the day that Bully Blake kicked Tom Benton
out of the office, he reëntered it as the company's
manager, and seated himself in the identical chair
Captain Blake had occupied that morning.

Tom Benton sits in the parlor of his well-appointed
home with his son Joe, a loquacious young man of

three years, upon his knee. He has just read a letter from jolly Captain Bradford, the Assam tea-planter, who writes that, in deference to his liver, he has put himself on half allowance of brandy 'and water *pawnee lao*.

Tom chucks his boy under the chin, passes his hand caressingly over his wife's glossy hair, and, with an affectionate glance toward Mrs. De Lacey in her easy chair by the fire, decides that, after all, Tom Benton's luck has not been so bad.

9 783743 389946